THE
CHILD
IN THE
PHOTO

BOOKS BY KERRY WILKINSON

Standalone Novels

Ten Birthdays
Two Sisters
The Girl Who Came Back
Last Night
The Death and Life of Eleanor Parker
The Wife's Secret
A Face in the Crowd
Close to You
After the Accident
The Child Across the Street
What My Husband Did
The Blame

The Jessica Daniel series

The Killer Inside (also published as *Locked In*)
Vigilante
The Woman in Black
Think of the Children
Playing with Fire
The Missing Dead (also published as *Thicker than Water*)
Behind Closed Doors
Crossing the Line
Scarred for Life

For Richer, For Poorer
Nothing But Trouble
Eye for an Eye
Silent Suspect
The Unlucky Ones
A Cry in the Night

The Jessica Daniel Short Stories

January
February
March
April

Silver Blackthorn

Reckoning
Renegade
Resurgence

The Andrew Hunter series

Something Wicked
Something Hidden
Something Buried

Other

Down Among the Dead Men
No Place Like Home
Watched

THE CHILD IN THE PHOTO

KERRY WILKINSON

Bookouture

Published by Bookouture in 2021

An imprint of Storyfire Ltd.
Carmelite House
50 Victoria Embankment
London EC4Y 0DZ

www.bookouture.com

ISBN: 978-1-80019-504-2
eBook ISBN: 978-1-80019-503-5

ONE

I don't think human beings have enough hands.

Opposable thumbs and the central nervous system is clearly right up there when it comes to usefulness – but I honestly think the next step *has* to be a third hand. The main argument in favour is that getting a weekly big shop from the car into the house should be easier than it currently is. I don't think anyone can dispute that Tesco stores are too big nowadays.

As I hobble the few steps along the driveway, I have a bag hooked over each shoulder, two more cutting into one hand – and then a final bag in the other. That leaves me a grand total of zero hands with which to go fishing into my *actual* bag for the key to get myself inside.

I end up putting all the shopping bags on the ground in order to find the aforementioned key, by which time three apples are making a break for the road.

After I've rescued them, unlocked and opened the front door, and then retrieved the shopping, I'm beginning to think that a *fourth* hand might actually be necessary – because then I'd be able to pick up the mail that's scattered across the welcome mat, before tapping in the code to the manically beeping burglar alarm.

I dump the shopping in the kitchen, then return to close the front door. After that, I tap the code into the burglar alarm, which makes the brain-frying beeping finally knock it on the head.

In the blissful relative silence, it doesn't take long to skim through the four letters on the welcome mat. When I was young, any form of letter addressed to me would bring a thrill that would likely be the highlight of my week. My grandma, who lived on the other side of town, and who I saw most days, once mailed me a sixth birthday card. I thought it was the most wondrous thing. I kept the envelope and everything inside for a good dozen years until I had a clear-out.

Now, more or less anything that comes through the door is destined for the recycling box with only a cursory look.

Today's mail consists of:

a) A letter from Barclays that mentions something about my overdraft rate going up.

b) A pamphlet from the Liberal Democrat party about an upcoming local election that may as well have 'feed me to the shredder' written all over it.

c) Something for my ex-boyfriend, which means I will have to text him again.

d) A plain envelope with no stamp and my name written on the front. 'HOPE TAYLOR' stands out in black biro on the white background. It's been written in very neat block capital letters, almost as if it's come from a printer. It's thin and feels empty.

I carry everything through to the kitchen and then edge around the floor-dumped shopping bags as I slip a fingernail underneath the envelope's flap and scratch it open.

At first, I really do think the envelope is bare. There's nothing immediately visible inside and it's only when I go digging to the bottom that I find the browning scrap of slightly crusty newspaper.

As soon as I pull it out, there's a gentle edge of musty-dustiness in the air. Like the back corners of a library where nobody goes.

The newspaper clipping has been sliced neatly along the middle of an advert for Whiskas cat food. There is a stack of small tins plus a cat sitting at the side with its head very tidily chopped off.

Except that isn't what the clipping is of.

When I flip it over, I realise it's a short news story.

POLICE are appealing for witnesses after a six-month-old baby was stolen from the back seat of a car in Lower Woolton yesterday.

Penny Craven left her daughter, Jane, in the back of her brown Vauxhall Cavalier, which was parked on Marston Close, near to the junction with Vicarage Hill.

She was in Marston Newsagents for approximately three minutes before returning to find that Jane was no longer in the car.

The article cuts off at a point where it feels like there was likely more to come. From the date at the top, it is thirty-four years old.

There's a picture of the baby, although I'm not sure how much use it might have been to anyone at the time. The dotted image is slightly fuzzy, with the monochrome bleeding into the background. To my untrained eye, the child looks like any other of a similar age. Jane has almost no hair, a slightly pudgy face and a squat nose. She's sort of smiling, although it's more that confused face that kids do as they're trying to figure out how their mouths work.

I read the story through a second time and then check inside the envelope again, wondering if I've missed something.

It's empty.

I look at the front of the envelope, then the back, except the only details are my own name. There's no return address, or anything to indicate who might have put it through the door.

I've never heard of Penny Craven, Jane Craven, or Lower Woolton. It all feels as if this has been delivered to the wrong person. Perhaps a different Hope Taylor, who'd know what any of this meant?

I put the article and the envelope down on the side and then send a reluctant text to Aki, telling him there's more mail for him if he wants to pick it up. After that, I put away the shopping, before returning to the article.

The third read offers no more clues than I had before. The snip along the bottom of the article isn't quite straight and there's a hint of a fourth paragraph that isn't there.

I put it down and then pick it up. Something about it feels familiar and yet it doesn't. The photo of the missing baby is grainy and greying. A reminder of how fast things have moved in my lifetime. Newspapers have gone from an inky black and white to colour to an anachronism.

The baby photo is the sort of posed picture that could have been taken in the old days by a professional at a shopping centre. Perhaps they still are? Jane has puffed-out cheeks and wide eyes. The poor thing is probably scared of the giant figure in front of her with a huge camera.

And then I see it.

I find myself touching my ear. The curved bit along the top is called the helix except, for me, there is no arch. It is a straight slice, almost as if someone once cut through it with scissors.

When I was young, I'd hate to look at myself in a mirror because the deformed ear was the only thing I'd ever see. One of my friends once got a pair of piercings through the helix of her ear and I always wondered if it was a subtle dig at me because that part of my ear doesn't exist. Boys, especially, would notice.

In recent times, that angle of my ear has been the least of my worries when it comes to health. I don't think about it too often any longer.

I'm thinking about it now, though.

I've seen myself in a mirror tens of thousands of times. I know exactly how my ear looks – and yet I hurry through to the hall and stand in front of the full-length mirror to stare at the side of my head, the article still in my hand. I tuck a strand of my short hair behind my ear and turn a little, so that I'm at the same angle as little Jane Craven in the picture.

The article is from thirty-four years ago. I'm thirty-four years old.

I look from Jane to me and back again.

The top part of my ear is missing. The top part of *her* ear is missing.

Mirror to photo to mirror… to photo. Which leaves me with one simple, yet horrifying, question.

Is this… *me?*

TWO

There are definitely other people on the planet who have an ear like mine. When I was younger and particularly down about things, Mum would comfort me by saying that I wasn't the only one. She'd point out that almost everyone looked the same ear-wise but that only someone who was special would be different.

I didn't want to be special *or* different. I wanted to be like everyone else.

The memory leaves me thinking of Mum. I could call and ask if she's ever heard of Jane Craven – except that it doesn't feel like the sort of thing that can be asked in a phone call. It definitely can't be asked in a text message.

It's not an in-person world nowadays, except that some things still have to be – and Mum is old-school when it comes to communication.

I return to the kitchen and slip the article back into the envelope, then I go back out the front door and hop the low fence until I'm standing outside my neighbour's door. There's no doorbell, so I knock on the glass and wait.

There's a ritual to the door being answered. First a call of 'yes' to acknowledge the knocking has been heard, then the hallway light going on – this happens regardless of time of day – and then a low grumbling until the door is eventually pulled inward.

A curious smile spreads across Mr Bonner's face, as he uses his walking stick to prop himself up.

'Hope, love,' he says.

Mr Bonner turned eighty on New Year's Day this year. He celebrated by eating roast potatoes with me in my kitchen and then inviting me back to his to get drunk on expensive whisky that he'd been hoarding since he turned seventy. He keeps insisting I call him 'Jack', although I was raised to call people older than me 'Mr' or 'Mrs'. It's been largely impossible to get out of the habit.

'What's wrong?' he adds. He has seemingly seen something in me that I didn't know was there.

'Nothing,' I reply quickly. 'I was just wondering if you saw anyone at my door during the day?'

Mr Bonner glances sideways towards my driveway. There's an ankle-high fence separating the two properties and my car is now parked back in its place.

'Only the postman,' he says.

'What time was that?'

'Around two. Same as always.'

He raises his eyebrows with a hint of expectedness.

I allow myself a smile: 'I bet you remember when there were two posts a day, don't you?'

The grin is infectious. 'Cheek!' he says. 'How's the leg?'

I lift my prosthetic leg, feeling the slight friction as my amputated limb rubs against the cup into which it's attached.

'I can still beat you in a race,' I reply.

He laughs, as he always does. The pensioner versus the amputee sounds like something ITV might commission for primetime. When it comes to me and my neighbour, it might happen one day – though I suspect we'll need a lot more expensive whisky first.

As I put my foot back onto the ground, I picture the pile of mail from inside my door. The one without the stamp was at the bottom, underneath the regular post.

'Was there anyone before the postman?' I ask.

A shake of the head. 'Not that I saw – but I was out the back for a bit.' There's a pause as his wrinkled eyes narrow. 'Is everything okay?'

I try to sound breezy and unconcerned as I tell him it's fine. I'm not sure he's listening because he wafts his free hand in the vague direction of the street.

'Did you hear about the break-in a week back?' he asks. 'Other side of town but makes you think.'

'Nobody broke in,' I reply. 'It's nothing really – but if you see anyone hanging around the house that you don't recognise, can you let me know?'

Mr Bonner digs into his trouser pocket and pulls out an old Nokia 3210. He holds it up proudly, as if showing off a trophy he's won. His daughter bought it for him from eBay two or three years back and he grins every time he shows it to me. He brags that he only has to charge it once a month.

'I've got your number in here,' he says.

'I've been wondering who keeps calling me and breathing heavily down the line.'

He laughs as he re-pockets the phone.

'Are you sure everything's all right?' he asks again.

'It's all fine,' I reply. 'You just let me know when you want someone to beat you at Scrabble again and I'll be right around. Then I'll race you round the park and beat you at that, too.'

The grin is back. 'You're on.'

THREE

I sit on a stool in the kitchen and reread the three paragraphs of the article. The paper feels brittle, as if it could crumble if I hold it too hard.

Someone has kept this for three decades. Someone who seemingly thinks I'm the girl in the photo… or someone who *knows* I am.

I'm not sure what's worse.

The more I stare at Jane and her ear, the more I see the similarity to myself. It's not only that the straight slice is on the same ear, it's that it's at the *same* angle. The light catches it in the same way. Everything is the same.

It's like looking in a curved mirror at the fairground, where everything is the same and yet it isn't. It has to be a coincidence.

I take my keys from the hook in the hall and then leave the house and get into the car. It's around a twenty-minute drive from where I live in Macklebury to where I grew up, in Elwood. They're both small towns that are surrounded by countryside. The sort of places where people either live their entire lives, or leave the moment they finish school. I suppose I'm an oddity in that I left one place but then moved to the other. I got out… but not really.

As I pass the Welcome To Elwood sign, there's a second banner a little past it with a large 'Save Our Jobs' slogan painted across it. A pair of men in bright orange vests wave their fists in a salute as I beep my horn in the customary fashion while I pass.

My home town never makes headlines for positive reasons. Last year, Elwood was in the news because of a hit-and-run where a young boy was left for dead. This year, it's all about how the large shoe factory in the centre is on the brink of closing for good. It's the place that employed a large number of men throughout the area, a factory around which the town itself was built. It's been downsizing for years and nobody seems quite sure what will be left of the town once it's gone.

I try to think of that instead of the article that came through the door but the picture of Jane with her damaged ear keeps drifting to the front of my thoughts. That and the date of the article. Jane and I would be the same age.

I navigate the streets of Elwood on autopilot. All roads through the town seemingly lead towards the shoe factory and I find myself easing past it, where there's a second protest happening close to the gates. More men in fluorescent tabards thrust a banner high and cheer as I beep my horn for them, too. I wonder if my support is to make them feel better, or me. We likely all know the truth that the factory is closing and that jobs aren't coming back. No amount of protests or honked horns are going to change that.

Elwood is not a large place and it's only a few more minutes until I'm parking outside Mum's house. I let myself into my childhood home without much thought, using the key I've had since I was eight or nine years old. The sort of thing I've also done tens of thousands of times before.

'It's me, Mum,' I call, as I close the door behind me.

She shouts back to say she's in the living room, not that there are many other places she might have been. If it wasn't there, it would have been the kitchen.

I poke my head around the living room door and she's in her chair, with the headrest back and her feet up. She motions to stand but doesn't make a real effort as I wave her back down. *Coronation Street* is frozen on the television but, from the time of day, it's either a rerun or a recording. Her relationship with Corrie is perhaps the longest with anything she's had in her life.

'I didn't know you were coming over,' she says.

'D'you want a brew?'

I give the universal hand-to-mouth sign while holding an invisible mug and Mum reaches for the empty Little Miss Wise cup that's already at her side.

'I'll do it.'

She doesn't move to stand as she says this, although we both know the ritual by now. I take her mug and then head through to the kitchen, where I fill the kettle and set it boiling. After that, I rinse out Mum's mug and then grab a couple of teabags from the cupboard.

Mum has already set her programme playing again in the living room, with the volume approaching sonic boom levels. She insists she doesn't have a hearing problem, although, if that's true, then 'What?', 'Pardon?' and 'Who?' must be her three favourite catchphrases.

I stand in the doorway that links the kitchen to the living room, slightly behind Mum where she can't see me.

In the two years since Dad died, she's changed almost nothing about this room. The walls are still covered with a succession of family photos that almost all contain the three of us. If not that, then it's me by myself. There are class photos from primary school, and then the posed photographs of me in school uniform with a discomforting number of bewildering haircuts that makes me think my ear was the least of my worries when I was young.

There are holiday photos from caravan parks and the seaside. Something from when I rode a donkey at Elwood Summer Fete when I was seven or eight. I'm at a wildlife park, then a water park, then Alton Towers. We visited Edinburgh when I was around twelve and there's a photo of me sitting on one of the cannons near the castle.

My entire childhood is chronicled on these walls.

The kettle clicks off and I move back into the kitchen, where I pour two cups of tea. Mum has a splash of milk and her customary three sugars, and then I carry everything back through to the living room.

Mum thanks me for hers as I put it on the small side-table next to her chair. She won't be touching it anytime soon as the only way she has hot drinks is when they're cold. Dad teased her about it for at least the thirty years I remember, and likely another decade before that.

It's those little thoughts, as simple as putting down a cup of tea, that bring the memories crashing back.

I sit across from her and cradle the mug in my fingers as Mum pauses the television again. The ear-crushing sound is gone in a flash, leaving only the relative silence of the unassuming house on an unassuming road.

'I didn't expect you today,' Mum says.

'I've been thinking about my ear.'

Mum's eyes narrow as she stares across the room towards me. 'Oh, love… what has someone been saying…?'

I shake my head. 'It's not that. I suppose it's been on my mind recently.'

'How come?'

'I'm not sure. I was wondering if you could tell me about it again.'

She wriggles in her seat, confused, which isn't a surprise. This is the story she used to tell me when I was much younger. She wanted me to understand why I was how I was. It's not something she's had to say out loud in anything close to twenty years.

'Are you—?'

'Sometimes I need to hear it, Mum.'

She straightens herself and clears her throat. Any eye contact is lost now as she stares off towards some of the photos on the wall. It's as if she's aged in front of me. She's suddenly frail and confused where, moments ago, she was confident and content.

Or perhaps I'm seeing something that isn't there.

'It was a complication with the umbilical cord,' she says with a slight cough. 'You were already partly out when they realised it was wrapped around your neck. All these people suddenly appeared from nowhere. Doctors, I guess – although I don't know for sure. It was so long ago. They managed to get you out but, in doing so, the cord ripped across part of your ear. If it wasn't for that, you probably would've choked to death.'

She reaches for her tea, hot or not, and sips from the top. It's the same thing I was told as a young teenager and, perhaps, as an even younger girl. I didn't know what an umbilical cord was when she first told me but finding out meant that I was ahead of the class when we first started doing biology.

I've never questioned it, because why would I? It feels like something that could have happened. Like something that *did* happen.

I take the envelope from my bag and then step across the room and hand it to Mum. She asks what it is but I don't answer as she reaches inside and removes the article. I watch her face but she's unmoving as she either skims the piece or pretends to.

She doesn't look up when she next speaks. 'Where did you get this?'

'I was given it.'

'Who by?'

I don't know the answer, although that's not why I remain quiet.

'Jane would be my age,' I say, ignoring the question. 'She's missing the same part of her ear.'

Mum continues to look at the clipping, perhaps at the photo itself. From nowhere a memory returns of me lying on my bed upstairs. I would have been fifteen or sixteen and obsessed with boys and acting older than I was. It occurred to me suddenly that

I didn't look much like either of my parents. My hair has always been a naturally mucky blonde, while both of theirs was dark. They had brown eyes, while mine were blue. I asked Dad about it once but he said something about getting genes from grandparents. It was the sort of conversation that was forgotten about until all these years later. So distant that I'm not certain it even happened at all.

Mum looks up from the article and blinks. All of a sudden, she's speaking quickly and decisively, as if telling me to clean my room and that she doesn't want any backchat.

'What's this got to do with anything?' she asks.

'I'm not sure.'

She pauses for another moment, her eyes squinting as if trying to figure out how to phrase whatever comes next.

'I remember giving birth to you,' she says. There's the hint of steel in her tone, as if she's disappointed in me. 'I don't know why you're showing me this.'

There's a hint of hurt, too, which I guess is understandable. A moment in which it feels like she might rip the article in half. Her fingers grip the two corners and her arms tense.

Instead, she stuffs it back into the envelope and then offers it to me. I step across the room and take it from her, before depositing it back into my bag. It suddenly feels important, as if nobody should touch it except me.

'I've never met anyone with an ear like mine,' I say. 'And she would be *my* age…'

There's silence for a good twenty or thirty seconds until Mum turns her attention back to the television. She starts her show playing once more, although the volume is muted. Her hand trembles on the remote as she presses a button to set subtitles blinking along the bottom. It could be age-related, except that I've never seen her tremble like this before. She might be feeling ill or, perhaps… it's something much, much worse.

FOUR

I'm back at home when it occurs to me that I should google Jane's name. Instead of measuring time with BC and AD, it should be Before Internet and After Internet. It's as if the sum total of our knowledge as a species is measured through what happened before and after we were able to record it online.

Almost no information exists through Google when it comes to Jane or Penny Craven. The disappearance happened when local news didn't necessarily become national. Before newspapers put all their content online and it was archived forever.

There is a single link from four years previous, which is a general piece from Mail Online about missing children. It profiles five kids from various time periods who were never found. There is one from the year the piece was written, then another from each of the previous decades.

Jane Craven is listed as part of the 'thirtieth anniversary' of her disappearance, as if that's something to be celebrated. It talks about her mother, 'now called Penny Morse' who 'works as a barmaid in her home town of Lower Woolton'.

That sends me searching for 'Penny barmaid Lower Woolton', which gets one more hit – a five-star review of the Black Sheep Pub on TripAdvisor. The person who left it says that the food is 'top-notch' and that she got 'great service from the barmaid Penny'.

I stare at the review for a while. The details of the pub are at the top of the review, with an address and phone number. The photo shows the outside of an old-fashioned building with a thatched roof and hanging rainbow flower baskets.

I scroll through the photos. There are a couple of the pub's outside lawn area, with picnic tables and a kids' slide. For the interior shots, there's a fireplace and a series of pictures showing the brewers' logos across the long tap pumps. It's the type of place that tourists would spot in a guidebook and then accidentally spend seven hours on a series of buses trying to find.

There are no photos of any individual working behind the bar and little else that can help.

I live alone and there is nobody to talk me out of doing something stupid, not that I'm convinced it *is* stupid.

It's a man's voice who answers the phone with a crisp and distracted 'Black Sheep…?', which he phrases as if it's a question.

My own voice falters. 'Can I talk to Penny, please?'

There's a momentary pause and a grunt. It sounds as if whoever's answered is in the middle of doing something else. It must only last a couple of seconds but a flurry of thoughts flood through me. He'll say that Penny doesn't work there any longer, or want to know why I'm bothering his staff. He'll tell me to get lost and not bother calling back.

Except that he doesn't.

There's a huffed and breathy sigh and then a somewhat muffled: 'Pen! Call for you.'

The line goes quiet for a while, with the only sound being the bustle of the pub in the background. There are glasses clinking and voices chattering to each other, plus a gentle undercurrent of music that I can't quite make out. Something rocky.

I can hear my heart beating. Something to which I've never paid attention before. It's steady but feels fast.

And then there's a woman's voice. She sounds unsure, perhaps confused as she gives a tentative: 'Hello…?'

My mouth is suddenly dry and when I try to speak, nothing comes out.

The woman repeats her 'Hello…?', although there's more of an edge this time.

'Is that Penny?' I ask. My voice croaks like a long-term smoker's. 'Penny Craven?'

'Used to be,' she replies. 'Who's asking?'

'Was your daughter stolen from your car?'

It's so direct, which is completely different from my usual personality. The shield and distance of the phone is giving me a courage I don't think I have.

There's a short pause, which turns into a really *long* pause. The only reason I know the call hasn't dropped is because I can still hear the hubbub of the pub in the background.

'Who did you say you were…?'

As soon as Penny finishes the sentence, I press the button on my mobile to hang up. It's instinctive and I immediately regret it, knowing I shouldn't have called in the first place. Knowing I shouldn't have asked about Jane.

I think of a woman standing in a hallway at the back of a bar, old-fashioned landline phone in her hand, as she stares at the receiver, wondering what's just happened.

I jump as my phone starts to vibrate. It's more or less on permanent silent mode, like any sane person, but the juddering is so unexpected that I almost drop it.

It's the pub's phone number on the screen. I stare at it but can't bring myself to press the green button. I watch as the call rings off but my phone almost immediately begins to vibrate as the pub calls me back a second time.

I should answer and offer an explanation. It's the right thing to do… except that I can't. Not now.

The call rings off again and I continue staring at my phone, waiting for it to buzz once more. If things were reversed, there's every chance I'd keep calling until someone either answered or blocked my number. If they did that, I'd get another number and try from that.

I never should have called Penny. I was wrong and I know it.

I'm not one of those people who thinks I'm right about everything. One of those psychopaths who bangs on about having no regrets because it makes me who I am, as if I'm the only person who counts.

Except I don't get an immediate chance to do anything about it – because that's when my doorbell sounds.

FIVE

The silhouette through the rippled glass lets me know who's on the other side of the front door before I open it. Aki, my ex-boyfriend, is a big guy, well over six foot and the sort of person that would definitely be called a 'gentle giant' by a newspaper if he ever got famous.

When I open the door, it's almost as if he's been taken by surprise. He was leaning against the wall but jumps into an upright position and slips his phone into his pocket.

We blink at each other for a moment, more like acquaintances than a former couple. That's probably why we're *not* a couple. No big fall-out, no ill feeling… more ambivalence than anything else. It was fun and then it wasn't. A grown-up ending to a not very grown-up relationship.

'You messaged me,' he says.

I'm immediately blank, wondering what he's on about, when he adds: 'Something about mail…?'

'Oh, right… do you want to come in?'

Aki straightens a little, standing unnecessarily taller as if the mildest of electric shocks has pulsed through him. The reason is immediately apparent as he takes a small step to the side to reveal the bundle of piled curls who is sitting and scowling in the car behind him.

His current girlfriend is named Angel, although I'm unsure if that's her real name, or self-given. What's more important than her name is that she can give a stare of such intense animosity that it's as if she's trying to strip wallpaper with the force of nothing but her own mind.

I momentarily feel the power of that glare until Aki shuffles his weight onto the other foot and blocks it.

'I've only got a minute,' he says – although what he's *really* saying is that he's only got a minute until Angel marches along the driveway and burns holes through us with her fiery death beam.

I lead him along the hall into the kitchen, where his letter is sitting on the table… or at least I *thought* that's where it was. What's there now is the article from the envelope, plus the yet-to-be-filed-in-the-bin Liberal Democrat flyer. Aki's letter has gone walkabout.

'It's somewhere around here,' I say, talking largely to myself as I start to look through my 'keep' pile of letters, which is next to the microwave. When I can't find Aki's letter there, I start flipping through the cookbooks, before checking the bin, in case I accidentally threw it away. It wouldn't be the first time.

By the time I find it on top of the microwave – which was essentially right in front of me – Aki has picked up the clipped article about Jane Craven.

'What's this?' he asks.

The slip of paper looks so tiny and delicate in between his massive fingers. I feel a nonsensical moment of worry that he might damage it, in the same way I had a second of fear when I thought Mum could tear it in half. It's more than a simple scrap.

'Nothing,' I reply.

'Where's it from?'

'I dunno. I found it in a drawer.'

I hold Aki's letter out towards him but he pays it no attention as he continues to scan the article. I wonder if he's spotted Jane's misshapen ear. I didn't at first but, once I'd seen it, it became the first thing upon which my eyes focused.

'Weird thing to find in a drawer,' he says. This time he picks up the envelope in which the article arrived. The one with my name on the front and no stamp.

I waft his letter towards him once more as Aki slowly returns the envelope and article to the table and then takes his mail from me.

'You'll have to change your address,' I reply.

'Did someone mail that to you?' he asks, with a nod towards the table.

'I told you I found it in a drawer.'

We're at an impasse where he must know I'm lying and yet I'm not prepared to give any ground.

'Change your address,' I say again, firmer this time.

He blinks away from the table until he's focused on me. 'I have. I did it online but there was something about their system being down. I tried calling but ended up in one of those loops where you're pressing "one" for this or "two" for that. It's impossible to actually talk to someone.'

There's a creak from the hallway and I immediately know what that means as Aki and I both turn to take in Angel. We didn't know one another before she and Aki got together and I suppose we don't particularly know one another now. I know the sort, though. A person for whom irrational jealousy and mistrust is the default setting, with volcanic anger only a little behind.

I'm not friends with her on Facebook but, if I were, I guarantee there'd be drama on a daily basis. She's a definite 'You OK, hun?'-type. There are smaller red flags outside the Chinese Embassy.

Angel purrs as she looks towards Aki. 'I was wondering where you were. You've been a while…'

At most, he's been two minutes – and considering we left the front door open, he was visible from the street at all times.

No sooner has that thought occurred to me, than it's as if Angel has read it. She spins towards me and growls a decidedly non-purred: 'What?'

'I didn't say anything.'

'You're always texting him, calling him, wanting him over.'

I can't prevent the sigh but I do stop myself from rolling my eyes – and that's an achievement in itself. 'I told him there was mail. I didn't say to come over. If he wanted me to open it and send him a picture, I'd have done that. If he told me to put it in the bin and never text him again, I'd do that. I can show you the message if you want. It was very simple.'

'Oh, I know what you sent him.'

I motion towards the letter in Aki's hand. 'What's the problem, then?'

Angel is coiled, ready to argue, as she points a long pink fingernail that surely qualifies as a weapon towards me. From the way Aki steps in between us, he knows it too. He says: 'We've got to get off' – although it's unclear which of us he's talking to.

'Change the address,' I tell him.

'I've tried!'

'Try harder.'

Aki bundles Angel back along the hallway and out the front door. He turns to give me something close to an apologetic raise of the eyebrows. I almost blow him a kiss, simply because I know it'll drive Angel wild. I might have done when I was younger; before The Bad Thing happened, before life had perspective.

'Change the address,' I repeat – and this time he doesn't answer.

SIX

My Saturdays all begin in a similar way – with an argument over an apostrophe. I know that sounds far too rock and roll for a person in their mid-thirties but my life is what it is.

This particular argument is more passive aggressive than anything else. The whiteboard at my side of the hall reads 'Creators' Club Paint Station', while the one across the way, at the side of my friend Stephen, reads 'Creator's Club Story Station'.

He catches my eye from across the room and gives a small smirk, knowing precisely what he's doing. It's the same thing he does every week.

The Creators' Club, as it's *definitely* known, is a twice-weekly group to help young people pick up arts and crafts. Growing up, there always seemed to be a lot of weekend options for kids who were into sports but almost nothing for those who wanted to make things. Because of that, Stephen and I decided to do something about it. We got a block booking on the biggest room at the community centre to put together our own club. Things started slowly but, two years on, our regular attendance is up to sixty young people from across the county – plus a handful of others who drop in depending on what our guest stations might be.

It's the sort of thing I wished was around when I was young.

At my station, there are eleven kids sitting in a circle, with a trio of soft toys on a table in the centre, which they're painting.

Stephen is helping a smaller group with constructing a short story. Elsewhere around the hall, one of the mothers is doing a make-up tutorial, while another is showing youngsters how to make and fix clothes. There's a long-running quilting corner, where a group of predominantly girls have been making blankets for months.

Our guest this week is a local musician, who's showing off some guitar chords to eight or nine young people.

I walk around the outside of the paint station, taking in everyone's evolving work. It's fair to say there is a differing level of ability – although that's largely the point. There are no marks at the end and no competition. Young people can turn up, pay their two quid, and decide whatever it is they want to spend their Saturday morning doing.

I stop behind Oliver, as I often do when he's at the paint station. He's thirteen and one of those kids who is seemingly a natural at whatever he wants to do. Stephen says he's comfortably the best storyteller when he spends a morning writing stories and, when he turned his hand to pottery for our guest slot a month or so ago, he was the only one who attempted something more complicated than a standard pot. The thin-necked jug he came up with off his own bat was something that even the instructor couldn't believe had been made by a novice.

Today, Oliver's watercolour is somehow both as realistic as a photograph and yet his own interpretation. The facial features of the soft toys have been exaggerated to make them appear more cartoon-like but it's managed to maintain the realism of being a toy.

When he realises I'm at his shoulder, Oliver half-turns and looks up to me. 'Is it okay?'

I almost laugh at him, because it's incredible he can have such raw talent and still wonder whether it's good enough. If he came from a rich family, he'd be filled with a misplaced sense of confidence that would have him thinking everything he ever tried was destined to come off and that, if it didn't, it was somebody else's fault.

He doesn't, though.

Oliver's clothes are at least two sizes too big for him. It doesn't matter if it's freezing or baking outside, he wears the same jeans with a hole in the knee, plus a raggedy red sweatshirt. I've always assumed they're hand-me-downs from an older brother I've never met, although it's a guess. He could be an only child. The battered olive green backpack at his feet has a large blue-black ink stain along the bottom and there's a half-tear through the flap at the top.

'It's excellent,' I say. 'As good as all your work.'

Oliver shrinks into himself a little, craving the praise but not sure what to do with it.

It's easy to make judgements about someone and their home life from the snapshot few hours I see them every week.

It was his third week at Creators' Club that Oliver sheepishly told me he'd forgotten his £2. Everybody is a volunteer and nobody makes a profit but it's a nominal fee to cover the cleaning costs from week to week.

I told him he could stay that week but then, when he nervously told me something similar the next week, it was clear that his memory wasn't the problem. His jeans are long enough to go over his shoes if he doesn't roll them up – and his bony, angular shoulders tell another story of their own.

I said not to bother about the money and have been covertly dropping coins into the bucket ever since to ensure everything adds up.

Oliver turns back to his painting and swishes a perfect stroke across the background. I crouch close and lean in, so that only he can hear.

'Don't rush off at the end,' I say. 'I've got something for you. Find me before you leave.'

He turns a little, frowning with confusion. 'What have you got?'

'I'll show you later.'

I push myself up into a standing position. It's a simple action but one of the exercises I had to do over and over when I was learning how to stand and walk after The Bad Thing. It's incredible what I used to take for granted.

The next hour and a half or so is spent doing laps of the hall, generally checking in on what everyone's doing. It's become such a machine over the past couple of years that, even if I was a micromanager, there'd be no need. Everyone knows what they're doing and gets on with it. The wildcard is always the guest – but the friendly guitar player has already taught the small group a short ditty, which they're happily repeating over and over.

I wait until Stephen's attention is taken up with one of the children and then change the placing of the apostrophe on his board before continuing as normal.

Parents start to mass near the doors a little before noon, ready to whisk their children away. I hang back at the far side of the hall, and Oliver finds me close to where the quilters were working. His bag is slung across his back and he looks so small in the oversized clothes, as if *he's* shrunken in the wash.

I pass him a plastic bag and then stand between him and the front of the hall, so that nobody can see what we're up to.

'What's inside?' he asks.

'Have a look.'

He unfolds the bag from the contents until he's revealed a sketchbook and a metal tin of coloured pencils.

'I had them lying around the house,' I say, hoping it doesn't sound too much like the lie that it is.

Oliver's eyes widen as he alternates between looking at the two items. 'Are these for me?'

'You'll get better use from them than I ever will.'

He twists the tin of pencils in his hand, showing off the price tag that I've forgotten to remove. I act quickly, momentarily taking it back as I peel away the sticker before returning it.

'You can put them in your bag,' I say, with a nod towards his backpack.

He glances past me towards the entrance and seemingly understands as he does precisely as I suggested.

'Are you sure you don't mind?' he asks.

'Positive.'

'Just to borrow, though...?'

I start to tell him that they're his to keep but then realise it's not really what he's asking.

'Mum might not let me have them,' he adds. Quieter this time.

'You can borrow them as long as you want,' I reply. 'If your mum needs to talk to me, then I'm here every week. I can explain that you're only borrowing the pad and pencils.'

As he re-zips his bag, the grin on Oliver's face spreads. He's never been one for eye contact but there's a moment in which he catches my gaze before he quickly looks away once more. That second of utter joy says more than he ever might out loud.

'I'll look after them,' he says.

'I know you will.'

'I've got to go.'

'See you next time.'

I stand and watch as Oliver ducks his head and hurries towards the doors. His mum is waiting just inside the hall, one hand jammed into her jacket pocket, the other scratching her head. The light catches one of the many rings on her fingers and glints its way towards me. Her stare is nothing quite as ferocious as Angel's but I feel it across the hall nonetheless.

'You're gonna get yourself in trouble one of these weeks...'

I blink around to see Stephen at my side.

'Doing what?' I reply.

'You know. I hope his mum doesn't mind.'

'It was only a pad and some pencils I had lying around the house.'

I find myself rolling the price sticker between my fingers, before dispatching it into the nearest bin. Stephen doesn't say anything about it but we stand together for a couple of minutes, watching as the hall empties.

'What's been up with you?' he asks.

The distraction of Creators' Club has been welcome but it was only ever going to be a few hours.

'What d'you mean?'

'You've been distant this morning. Not as annoying as usual.'

I resist the smile, not wanting him to know he's got me.

'Something got posted through my door,' I say. 'An old newspaper article.'

'What about?'

'It was a story about a six-month-old girl who was stolen from the back of a car.'

'Recently?'

I turn to take him in. There's confusion on Stephen's face as he wonders why I'm telling him this.

'The stolen girl had an ear like mine,' I say. 'Not a bit like mine but *exactly* like mine.' A pause. 'She was stolen thirty-four years ago…'

I dig into my bag for the article and hand it to him, watching as his brow ripples while he skims the content. He blinks because we went out drinking in town for my thirty-fourth birthday. He always teases me because he's younger than me by a month and he wants me to know that I'll always be the oldest.

Stephen opens his mouth to speak but nothing emerges, so he closes it again. He passes me back the clipping and, when he does manage to get the words out, there's a degree of surprise, although not the outright stunned amazement that I might have expected.

'That's quite the coincidence,' he says.

'I talked to Mum about it.'

'What did she say?'

'She was weird about it. She said she remembered giving birth to me and didn't get why I was bringing it to her.'

'She was probably as shocked as you.' He pauses, waiting for me to reply. When I don't, he adds: 'Are things all right between you?'

I gulp, not sure how to reply. Stephen knows the only family I have is Mum. We've seen more of one another since Dad died than we ever did in the years before that.

'I guess,' I reply. 'We didn't talk much after I asked her about the article.'

'It is an odd thing. She might have felt like you're accusing her of something.'

'I figured out that much. I didn't know how else to ask her about it.'

Stephen mumbles something under his breath that might have been a 'Right…'

I tell him about Lower Woolton, of which he's never heard either. Then there's the Black Sheep and my aborted phone call. Stephen and I know each other well enough that I half expect a disapproving stare, though it never comes. Perhaps he knows me even better than I think?

'Why don't we just go there?' he says.

'Where?'

'Lower Woolton, or whatever it's called.' He takes his phone from his pocket, types something into it, and then turns it around so that I can see the map. 'It's only two hours to get there,' he adds. 'What else have we got to do this afternoon?'

I start to argue, except that he makes it sound so obvious and simple. Lower Woolton is a couple of counties away. Not down the road but not exactly the Scottish Highlands, either.

'I'll drive,' he says.

'I don't—'

'There's no point in sitting around worrying about it. Let's go find out.'

'But what if…?'

He fishes around his pockets for car keys. When he finds them, he tosses them from one hand to the other. 'You're not the only one with news,' he says. 'Let's go for a drive in the country and we can talk.'

'What's your news?'

'I'll tell you later. Let's go.'

He takes a few steps across the hall and then turns to make sure I'm following. He really does know me this well. If it was on me, I'd spend days or weeks worrying about this instead of making a relatively short drive and seeing what I can find out.

As we're on our way out, the cleaners are on their way in. Considering we pack everything away that we use, there's not too much to do – although it was part of the contract with the community centre that we have a handover each week. We say our usual hello-goodbyes and then cross the road to Stephen's car.

It's the sort of day where the sky is an endless grey and it feels as if the sun might never rise again. I pull my jacket tighter as a bone-chilling wind sends the tree branches rattling.

Stephen has stopped to tie his lace and as I turn to complain about him making me wait in the cold, I notice a woman in a short red coat waiting at the bottom of the community centre steps. I would have almost certainly walked past her without a second glance – but she's spotted me and doesn't bother to mask the way she's staring across the road.

I turn towards the car as it plips open but, when I twist back, the woman is still watching.

She has long brown hair with a reddish tinge and is probably somewhere in her late-twenties or early thirties. She's too far away for any other features to be overly identifiable. I have no idea who she is.

I clamber into the passenger seat and the car dips and Stephen plonks himself into the driver's side and starts the engine.

'Do you know that woman?' I ask.

Stephen is about to lower the handbrake but stops himself as he ducks a little to look in the direction I'm pointing.

'Red jacket?'

'Yes.'

'Not a clue.' A pause. 'Why?'

'She was watching me.'

He crunches down the brake and then shifts the car into first. Every time he does this, it reminds me of how he refuses to drive my automatic. 'Probably wondering how long you've had your skirt tucked into your knickers.'

I immediately shuffle in the seat, reaching around to my back – which sends Stephen into a cacophony of giggles.

He pulls away and almost immediately shifts the car into second. By the time I manage to peer around him back towards the hall, the woman has gone.

SEVEN

In a straight line, Lower Woolton is around eighty miles from Macklebury. If there was a motorway between the two places, it would be close to an hour's journey – though that would be to underestimate quite how out of the way both places are.

Macklebury is nestled in the countryside, part of a series of nowhere towns and villages that are linked by narrow, winding lanes which are – at best – wide enough for two vehicles. Hedges grow high and verges sink low, while tractors trail slicks of mud that will sit barely touched on the road surface from season to season.

There is a wider, faster A-road close to Macklebury but that heads in the opposite direction, leaving Stephen and me stuck on the country lanes at an absolute maximum of fifty miles an hour. And that only happens on the straights.

Speed scares me – and Stephen knows that.

These are the sorts of roads where at least one car will end up in the ditch every time winter turns into spring and sunshine fuels the urge I've never felt to race and compete.

Stephen and I chat about our morning with the children as he drives and, as ever when we're together, time seems to travel at a faster pace. I would have sworn we'd only been talking for ten minutes but an hour has passed when we hit our first momentary pause in conversation.

To my shame, I'd forgotten about Stephen's promise of 'news' but it comes back as he clears his throat with a gentle cough.

'I have a date tomorrow,' he says.

'It's not someone from one of your dodgy apps again, is it?'

'All right, Grandma. Everyone meets online nowadays.'

'I'm not against meeting someone from the internet, it's more your apps that worry me.'

'Didn't you and Aki meet in a curry place? I don't think you're one to criticise.'

He says this with his usual tone which, if I didn't know him better, might make me think he was being serious. There's a fine line between joking and mean and Stephen runs it tight.

'That's a fair point,' I reply. 'I'm never going out with anyone I meet at a curry house in future.'

Stephen isn't listening: 'We're going out tomorrow afternoon. I figured it was calmer on a Sunday. I like daytime dates. Less pressure.'

There's a hint of excitement in his tone, which isn't really like him. He's too good at keeping things close to his chest and using humour to deflect. I wait for a punchline that doesn't come.

'Who's the lucky guy?' I ask.

'Justin-something. He's training to be a doctor.'

'I knew it'd be someone who has to wear a uniform for his job. Couldn't you find a suitable fireman?'

Stephen grins. I know him too well.

He slows and pulls into the verge as he allows a car coming the other way along the narrow lane to pass. We chat but it's the sort of talk that's there and gone, not because it's inconsequential but because that's what it's like with true friends. We've spent entire nights in one another's company when I've woken up the next morning and realised that hours and hours had flown by.

Country lane twists into country lane and, aside from getting stuck behind some cyclists for a few minutes, the rest of the journey is uneventful.

The sign for Lower Woolton is coated with a greeny-brown moss and someone has drawn a cock and balls in the corner. Stephen slows as we pass, saying the balls are too hairy for his liking.

As we enter Lower Woolton, there are rows of semi-detacheds and then a shuttered post office that's next to a Londis. There are boarded-up shops and an off-licence with an A-frame board outside advertising a deal on twelve-packs of Carling. A group of half a dozen tweens are hanging around outside, passing a cigarette or vape thing between them. I assume they're waiting to see if someone might buy them booze, though that might say more about me than them.

In the middle of the town there's a big church, plus fluorescent boards on the opposite side, next to a hall, that are advertising the local am-dram performance of *Pirates Of Penzance*.

I'm not sure what I was expecting from the town but it feels incredibly familiar. It's not a sense of déjà vu, or of having been here before, it's that this could be Elwood or Macklebury. The place I grew up, or the place I live. The names are different but the places are the same.

Stephen has gone quiet ever since we passed the welcome sign, which adds to a sense of growing unease that's building inside me. I want to tell him to turn around and drive us home – and yet I want him to keep going. I think of Mum in her chair and the aggrieved, betrayed tone to her voice as she said she remembered giving birth to me.

I shouldn't be here.

I open my mouth to tell Stephen to stop, except the words don't come. We pass another row of houses and then he slows to take a turn that sends us past a large green with huge white cricket screens on either side. There's a man on a ride-on mower zipping around the edges of the field, sending a spray of clippings into the air behind him.

There is no traffic in either direction but we reach a red light of a pelican crossing and so Stephen slows to a stop. Nobody is crossing but there is a pair of seven- or eight-year-old boys sitting on a wall close to the crossing who are making no attempt to hide

how funny they find this. As soon as the light turns green and
Stephen pulls away, I twist to watch one of them dart from the
wall to press the button once again.

When I turn back, the Black Sheep is in front of us. I spot the
flower baskets first. They're hanging as they were in the TripAdvisor
pictures, kaleidoscopes of colour sprouting from the tops.

Stephen pulls into the pub car park and reverses into a space, all
without saying a word. In front of us a man, woman and child get
out of their car. The man pats his pockets and mutters something
to his wife as their kid bounds ahead, clearly knowing where he's
going. The adults play catch-up as they head around into the beer
garden at the side of the pub. It's too cold to be outside and, within
another moment, they're through the doors and out of sight.

'Are we going in?'

It's the first thing either of us has said since we passed the
town's sign. Stephen leaves it hanging and I neither reply, nor
move. Not right away.

'What if Penny's inside?' I say eventually.

'Then we'll say hello.'

'But who will I say I am?'

'We'll figure it out. Show her your ear.'

The idea sends a shiver through me. There's a sense that I
suddenly don't know who I am. That walking into the pub and
announcing myself might unleash something that can't be put
away again, regardless of what comes from it.

Stephen opens his door. 'I'm going inside,' he says.

'Don't—'

It's too late because he knows I won't make the decision by
myself. He's already halfway across the car park before I've got off
my seat belt and opened the door.

Unlike the family from before, he heads around to the front,
waiting for me to catch him and then theatrically pressing the
button on his fob to lock the car from afar.

'No going back now,' he says.

He waits, wondering if I really will stop him. When I don't, he pushes through the door into the main part of the pub. There's a burst of sound – the same voices, clinking glasses and music that I heard in the background of my aborted phone call.

The pub is wider and more open than any of the photos made it appear. There are booths tucked around the walls and a smattering of tables between those and the long bar. A pool table is on one side, with half a dozen blokes hanging around offering unwanted advice to one another.

So, *so* familiar.

'You're limping.'

I look up to realise Stephen is a few paces ahead of me. There are ripples of concern across his forehead.

I straighten myself and stretch down below my knee to make sure the compressed part of my prosthetic limb is still in place. When I realise that it is, I slot a pair of fingers into the small gap around the cup in which my residual limb sits, making sure the foam pad hasn't become squashed on the journey.

Everything's in place.

'Are you okay?' he asks.

'I think so.'

'I didn't really mean it when I said no going back. We don't have to be here.'

He says this a little more quietly and I want to tell him that I sometimes find myself limping when I'm reluctant to do something. It's a quirk that nobody else knows about. An unconscious habit I keep to myself.

'We're here now,' I reply.

Stephen turns and we stand next to one another looking towards the bar. There's only one man serving and I remember the voice who answered the phone the day before. It's probably the same person. He looks like a barman probably should, with thick forearms and no-nonsense, alert eyes that make it look like he could spot trouble from a couple of hundred metres away. He certainly spots Stephen and me as he scans across us, silently wondering why we're standing around not doing anything.

I look around the pub, wondering if Penny might be clearing glasses, not that I know what she looks like.

In the end, and with me seemingly frozen to the spot, Stephen takes the initiative by striding across to the bar. I slot in behind him, sensing the hairs on the back of my neck standing on end.

'Is Penny here?'

Stephen sounds confident, as if he's asking about a friend or neighbour.

I half expect the barman to frown and ask who we are, or perhaps even chuck us out.

He doesn't, though.

He half turns towards the open door behind him, as if he's about to shout for someone.

EIGHT

The shout never comes. The barman licks his lips and then turns back to us with a blink, as if he's only just remembered something.

'It's her day off,' he says.

Stephen handles this far more confidently than I would have done. The reply is instant, without any sort of hesitation. 'Do you know when she's back in?'

'Tomorrow.'

I expect that to be that – we tried – except that Stephen must have lost his mind. He's suddenly some sort of investigative journalist desperate for the truth.

'I don't suppose you could tell us where she lives…?'

I try my best to stand up straight and stoic, as if this is a normal thing to be asking.

There's definitely a scowl on the barman's face this time as he looks between us, perhaps wondering if we're people he should know.

'Who's asking?'

'We're friends of hers.'

'If you were friends, you'd know where she lives.'

He has us there.

Stephen starts to reply with something about not having been here in a while – but the barman has heard enough. A man is standing close to the till and wafting a £10 note in the air, as if he's an Eton student about to burn it in front of some homeless guy. The barman shuffles across and asks the man what he's after before giving us another glare and then reaching for a pint glass.

I'm about to question Stephen about his potential loss of sanity when my phone begins to buzz. Mr Bonner's name is on the screen, so I hold the phone up to show Stephen and then hurry outside to answer it.

'Is that Hope?' he asks.

'It's me.'

'It's Jack Bonner, from next door.'

There's something wonderfully sweet about the way he introduces himself on the phone. He's called me a handful of times in recent months: often about trivial things, such as to say that he's brought my bins in for me, or that he signed for a parcel. I don't think texts are his thing and every call will come with the same introduction.

I have to resist the urge to call him 'Mr Bonner'.

'Hi, Jack,' I say.

'There was a woman out front earlier. I thought you should know.' A momentary pause and then: 'You told me to call if I saw anyone hanging around the house.'

'Did you recognise her?' I ask.

'No idea, love. She was about your age, in a red coat. I didn't know if she was one of your friends. I thought you'd want to know.'

I picture him in his living room, twitching every time he sees movement at the end of the drive, in case it's someone about to head towards my door. I shouldn't have asked him. It was too much of an imposition.

Except there *was* a woman in red jacket waiting outside the community centre earlier who I thought was watching me.

'Did she knock on my door?' I ask.

'I don't think so. I saw her walking past a good three or four times. She'd stop and look at your place and then carry on. I opened my door the final time and she walked off before I could say anything.'

I'm torn between the guilt of picturing Mr Bonner getting off his sofa and then hurrying through the house as best he could, all for me – and the curiosity of the mystery woman's identity.

'I'm a couple of hours away,' I tell him. 'Thank you for calling. Hopefully everything's fine.'

'Right y'are, love. I'll let you know if she comes back. Can't be too careful nowadays.'

There's a clunk and then a muttered, barely audible grumble as I sense he's unclear whether he's hung up. I do it for him, pressing the red button and then dispatching my phone back into my bag. As I do that, Stephen emerges from the pub.

'Barman's not having it,' he says.

'I'm not surprised.'

'We could come back tomorrow.'

'Don't you have that date?'

'I'll move it.'

'No you won't.'

He turns and half looks backwards, twisting between me and the pub. 'We could ask around today,' he says. 'Some locals are bound to know who Penny Craven is.'

'I don't think that's her name any more. When I said that to her on the phone, she said that used to be her name. I think it's Morse.'

'We could ask about Penny…?'

I shake my head. 'You might be that much of a stalker but I'm not. Besides, even if we found her, I don't think it's a good thing to go knocking on her door to say that someone gave me an article about her baby that was stolen thirty-odd years ago.'

Stephen nods at this. 'Good point.' He twists between me and the pub again. 'What do you want to do?'

The air bites at my throat and standing still isn't an option on a day like today. I take out my phone and look at the photograph I took of the article, before showing it to Stephen.

'We could look for Marston Close,' I say. 'That's where Jane Craven was taken from.'

Stephen pulls his coat tighter and does up his top button. He has out his own phone and has typed in the details before I have the chance.

'It's about a mile away,' he says. 'Shall we drive?'

'I don't mind a walk. We can get a better idea of the town on foot.'

He turns a little on the spot and I know he's wondering whether I'm up to this with my prosthetic. He's the person I've talked to most about what it's like to learn to walk again – but it's still our elephant in the room. The fact he caught me limping seems to have thrown him off.

'I'm not an invalid,' I say.

'I didn't mean that – but I can drive.'

'Just because *you* hate the environment and want to cause flooding on a global scale, doesn't mean I do.'

Stephen hesitates but only for a moment, before he leads the way. He's holding his phone out in front of him at arm's length like my dad used to when he was trying to read a label without his glasses.

Being cold is one of the things that will make my residual limb ache at the end of a day. The therapist explained that it can be like a person's fingers or toes, in that it swells and shrinks based upon the temperature. A hot day is worse than a cold day – but neither is ideal.

We head past the pub and keep going along what turns out to be a short high street. There's a part of me that wants to picture it how it might have been thirty-four years ago. Now, there are cars parked nose-to-tail along both sides of the street and intermittent signs telling people not to park here on a Wednesday because there's a market.

Everything else seems to be part of a chain. There's a Tesco Metro at one end and a Sainsbury's Local at the other. In between, there's a Starbucks, a Costa, a Greggs and a mishmash of banks and charity shops.

It could be Macklebury.

We get to the end of the High Street and then Stephen leads us around a corner, past a row of terraced houses. I have no idea in which direction we're heading but, whatever it is, there is more of a natural shield from the wind this way.

'My dad used to have a Vauxhall Cavalier,' Stephen says.

It takes me a moment to work out why he's said this but then I remember the article and that Jane was taken from a Cavalier. He skimmed it before we set off – though he must have taken in more than I thought.

'We never had a car,' I say. 'I used to get the bus, or Dad would ask Mr Hawthorne next door to give me a lift. Either that, or I'd walk. I walked everywhere up until… well…'

I don't finish the sentence. Sometimes I would but Stephen pointing out the limp has left me self-conscious.

There's a moment of silence and then Stephen replies: 'Everyone seemed to have a brown car when we were kids.'

He leaves that hanging but I'm not sure how to respond.

We're out of the town centre now and an ominous sense of discomfort is beginning to creep into my thoughts. I only realise Stephen has stopped walking when he calls my name. I'm a few steps past him and then realise I'm at a corner where there's a sign for 'Marston Close' attached to the wall of the nearest house. Over the road on the perpendicular street is a similar board that reads: 'Vicarage Hill'.

'I think it's here,' Stephen says.

I move back towards him and we stand close to the corner looking up and down the street.

'There's no newsagent any longer,' I say.

The street is lined with three- and four-storey houses, the sort of places that might have been converted into an upmarket office for a dentist, solicitor or accountant. Either that or a house that almost nobody could afford to buy any longer.

Stephen points towards the outlier. There's a sign for a funeral director on a small patch of grass and behind that is the only building that's different to everything else. It's a single storey with a low roof and space for a couple of cars at the side.

'It could have been there,' he says.

He's right in that it's the only building anywhere near that doesn't look like a house. Many of the places have tall gates across the front, along with high walls or towering leylandii. On a middle-of-nowhere street, in a middle-of-nowhere town, the security measures feel like ludicrous overkill.

There are far fewer cars parked on the street here, with each property having a large driveway at the side. The article said that Penny's brown Vauxhall Cavalier was parked close to this corner and, with the wide street, I can almost picture it outside what is now the funeral director's.

We're distracted by the click-clacking of an old woman heading along the street, wheeling a shopping carrier behind her. She gives us a quick glance and then keeps going – except she doesn't get past because Stephen calls a friendly 'hello' in her direction.

She stops and turns, taking us both in properly.

Stephen nods towards the funeral director's place. 'Do you know if that used to be a newsagent?' he asks.

The woman is momentarily hesitant but then she starts to nod. 'Years ago,' she says.

'How long ago did it shut?'

She puffs out a long breath, which sends a cloud up into the air. 'Five years? Ten? Ages. Used to get all my magazines there but there's nowhere now.' She pauses for a moment and then adds: 'Did you used to live round here?'

Stephen glances to me and, just for a moment, I think he's about to say that I did.

'Not really,' he says. 'I think I might have visited a few years ago.'

The woman opens her mouth but then closes it again without saying anything. Stephen thanks her and then she turns and continues clicking along the pavement.

Stephen and I stand together for a moment, looking towards the other side of the street. It feels like such a serene area, the type of place where nothing bad ever happens. I can't picture where someone might have gone with a snatched child. If Penny was only away from the car for three minutes, whoever took Jane would have either had to have their own car or must have run off at quite the rate. If not that, they would have had to run into the grounds of a nearby house. The two intersecting roads are long and straight, not like the newer estates with their mazes of cut-throughs and shortcuts.

Was that child… me?

'I don't know what to say,' Stephen begins. He is watching me with his arms folded. I can see his breath now, too, and it's as if someone's opened a freezer.

'Thank you for driving out here,' I say.

A hint of a smile appears on Stephen's face as he offers me his hand, which I take. 'Is that a thinly disguised way of saying that you're ready to go home?' he asks.

'You know me too well,' I reply.

NINE

Stephen drops me off outside my house and we sit together for a short while, enjoying the heat from the car vents.

'Let me know how your date goes tomorrow,' I tell him.

'What are you going to do about Lower Woolton?'

'I don't know. Maybe leave it.'

I can tell from the pause that Stephen isn't sure about this. 'If you need to talk…'

'Thanks for the lift.'

As soon as I open the door, the frosty air blusters inside. I get out quickly and then, as Stephen pulls away, I head to Mr Bonner's door. I knock on the rippled glass and wait for the call of 'yes' to be shortly followed by the internal light being switched on.

When he opens the door, Mr Bonner breaks into a smile. 'Chilly, isn't it?' he says. 'It's usually warmer by this time of year.'

'Not like this in your day, huh?'

He laughs at this and then the smile settles. 'She's not been back,' he adds. 'I've been watching but I must've scared her off. If she turns out to be one of your friends then make sure you apologise for me.'

'You are kinda scary.'

Another smile before he turns serious. 'Did I do the right thing? I wasn't sure.'

'You were great. Thank you very much.'

He nods towards the inside of his house. 'I know it's Saturday night and that you've probably got somewhere to go – but if you fancy that game of Scrabble…?'

It's a friendly question but there's something under the surface, too. A sense of… loneliness, perhaps.

'I would, it's just—'

'Oh, it's fine.' Mr Bonner speaks quickly, over the top of me. 'Just a suggestion,' he adds. 'Maybe another night.'

I motion towards the low fence, ready to step across. When Mr Bonner found out about my leg, he offered to remove the fence entirely, meaning I could walk from my house to his if that suited me. I told him that stepping over it would be good practice but I wondered afterwards if I'd somehow misread the intentions. He was trying to be nice, after all.

It's impossible not to feel bad about saying no to him.

'I'll see what time I get in later,' I say. 'I have to go out for a bit.'

'No worries, love. You have a good time. I'll be here if you change your mind.'

He hovers in the doorway and I almost *do* change my mind… except that forgetting about the article isn't an option. After the disappointment of Lower Woolton, it feels as if I have unfinished business tonight.

I wait until Mr Bonner has closed the door and then step across the fence onto my driveway. I dig through my bag until I find my keys and then I unlock my car.

I drive to Mum's house without considering the route too much. I've been thinking about her reaction to the article all day, how she said that she remembered giving birth to me. The more time that's passed since she said it, the odder it feels. But perhaps it's because I was too direct and harsh. She didn't deserve the way I spoke to her.

After parking outside, I let myself into the house and call out to let her know it's me. I expect her voice to sound back from the living room, letting me know she's in there – except that there's silence. Not even the television is blaring.

To say this is unusual is an understatement. I can barely remember the last time I entered this house to be met with silence. It's probably when Mum and Dad last went on holiday together and I would come around to water the plants. That would have been five or six years back.

'Mum...?'

There's no answer.

I poke my head into the living room, but Mum's seat is empty. A mug sits at the side of her chair, half-filled with stone-cold tea. The remote control, usually welded to her hand, is abandoned on the coffee table.

There is nobody in the kitchen, so I head back to the front of the stairs and start to go up.

'Mum...?'

I call louder this time but my voice echoes unanswered around the house and back to me.

The bed in Mum's room is made immaculately, as it always is. There were times when I'd swear she and Dad slept on top of the covers in order to not mess them up. She used to tell me that no matter how good or bad a day might have gone, getting to sleep in a well-made bed would make everything feel better. I understood the sentiment – but it was still a pain to be sitting downstairs waiting for the toaster to pop, only for Mum to repeat the same thing she said every day.

There's no sign of Mum in the bathroom and it's as I'm on my way downstairs that I smell the faint whiff of something burning. It's not strong, more the sort of scorched charring from a grill that would set off an overenthusiastic smoke alarm.

I head back into the kitchen, following my nose – except that the stove hasn't been left on, and neither has the toaster or cooker.

'Mum...?'

There's a chill that shouldn't be in the house. Dad always liked everything to be warm and he would crank the thermostat up to Death Valley in July levels. Mum once told me it was because he hadn't had any sort of heating in the place where he grew up – but that was one extreme and this was another. I'd frequently spend winters sitting indoors in shorts and T-shirts before having to change completely to go out into the cold. Mum has kept that going since Dad died… except that a breeze is bristling through a slim gap from where the back door isn't quite closed.

I pull it inwards and am met by a blast of cold that smacks me in the face like an open hand. My skin stings from the needles but the smell of burning is strong now.

The lights at the back are on, with a ringed cascade of white looping around the edge of the patio. It used to be a full lawn but Dad had the whole thing paved over a decade or so back. He said it would make it easier to entertain but the truth was that his knees weren't up to dragging around the mower any longer.

I see Mum now, standing with her back to the house, staring at what I first think is the fence. The lights from above have cast something close to a halo around her shape.

It's only as I say 'Mum' that she jumps in surprise and shrieks my name.

'You scared the life out of me,' she says – although that's far from the most disturbing thing.

There's a hose in her hand, with water dribbling into the grate at the bottom of the guttering. The way she moves quickly to block my view of what she's doing would be suspicious even if she wasn't so clumsily transparent in doing it.

I head across to where she's standing and squint down to the grate, where there's a scattering of blackened ashes in the process of disappearing into the sewer. The burning smell is particularly strong now – and I look around to spot the open barbecue smouldering.

At first I think she must have decided to cook outside, which would be out of character for her, even if it wasn't this cold.

There's no food on top of the grill, though. Not tonight.

Something else is burning. Something far more worrying.

I step around my mother until I'm directly in front of the grill where, flickering from white to orange to black, is a small stack of paper.

TEN

'What are you doing?'

There's no attempt to hide the accusing tone of my voice this time. I reach for the paper but the pages are too hot and the corner I do manage to grab crumbles to flakes of charcoal.

Mum is staring at me, apparently unable to talk. I move past her quickly, heading to the tap on the wall, which I turn off. The flow of water from the hose she's still holding slows and then stops, until spotted dots are left dripping into the gutter. By the time I get back to the gutter, whatever she was washing away has long gone.

'What were you burning?' I ask.

She shakes her head and blinks at me, as if not quite believing I'm in front of her. 'I didn't know you'd be round,' she says.

'What are you burning, Mum?'

Another blink and then her eyes are wide and unfocused. She drops the hose onto the ground, where it flops like a decapitated snake.

'Bank statements,' she says.

'You've got a shredder. I bought it for you.'

Her gaze flicks to the house and back again. The last time I saw her confused like this was after Dad's funeral, after the wake, when everyone had gone home and it was all final. I drove her home and it was impossible not to see her muddled wondering of what life would be like from now on. Of not knowing which of his old errands and jobs would be hers and which would go undone. She told me a few days later that she wasn't sure which side of the bed she should sleep on any longer, because it didn't feel right being on hers without a presence at her side.

She has that same haunted look now.

'The shredder's jammed,' she says.

'You never said anything.'

'I forgot. It's happened before and it sometimes fixes itself.'

I nod towards the grill, where a soft orange continues to glow in the coals at the bottom of the tray. At the side, I now notice the bottle of flame accelerant and the ignition wand that usually sits in the drawer next to the cooker.

'Why the hurry to burn bank statements?'

'I was, um…' She pauses for a second or two and then concludes with: 'I was after something to do.'

We stand for a moment, staring at each other as our breaths pool into one another's and swirl up and into the night.

I glance to the barbecue again and, though there are corners of white paper, whatever was in the middle has been cremated into cinders. There's no sign of any bank logos.

Mum suddenly becomes herself, taking a couple of steps around and ushering me towards the house. 'Let's get inside,' she says. 'It's so much colder than it usually is at this time of year. We'll both catch our death.'

I allow myself to be shepherded into the kitchen and then Mum locks the back door. She picks up the kettle and carries it across to the sink, where she fills it from the tap.

'Have you got time for a brew?' she asks.

'I suppose.'

She puts the kettle on its stand and clicks the button, before busying herself around the room. She re-coils the kitchen roll so that there's no hanging flap – and then starts to reorder the cutlery drawer for no apparent reason.

'How come you came over?' she asks.

I don't answer immediately, watching as she continues to shift forks from one side of the drawer to another.

'I was in the area,' I say.

Mum makes a mix of a 'hrrm' and an 'mmm' sound. More of an acknowledgement that I've spoken as opposed to anything else. She has her back to me as she continues to fiddle.

I'd come over to tell her about visiting Lower Woolton and say that I was sorry for the suspicion with which I spoke to her the previous day. That all feels stuck now. Words that won't be said. For the first time ever, I find myself wondering if I can trust her.

It's a feeling that's so startling, it sends me spiralling back to childhood. The closest thing I can remember is being six years old, when Karen at school told me that Santa didn't exist. The fact that he was real had never been in doubt for me but, in that moment, from nowhere, I wasn't one hundred per cent sure.

I feel that now. The denial and the confusion, which is mixed by a teeny-tiny voice inside telling me that I know the *real* truth.

'I need to pop upstairs,' I say.

Mum continues rattling through the drawers as I head back through the hallway. 'Pop upstairs' has always been our code for needing the toilet. One of my friends at primary school had their bathroom downstairs and, the first time I went to their house, I got a blank stare from her mum when I said I needed to pop upstairs. I hadn't realised it was an odd thing to say until then.

When I get upstairs now, I don't head into the bathroom. I should have checked before, when I was looking for Mum, but I do it now instead.

My old room is not how it used to be. Gone are the posters, the bookshelves and the boxes of assorted tat that used to live under my bed. There were empty journals, cinema tickets, braided wristbands, an old school tie, plus so many photographs all piled on top of one another. Trinkets I couldn't face throwing out until the day it all went on a whim that I still regret. The room had character then. It was an expression of who I was and, though I've not lived in this house for fifteen years or so, there's never a time when I open the door and don't feel a degree of having lost something.

It's now a bordered, boring cream-coated guest room, in which I don't think Mum has ever hosted a guest. It's an Ed Sheeran B-side in a world of rock and roll.

I'm not sure how I knew what I was going to find in here – but it's right in front of me. The hatch that leads up to the attic is open, with the foldaway ladder stretched down to the floor. Even though the only access was via my room, the attic always used to be Dad's domain. The Christmas decorations and fake tree would be kept up there and he would make a big song and dance of going up to get them at the end of November every year. He'd say he liked to make the house look festive for any visitors but it was always for himself. I think he enjoyed Christmas more than any of us and, because of that, I still feel a twinge when Christmas trees start to appear in people's windows.

In the entire time I lived here, I never once knew of Mum going into the attic… except that she definitely has now. Despite her knees and the pain in her shoulders and back, she's come upstairs, stretched up with a pole to pull down the hatch, and then clambered into the loft.

The wooden stairs creak as they take my weight. When I was relearning everything, steps were one of the hardest hurdles to get over. Literally, I suppose. For a long time, it would be one stair at a time. I wouldn't trust my body to be able to put one foot in front of the other. I do now, though.

The squeaks and groans from the wood get louder as I reach the top – and then I'm blinking into the darkness. It's as cold up here as it was outside and, though I can't see my breath, I can sense it dissipating into the air.

I use the light on my phone to send a white glare around the space. Despite the chill, there are puffs of feathery yellow insulation laid flat in between the beams.

There's a Christmas tree, too.

It's on its side, the plasticky branches clamped tight to the stump with a series of cable ties that I can still picture Dad attaching shortly after New Year. That was when he'd admit with a sigh that it was time for everything to come down.

Mum hasn't had a Christmas tree since he died and I suppose there was no reason for the one up here to have been thrown out. The sight of it still momentarily leaves me like a statue. It's from a time when life was... *different*. Maybe better, maybe not – but certainly easier.

I really miss him.

I think I stare at that tree for a few seconds but it's hard to know.

There's a battered box next to it that has 'DECORATIONS' scrawled on the side in black marker. Dad's handwriting.

I make myself turn away because, if I don't, it feels as if I'd never move again.

On the other side of the attic is more fluffy yellow insulation, a couple of boxes in the furthest corner, and then, almost within touching distance, another box with 'KEEP' written on the side.

Still Dad's handwriting.

The flaps are open at the top. Mum must have been in it recently.

I stretch towards it, wanting to pull it towards me, but that's when there's a loud, echoing creak from below. I look down, through the hatch in which I'm half standing, to where Mum is at the base of the steps squinting up through the gloom.

'What are you looking for?' she asks.

'Nothing. The hatch was open, so I thought I'd have a look.' A beat. 'Why were *you* up here…?'

It's Mum's house and she has every right to be up here. She brushes away something from her top and takes a small step away from the ladder.

'Bank statements,' she says. 'I told you. You can help put the ladder away if you can manage it.'

She takes another step back and I'm stuck. The open box with 'KEEP' on the side is almost within reach, except there's no way to look through it without having to do so in front of Mum.

I make a decision on the spot, stretching and grabbing the box, before nudging it onto its side.

It's empty.

Whatever was inside – bank statements or not – they are now crisped ashes that Mum washed down the drain.

I clamber back down the stairs, carefully avoiding anything that might be eye contact with my mother. She would have seen me tip the box onto its side. She'll also be worrying about me climbing with my leg – because that's what she does.

At the bottom, I pick up the rod that was leaning against the bed and then use that to lever the stairs back into the hatch above. Mum is standing in the doorway, watching me, though not saying anything.

'I still need to use the bathroom,' I say.

She shuffles backwards onto the landing and then waits at the top of the stairs as I disappear through the door at the end of the hall. I lock it behind me and then sit on the closed toilet seat.

Everything feels wrong.

That box… Dad's handwriting… the paper barbecue.

I listen, wondering if Mum might still be standing on the landing for some reason. I haven't heard her go down the stairs but it would be odd if she's still up here. In the old, old days, we'd have arguments through this door about the length of time I'd spend getting ready in the mornings. They feel like such quaint disagreements now. So inconsequential.

I flush the toilet and then let the taps run for a few seconds. When I leave the bathroom, the hall is empty, although there's still no sound of the television from downstairs. I step gently across to Mum's bedroom door and then nudge it open.

There's nobody inside except, sitting in the corner, where it's been since the day I bought it, is the shredder. I could never understand why Dad kept it in their bedroom, as opposed to anywhere else – but Mum said it was something about the noise. I said it would make the same sound regardless of where it was kept and she shrugged in the way she always did when she didn't understand something Dad had done.

The plastic container underneath the shredding unit is a third full. It is mainly scraps of monochrome black print on white – but there is a distinct sliced-up HSBC logo on one of the scraps. I sift through the rest of the confetti and conclude from the mishmash of currency symbols and numbers that it's probably a series of bank statements. Statements which clearly haven't been burned.

I pick up a few of the scraps and then put everything back together before feeding the slivers of paper into the shredder jaws. There's not even a hint of a delay, let alone a blockage, as it burrs and slices the paper into even smaller pieces. The grinding booms around the room and possibly through the house. It only lasts a couple of seconds and then it's gone. Silence reigns again.

I wonder if Mum's heard – and then, coldly, I wonder if I should care.

ELEVEN

Mr Bonner's lights are off when I pull back onto my driveway. I wouldn't be in the mood for playing a game anyway but I still feel a twinge of sadness at letting him down.

I tap in the alarm code as I get into my house, waiting for the final beep to stop as I realise the heating has kicked into gear while I've been out. The house is toasty, although I'm not sure it feels welcoming. I head through the hall into the kitchen, where I dump my bag and keys – and then take the article and envelope out of my bag. I know exactly what it says without needing to look.

Distant and imprecise music hangs on the air and there are loud, happy voices shouting, joking and singing. Someone's having a party at the back of the house. It's not directly behind but perhaps a street away. It won't be long until someone closer to the noise calls the police and then there will be the inevitable fall-out on the town's Facebook page tomorrow. Someone will ask where all the noise was coming from and then someone else will wonder who called the police. Then the name-calling will start and then the local newspaper website will pick up on it.

I stand in the gloom for a while, watching the lights dance through the half-closed blinds.

Catching a parent in a lie is a strange feeling. A child thinks that a parent is all-knowing. It's only when someone becomes an adult themselves that they realise everyone's making it up as they go along and hoping for the best.

There's a clunk from the boiler that brings me back into the room – and I suddenly know what I'm going to do.

I head upstairs and into the spare bedroom. Unlike the one at Mum's house, my own spare bedroom does get used – mainly by Stephen. He'll come over for a brew and a catch-up, which often turns into a wine and whining session. He'll be too drunk to go home, so will bunk down until we both emerge for some toast at close to noon the next day.

There's a bed against the back wall and an IKEA dresser that Stephen and I spent almost three hours trying to put together. If two people can get through that and come out the other side without a casual manslaughter or two, then they can get through anything.

As well as that, there are five or six plastic crates stacked in the corner. The ones at the top are filled with boring necessities, such as bank documents, various legal documents, proof of insurance, and the like. Below that is a box filled with a series of mementoes that I started to keep after getting rid of everything I had at my parents' place. There are tickets and programmes from gigs, theatre shows, festivals, the panto and other things that Stephen and I have dragged one another to. I doubt I'll ever look through any of it again but I can't face throwing it all away once more.

It's the bottom crate I'm after.

I have to manoeuvre everything around until I'm able to drag it into the centre of the room. When Dad died, Mum said I could take whatever I wanted of his possessions by which to remember him. I went through his wardrobe and thought about keeping one of his ties, or something like that. Mum said I could have his watch, or his rings – but none of that would have meant anything. Neither would one of his ties, of course.

I almost told her that I didn't want any of the possessions but it felt disrespectful, so I ended up taking his scrapbook. I keep meaning to go through it properly but have only ever skimmed the contents. Last time I tried, I managed two pages before it was too much. It was always too close to his death.

Over the course of a few decades, he pasted together a series of large photo albums and then stuck in various things that either interested or involved him. Everything has a neat caption underneath, another striking reminder of his handwriting.

The first page of the book is a grainy photo from a newspaper announcing his and Mum's wedding. It's more of a notice than an article, saying that Barbara Paisley has married Ged Taylor, before listing the date and name of the register office. Both of them are smiling awkwardly at the picture-taker, as if they'd never seen a camera. Mum's dress is simple and light, less flashy than most people would wear for a night out nowadays, let alone for a wedding. Dad's suit is too big for him and I vaguely remember Mum once telling me that it was a hand-me-down from his own father. It was part of a general rant – or 'conversation', in her words – about how little my teenage self looked after *my* clothes.

As well as a wedding photo, there is a goldmine of things that Dad kept. He has payslips from one of his early jobs, back before the country was decimalised and there were a hundred pennies in a pound. If I'm reading it right, he made £29 a week. There's a letter from British Telecom confirming his first-ever phone number and a monochrome television licence, which cost him £7.

My stomach jumps as I flip to the next page, where he's stuck gig tickets and stubs from the movies. It's something we had in common: perhaps something he passed on to me. He went to watch *Jaws* at the cinema, plus *One Flew Over the Cuckoo's Nest*.

There's a receipt from a record shop and a programme for the Silver Jubilee celebrations. Into the eighties and there's some sort of commemorative magazine for Charles and Diana's wedding. He has a clipping about the Falklands and then a letter he received about being summoned for jury service. There's a faded receipt for a car he bought, where the word 'cash' is underlined four times.

There are tickets for Longleat Safari Park and a lolly stick that has 'Weston-Super-Mare' imprinted on the wood.

Before I know it, I'm towards the back, scanning the tickets Mum and Dad had for a cruise they took a few years ago. Dad kept an itinerary of the various tribute singers and it's hard not to think that if I had to put up with a fake Mick Hucknall one night, a fake Neil Diamond the next, then I might have hurled myself overboard.

It's as I'm thinking that that I remember I came upstairs to look for anything around the time I was born.

The book isn't quite in chronological order. It's more groupings, as if Dad would remember to put some items aside every three or four years and then he'd update the book.

I flip back towards the beginning and then start again but this time pay more attention to the details.

I've already missed it once and almost do a second time. I've turned the page when I go back and focus on the receipt for the car.

It's grouped with items from around the time I was born – except we didn't *have* a car when I was young. There were buses and taxis. The begged lifts from Mr Hawthorne.

There's an address of a garage on the top, with the blank ink faded to a grim grey. The details of the car are handwritten below. The writing isn't great but I think it says 'Talbot –£220 – cash', with the heavy underlining underneath. It's the sort of thing that, in the days of credit cards and online banking, probably wouldn't happen nowadays.

It's not a complete mystery. My parents could have bought a car and then decided it was too expensive to run. They might have even told me that and I forgot because it was so long ago.

Except…

The address of the garage isn't from Elwood, where I grew up – and it's not from any of the surrounding towns and villages.

It's from Higher Woolton.

The room is suddenly cold.

I've never heard of a Higher Woolton – but it was barely a few hours before that I was in *Lower* Woolton, looking for Penny Craven and standing opposite the old newsagent from where Jane was stolen.

I get out my phone and type the name into the Maps app. The screen freezes momentarily and then spins out, before swirling back in once more.

Higher Woolton sits approximately five miles from Lower Woolton. If Stephen and I had continued walking for another hour or so, we'd have been able to go from one town to the next. From what I can see, they're separated by a river, with the outskirts bleeding into one another.

Back in the scrapbook, there's a date at the top of the receipt. It's been written by hand: day/month/year.

I remove the receipt from the page. The tackiness of the decades-old glue grips my fingers and the slip almost rips as it comes away.

I already know the date of the article in the kitchen but rush downstairs anyway and place the two pieces next to each other.

It can't be true, except that it is.

Four days before Jane Craven was kidnapped, my father was buying a car barely five miles away in the neighbouring town.

TWELVE

SUNDAY

I barely sleep. I try but even when my exhausted eyes are closed, I twist myself around the bedcovers and think about those dates. Mum and Dad have lived in Elwood their entire lives. Even in today's vehicles, it's a couple of hours' journey to reach Higher Woolton. It's not an easy place to get to – and yet, thirty-four years ago, Dad travelled that distance to buy a car.

Four days after that, a short distance away, Jane Craven, with the straight slice across her ear, was snatched and never seen again.

Thirty-four years later, someone has put an article through my door to make sure I know.

Those details swirl as I try to think of an explanation that isn't the obvious.

I finally give up on sleep just after four and spend a little time reattaching my prosthetic, before taking Dad's scrapbook down to the kitchen.

Whoever was partying at the back of the house has finished now. I never fully closed the blinds and the white of the moon bleeds like a spotlight through the darkness onto the draining board and across the floor.

I fill the coffee machine with grounds and water and then set it bubbling as I settle at the table with the scrapbook. This time, I linger over everything, reading each word in case there's something I missed. I look for anything relating to the name 'Craven', or either of Higher and Lower Woolton. I check every photo, wondering if this Talbot car Dad bought might be somewhere in the background.

There's nothing.

The only reason I can come up with for Dad keeping the car receipt is that it was probably the first car he bought. I think that's likely true of the other bits, too. First payslip, first TV licence, first flight, first cruise. It feels like the sort of person he was.

Except I'm left wondering if I really know who either of my parents are.

The pot of coffee disappears at such a rate I almost worry there's someone else drinking it with me. I feel my stomach churning and thoughts buzzing.

Four o'clock has become five and then six.

The sun is on its way up, with an orange haze causing a crescent over the houses at the back. Birds are chirping to signal the beginning of something I'm not sure I want to face. I think about calling Stephen to tell him everything I've found. He probably wouldn't mind about the time, except there's a part of me that feels as if it has to be me and only me who deals with this.

Six o'clock becomes seven.

I've already given Mum a couple of chances to talk to me but, if anything, she is doing the opposite, burning things.

Seven o'clock becomes eight.

There's only one thing for it and so I go through the motions of showering and dressing before heading out to my car. I've already unlocked it and opened the driver's door when I notice what I should have seen immediately. There are a series of scratches etched into the paint running from the petrol cap across the back and front doors. I crouch to get a closer look – but all I can make out is that whatever tool was used to do this must have had a sharp blade. The scratches haven't simply removed the paint, they've gone all the way down to whatever the door is made from.

The lights are on inside Mr Bonner's house, so I step across the fence and knock on his door. He opens it shortly after and leans on his stick as he takes me in. The smell of tea and buttered toast drifts from behind him.

'Didn't fancy a Scrabble whooping last night, then?' he asks.

'I got in late,' I reply. 'I'd been to visit Mum and we got talking. It was after ten when I got back.'

He smiles gently. 'I'm only teasing, love.'

I step to the side and angle towards my car. 'I don't suppose you heard anything overnight, did you?'

Mr Bonner reaches into his pocket and pulls out a glasses case. He pushes the glasses on his face and peers past me towards the car. 'I can't see anything from this far.'

He steps off the porch onto his path and then moves across to the fence, where he stoops forward and squints towards my car.

'Who did that?' he asks.

'No idea. It wasn't like that when I got home last night.'

He steps back and takes off his glasses, before turning to take me in. 'I didn't hear a thing. I wish I had.'

'I didn't hear anything, either – but I thought I'd ask.'

'Who'd want to do something like that?'

My instant thought is Angel, although it's probably not the best thing to articulate out loud.

'I don't know,' I say.

'D'you think it was that woman in the red jacket from yesterday?'

I pause with a reply because I'd somehow forgotten about her.

Mr Bonner is already far ahead of anywhere I might be. 'I can probably describe her to the police if you want to call,' he says. 'She had long hair and that jacket. I reckon I could pick her out of a line-up…'

I almost laugh, not at him, more at the sudden eagerness.

'I doubt the police would even come out,' I say. 'They normally just give you a reference number for the insurance if it's this sort of thing.'

Mr Bonner's face falls slightly. 'Aye, you're probably right. Still, that's what people voted for. That's what they wanted, so that's what they got.'

He stares past me for a moment and then heads back towards his door before taking me in again. 'Did you hear someone having a party out the back last night? That's probably why I never heard anyone out here.'

'I heard something.'

'Lights, music, the whole lot. I thought about going round there this morning and playing my music loud enough to wake them all up. See how *they* like it.'

'How were you going to carry a gramophone round there…?'

He's almost off on more of a rant until he realises what I've said. He stops and there's a laugh of acknowledgement.

'I don't have to put up with this ageist abuse.'

We grin to one another and I feel like I could bicker back and forth with him all day. I know I'm using him as a replacement for Dad and perhaps he does, too.

Except it's difficult to think of my father in the moment. Mum, too. If a part of me is doubting who I am, then a bigger part is doubting who *they* are.

'You all right, love?'

I realise I've been standing there silently. Mr Bonner sees it in me and he reaches out a comforting hand to touch my shoulder.

'I have a few things going on right now.'

He nods and bites his lip. He doesn't have to tell me that he's there to listen if I want, because I already know. Sometimes the things unsaid are more important than the ones which are.

'I've got proper sausages in, if you fancy it,' he says. 'From the butcher. Not the supermarket stuff.'

'I'm really sorry. I have somewhere to be.'

He smiles kindly. 'You look after yourself, in that case. You still owe me a race around the park – and don't think I've forgotten about it.'

'Maybe later,' I say – and then I head to my car.

THIRTEEN

I take the long way around to get to Lower Woolton, driving a slightly different route to the one Stephen took yesterday. This time, I make sure I go through Higher Woolton first.

It's not much of a surprise but the garage at which Dad bought the Talbot thirty-four years ago has long gone. In its place is an Indian restaurant. There's a string of lights around the roof and a huge pink and black flashing neon sign advertising that poppadoms are half-price before six.

I wasn't hungry before but am suddenly ravenous at the idea of mango chutney. It's late on Sunday morning but I've been up for so long that I'm in the mood for anything.

The thought is broken by a man in a waistcoat who's letting himself in to the building through a side door. He stops and stares towards me, wondering why I'm the only car in the parking area at this time of a Sunday morning. That sends me setting off along the road and over the river that leads first to the funeral director's and then, eventually, Lower Woolton itself.

The Black Sheep has not long opened for the day. There's an A-frame at the front proclaiming that they now do breakfast, which it describes as 'eggscellent'.

I sit in the car park, a few spaces down from where I was with Stephen less than a day ago. Families arrive at regular intervals, piling out of their vehicles and off towards the pub. The barman told us that Penny would be in today and I know that the choice I make now is one that can't be undone. I could drive home, play

Scrabble with Mr Bonner, and do my best to forget everything from the past forty-eight hours.

In so many ways, everything would be easier.

I get out of the car and follow a family of four into the pub. It might be earlier than Stephen and I were here yesterday but the place is rocking. A cacophony of sound erupts from all corners, with voices drowning out other voices as everyone talks over the top of one another. There's music underneath all that, not that I can make out anything identifiable above the rest of the din.

The family who entered before me walk in a small circle, until the young boy points off to the furthest corner. Like a politician spotting a bandwagon, they race in the direction indicated, before throwing themselves at what seems to be the only free table.

I press myself into a corner close to the pool table and watch the woman behind the bar multitask like I've never seen anyone before. She's simultaneously punching one customer's order into the till, pouring a coffee for another, sorting out a card payment for the first and then pointing another person towards the bank of cutlery against the patio doors. It all seems to happen at once – and then she seamlessly moves onto the next customer in line.

I don't know if this is Penny, although she's likely the right age. She's probably mid- to late-fifties, with dyed blonde hair and the general sense of a person who's been doing something so long that they could do it blindfolded. She could be one of the people Mum watches, behind the bar on *Coronation Street*.

There are a couple of other people darting around to collect and deliver plates to various tables – but they're either men or too young to be Penny.

Everything the barmaid does is with an efficient flourish. She calls people 'my love', or 'my sweet'. A young boy gets a wink and a nod as he asks if there's more ketchup because the one on his table is empty. She'll be in the middle of a conversation with someone through the door behind her and out of sight, while also asking a customer how their morning has been.

It's been around five minutes and I haven't moved. I feel breathless just watching her. The queue to order and pay has diminished to a single guy with pepper-pot hair, who is fiddling on his phone when he realises he's now by himself.

'You all right, Pen?' he asks cheerily. 'How's your morning?'

She smiles at him. 'Busy. What can I get you?'

I don't hear what comes next. This is truly her. I wait and watch as she puts the man's order through the till and then hands him a large wooden spoon with a number painted on it. He heads off to a table in a distant booth and then, finally, Penny stands alone. She takes a large breath and then leans against the counter as she takes a sip from a mug that's under the bar. One of the younger servers passes her, carrying a tray laden with plates. They exchange a few words and then Penny picks up the mug again and heads through the door at the back of the bar. I shift around the pub, trying to keep an eye on her, and move just in time to see her disappearing along a hallway and out through another door that leads to whatever's at the rear of the pub.

I am suddenly decisive as I leave the pub via the front door. I follow the line of the building along the pavement and then away from the road until I arrive at a small courtyard at the rear. Penny is there, standing by herself close to a grubby once-white plastic table. She has a cigarette in one hand and her phone in the other, still multitasking.

It's creepy, I know, but I find myself watching her again. She slips her phone into her bra and then pulls out a lighter from the other side, which she flicks over and over, trying to get it to catch.

Perhaps I move, or maybe she senses my presence but Penny turns and takes me in with the gentlest of frowns before she holds up the lighter.

'Don't suppose you've got one, have you?'

I edge across the courtyard towards her until she's standing in front of me. We're eye to eye, the same height.

'I don't smoke,' I say.

'I shouldn't either. It's so good, though. Like all the things that are bad for you.'

She sighs momentarily as she continues trying to get the lighter to catch. It eventually strikes a small flame, which she instantly transfers to the cigarette. The lighter is dispatched back into her bra and she sucks a deep breath before taking me in again.

'Do I know you?' She sounds hesitant, as if she thinks I might be a semi-regular customer.

'No... I mean... maybe.'

I feel the weight of her stare and then, as if this is something ingrained into her when meeting a new person, her gaze drifts in on the side of my head, onto my ear.

There's a moment, probably less than a second, when it feels as if everything stops. The breeze drops, the car that's passing is silent, the birds are still.

Everything freezes.

Then Penny's eyes flare wide and her mouth bobs open. The cigarette drops to the floor as I angle away, letting her see properly.

Penny's voice is an uncertain croak: 'You... you called on Friday...?'

'Yes but I didn't know what to say.'

She shuffles backwards, resting on the grimy table for support. Her stare never once leaves me.

'How'd you find me...? How'd you know...?'

It's too late to back away now. I've given myself to whatever this is.

'I was given an old article about Jane Craven being taken,' I reply. 'There was a picture of her. I typed her name into Google and there was an article from a few years back about—'

'—kids who were never found…' Penny finishes my sentence and then she reaches out to touch my arm, making sure I'm real. She looks at me with wonder, like a dog seeing snow for the first time. She blinks and stares, mouth still open. 'I always hoped Jane would see that piece,' she says. 'I always believed.'

I'm unsure how to reply. There's an uncertainty in the air, like that moment when a lift first starts to move and gravity is defeated.

'Where have you been?' she adds.

I almost start to reply but then notice the 'you', instead of 'Jane'. We both mentioned Jane before but there was a disconnect, as if Jane is a third person in all this.

'I might not be—'

'It's you, though. I know it is.'

I'm not sure what to tell her. A part of me wants this to be real but another, perhaps bigger, part can't face the fact that it might be.

Something catches my eye and I look down, taking in Penny's smouldering cigarette that's burning itself out at my foot. I consider standing on it but then wonder if she still might want it. I've never smoked and don't know the etiquette.

I look back up to ask – except that, from nowhere, Penny's eyes have rolled back into her head. She grunts, breathes out loudly – and then collapses into my arms.

FOURTEEN

The side of Penny's face knocks into my shoulder as I feel the join of my prosthetic leg buckle under the unexpected weight. I stumble backwards a step managing to hold her as, luckily, Penny regains her senses almost immediately. She rights herself, reaching for the table to hold herself up and then blinks half a dozen times.

'I have no idea what just happened,' she says.

'I think you fainted.'

My residual limb is suddenly sore and I'm left wondering if the padding has slipped – while simultaneously trying to act as if nothing has happened.

'Shall I call an ambulance?'

Penny is agog at the suggestion. 'Absolutely not,' she says. 'Just low blood pressure or not enough water, something like that. I didn't sleep well last night and this is all a bit…'

She doesn't finish the sentence, although I know what she means.

Penny reaches to the floor and picks up the still smoking cigarette. She brushes away a fleck of grit, examines the cigarette, and then inhales long and deep from it.

'Are you sure you don't fancy one?' she asks.

'I've not smoked since I was sixteen. Me and one of my friends at school used to get fags off the boys because we wanted to look grown up. It's a hard look to pull off when you can't stop coughing.'

Penny's eyes narrow and, for the first time, I'm an imposter under her stare. I realise it's because I'm talking about a life she doesn't know. She draws from the cigarette again and then turns her head to exhale the smoke away from me.

I can see her hand shaking as she cradles the cigarette close. Her voice trembles. 'How did you know to find me here, Jane?'

'It's Hope,' I reply.

'What's hope?'

'That's my name.'

She starts to breathe quickly and self-medicates with another puff from the cigarette. She's still trembling.

'There was a TripAdvisor review,' I say. 'It mentioned Penny and this pub. I didn't know it was you but Lower Woolton is a small place. I figured there couldn't be many people named Penny.'

She takes this in with a small nod and a twitch of the eye. I can't tell if I've offended her. 'It's why I never moved,' she says. 'We were thinking about getting a cottage out on the coast a few years back. There was this rental place that would've been perfect but I couldn't do it in the end. I wanted Jane to know I was here just in case.'

Penny turns away, gulping back thirty-four years of uncertainty. I want to tell her that I might not be Jane, that this could all be something different, except that I don't know. She's blinking quickly, fighting back tears but I can't pretend that I'm feeling sad or upset. All I have is confusion. Being here, giving her hope, could be the worst thing I've ever done.

'Who named you Hope?'

The question catches me by surprise, although I guess it should have been expected. I almost say 'Mum' as a reflex but pull it back just in time. Mum used to tell me that she'd once seen a photograph of a place called Hope in Canada. I've seen it, too. There's a raging river on one side and then the town sits low, surrounded by soaring mountains on all the others. When it snows, they have to close the roads, meaning that the people living there can be cut off for days at a time.

Mum always wanted to go, to stand in the centre of town and feel those mountains towering above her. It was something she said she'd do in retirement – but then Dad died and everything changed. For me, I ended up having the name of a place I've never visited.

I don't answer Penny's question because there's no good to be had from giving it.

'This is all new to me,' I say instead, wanting her to understand. 'Someone put an article about Jane Craven through my door on Friday. It was only two days ago and I… I haven't wrapped my head around it yet.'

Penny's eyes narrow. 'Who sent the article?'

'I don't know. It was in an envelope with my name on the front and that's it.'

Penny frowns momentarily. There are enough mysteries for one day and another is taking things too far.

'Where do you live?' she asks.

'Macklebury.'

She bites her bottom lip: 'I think I've heard of that.'

'It's not a big place.'

'Where's it near?'

'Elwood, Stoneridge—'

'Stoneridge?' Penny snaps the word back to me. 'I know that place.'

'It was in the news last year.'

I don't want to say why but I can see the moment that Penny remembers for herself. 'There was that girl,' she says. 'She was stolen from a garden and then went home to her mum twenty years later. I remember reading about it and wondering if you would ever come back. Chris said I'd never recognise her even if she did but I *knew* your ear would always be the same.'

I don't ask who Chris is.

Penny finishes her cigarette and then crushes it into the pan on top of a nearby bin.

'I used to walk around places looking at strangers' ears,' she says. 'I'd keep in mind roughly how old you'd be. At first, I was looking for young kids but then it was teenagers and then twenty-somethings. Chris said I had to stop because I was doing it when we were in Ibiza one time. Some woman got freaked out when she caught me staring. He said you'd never be out there – but I *knew* you'd be somewhere.'

I force myself not to edge away. The way Penny keeps saying 'you' riddles me with unease.

Mum's story about the umbilical cord and how my ear was torn rewinds and plays itself in my mind. It always sounded plausible, although I never looked into it to figure out if it *was* plausible. I had no reason to. Perhaps I still don't?

'How did Jane's ear get torn?' It feels dangerous to ask.

The wind has whipped up out of nothing. It swirls around the courtyard, sending chills along my back.

Penny touches her abdomen. 'Something in the womb,' she says. 'Your ear was like that when you came out. The doctors were never completely sure what happened – but it was all before the equipment got so modern. They might have been able to do tests nowadays, perhaps seen if there was a problem before I went into labour. The midwife thought it was something to do with you twisting while in the foetal position. They talked about reconstruction but you were really young – and then…' She stops to breathe, which turns into a sigh. 'And then you were gone and there was never the chance.'

I realise I'm touching the angled part of my ear. I don't remember anyone ever discussing reconstruction as an option when I was young. I'm used to it now, and wouldn't want it to be any other way, but, when I was a teenager, I'd have definitely wanted my ear to look like everyone else's.

Penny is watching me, watching the ear. 'What story were you told?'

I turn away, knowing I can't answer this either. I have no idea what's the truth.

Penny looks towards the rear door of the pub and then back to me. I think she knows there are things I can't answer.

'How long have you lived in Macklebury?' she asks.

'Around ten years. I grew up in a place called Elwood, which is a few miles from Macklebury. I guess that's where I think of as home.'

I realise what I've said the moment it's out of my mouth. It was more of a general point about moving away from a place but still thinking of it as home – except that Penny is appalled. Her eyebrow is twitching but not from nervousness. An anger has been bubbling and it now feels as if it might erupt.

'*This* is your home,' she snaps. 'This has *always* been your home.'

There's no answer to this, except the floodgates are open now.

Her top lip curls and the next question is a snarl: 'Who stole you?'

'It's not that simple.'

'But someone raised you. Someone must have known you were stolen?'

I can't speak. I picture Mum sitting alone in her house, in her chair, watching her shows, without Dad. I remember the blankness in her stare after the funeral, asking silent questions about what her future would hold, with neither of us knowing the answer.

And then, perhaps for the first time, it pops into my mind that I could have been calling the wrong person 'Mum' my entire life.

'Whoever raised you, stole you,' Penny says.

'No.'

'It's true. You might not want to believe it but it's true.'

I shake my head.

'They stole you and raised you as their own.'

'No.'

Penny reaches out and takes my hand. I let her. Her skin is cool and rough. The touch of a person who's worked for a living. 'You're my Jane,' she says. 'You're my Jane and you've come back to me.'

FIFTEEN

I'm trying not to shake as Penny strides out of the pub with her jacket buttoned tightly and her bag over her shoulder. She looks both ways along the street and I see the moment of panic as she fails to spot me first time. She stands up straighter, like a meerkat, until I pull myself up from the wall and give her a wave, showing I've not disappeared.

I don't know what to think. It's like seeing one of those optical illusions where it turns out a massive square is the same size as a smaller one that's right next to it. Perhaps my ear is the proof of something being true… and yet it doesn't feel like it.

I completely believe something that I don't believe at all.

For now, Penny's enthusiasm is enough to carry me along to wherever she wants to go.

She sighs with relief and then hurries across to me. 'I told my boss I've got a family emergency and needed to go home,' she says. 'At least I didn't have to lie…'

I don't respond to that but she doesn't seem to mind as she nods towards the other side of the street.

'Come on, I'll show you the house.'

I poke a thumb towards the car park. 'I'm parked here. I could drive.'

'I'm only two streets away and there's never anywhere to park. We might as well walk.'

Penny steps onto the empty road and then turns behind to make sure I'm following. She moves far quicker than my usual pace as I realise that I only walk places either by myself, or with Stephen, who knows me. When we get to the other side of the street, Penny stops and nods towards me.

'You okay?' she asks. 'You're limping. Have you hurt your leg, or something?'

'Something,' I say. 'I'll be all right.'

Probably because of this, she slows as we head along the road that runs opposite the pub.

She's true to her word as we reach the second street and then cut along it. It's a different world from the huge houses out by the old newsagent. Those are three or four storeys and surrounded by steepling fences and hedges. This is a long row of red-brick terraces that all look broadly the same. Cars are parked nose-to-tail along the street, with only a narrow space through the middle for single vehicles to pass.

'They should make this one-way,' Penny says. She speaks with the sense of someone who tells this to anyone she ever brings here.

She stops in front of a house roughly halfway along the rank and then fumbles through her bag, looking for a key. Before she puts it in the door, she hovers with it close to the lock.

'You'll have to excuse the mess when you get inside,' she says.

'I'm sure it's fine.'

I picture Mum's house, where everything's in its place. Where Dad used to say 'coaster' before I'd even motioned to put down a drink.

As it is, Penny's house doesn't appear particularly messy. There is a row of coats hanging on the wall close to the front door, although one has dropped to the ground. Aside from that, it doesn't seem as if anything is out of place.

Penny picks up the errant jacket, takes off her own, and then removes her shoes, which she puts on a rack next to a 'Bless This Mess' welcome mat. I copy and add mine to the row of what mainly appears to be men's footwear. I leave on my socks, which cover the moulded foot that's attached to my prosthetic.

There are framed photos on the wall of the hall. The first is of Penny in her younger days, tanned and in sunglasses, while standing on a beach next to a man whose skin is tomato red. I try to figure out when it might have been taken, based upon Penny's current look. More than ten years back but likely not as many as twenty. I wonder if it's her husband and, if so, how long they've been married.

Whether it could be my father…

Penny is already a few steps up the staircase. She stands over me and peers down, nodding me away from the rest of the photos.

'Up here…'

I follow her around the banister and then up the stairs. I need to stop at some point and check the binding of my leg because each step only re-emphasises that something doesn't feel quite right. My residual limb stings in the way it only does when the padding is loose.

The upstairs hall is as tidy as the one downstairs. There's a clothes hamper in a corner and a series of anonymous watercolour prints; the sort of thing that would have been mass-produced and probably sits in thousands of houses. There's a window at the end, with the greying sky casting a faint light across the pink carpet.

Penny opens one of the doors and then beckons me inside. There's a queen-sized bed in the centre of the room that's neatly made with a patterned light brown bedspread. Penny kneels next to the bed and lifts the hanging covers, before she pulls out a large, low plastic tray. It's the type of storage item that's piled high and sold cheaply in pound shops across the land. Scattered across the space of the tray is a selection of photo albums, much like Dad's scrapbook. I count four – and there could be more hidden underneath a folded blanket that takes up part of the space.

Penny sits on the edge of the bed and picks up one of the books. I take a spot next to her, with a degree of reluctance, as she opens the cover and points to a newspaper article.

'I kept everything,' she says. 'There are thirty years of articles and photos in here. Chris wanted to throw everything out but I wouldn't let him. I thought I'd end up being buried with them.'

She shuffles the book onto my lap – and the first article is immediately recognisable. The initial three paragraphs, along with Jane's photo, is the exact same thing that was put through my door. As I suspected, there is more to the piece below the extract I was given. I scan it through, although there's nothing more than I already knew.

Penny's copy has been looked after a lot better than the one posted to me. The paper is almost its original white-grey and has a lot more flexibility than the brittle one that still sits on my kitchen table.

Penny is keen for me to read on and flips the pages as I let her. There is more or less an article a day for the first week following Jane's disappearance. It really does look as if she's kept everything. It's not only local papers, there are smaller clippings from the nationals, plus a couple of different 'have you seen?'-posters with a slightly different photograph of Jane. This one makes her ear seem more apparent, playing on the fact that, if anyone sees an infant with a similar sort of marking, then they should call the police.

After a couple of weeks, the frequency of the articles drops off – and it quickly becomes obvious that, after around a month, there is almost nothing new. It's little surprise given the repetitive nature of everything Penny has kept. The articles reprint the same photo, with the same details. There are appeals for witnesses, hints about leads or breakthroughs, and then, ultimately, nothing.

She takes back the first book and closes the cover.

'There were a couple of sightings,' Penny says. 'My number was in the phone book at the time and people would call the house, saying they'd seen you in some place or another. I'd head off in a mad rush and then find out it was a hoax, or a misunderstanding.'

'How many times did that happen?'

She lets out a gentle sigh. 'Maybe twenty.'

I don't know what to say. My stomach feels as if it's doing flips. Even when The Bad Thing happened, when I had a sense of loss that was both literal and internal, I'm not sure I ever spoke with the shattered sadness that's etched into Penny's voice. I can see her dashing off to a place she's never been, trying to follow a map, or vague directions given on the phone. She'd arrive desperate and hopeful, only to be let down time and again. She might resolve to learn from what happened – but then another call would come in and she'd be off again.

It's horrifying.

Penny picks up a second album and opens the cover. She laughs as she twists the page so I can see.

'This was for the twentieth anniversary,' she says. 'They wrote an article about unsolved cases and commissioned an artist to come up with an impression of what you might look like after all that time.'

There's suddenly a lightness to the atmosphere as I have a look at the artist's version of how Jane would appear. They wouldn't have had much to go on, so the image is a pudgy-faced young woman, with combed-back dark hair and – of course – the ear without a helix.

It looks nothing like me. Perhaps nothing like any human who's ever lived.

'They gave you a lazy eye. I never knew why.'

I have a closer look at the image and Penny is right. 'How did the artist decide that based upon a photo of a six-month-old?'

Penny laughs again. 'I have no idea. The first time I saw it was when it was already in print.' She pauses, possibly weighing up the mood. 'I wondered if they thought the ear disfigurement might've spread to your eye…?'

She giggles nervously, wondering if this is okay to say. I laugh with her, letting it stick – for her, not me.

When we're done, there's a second or two of uncomfortable silence. It's almost as if we're on the weirdest of weird dates. Two strangers sizing up one another, wondering how far our personalities might stretch until it's too much for the other.

Penny reaches out again, touching my knee this time – the one not covered by support straps.

'Making sure you're real,' she says. She pulls out her phone and holds it up. 'Can we take a photo? The two of us together.'

I want to say 'no' but it doesn't feel fair to deny Penny anything today.

We shuffle closer and she holds her phone at arm's length, with the screen facing towards us for the selfie. She breaks into a slim smile and I copy her until the screen freezes to signify the moment that's now etched into an ever long reality.

Penny lowers her arm and stares at the picture, before tilting the device so I can see it, too.

'We have the same eyes…'

I squint towards the image, wanting her to be wrong, except that she's not. Penny and I share the same shade of blue eyes.

She lowers her phone and then twists sideways to take me.

'Is that your natural colour?'

I'm suddenly self-conscious about my appearance.

She takes my silence as an answer and holds out a strand of her own hair.

'I get mine lightened but it's a dark blonde, like yours.'

I try to ignore this but a fact is a fact. Mum and Dad had brown hair and brown eyes. I was dark blonde, with blue eyes… like Penny.

We sit in silence for a little while and I listen as Penny breathes in through her slightly blocked nose. I feel her body rise, sense the anticipation that she's about to talk.

'I don't know what to say to you,' she begins. 'There's so much I want to – but it all seems so small. How can you sum up all these years in a few sentences?'

We sit in silence again. Breathe the same air. I don't know what to say to her, either. It still doesn't feel real and I'm still not certain I should have come.

Penny breaks the impasse a second time. It feels as if she's been on the border of melancholy and barely controlled fury since she first saw my ear. The anger's back now. Her jaw is clenched, fists balled.

'Someone else raised you. All these years…'

I really can't speak now. There's a lump in my throat and, worse than that, an awful, barely comprehensible, sense that my parents aren't mine.

A growing, horrific sense that, maybe, just maybe… they're monsters.

SIXTEEN

There's a loud clunk from downstairs and Penny immediately sits rigidly tall. I'm not sure what's happening at first but then a man's voice calls 'Pen?!' from somewhere below.

'Wait here.'

Penny scurries from the room and I hear her darting along the hall and then down the stairs. There are muffled, angsty voices and then a man's voice clearly says: 'This is my house' before Penny's reply is drowned out by a gull that's howling outside the bedroom window.

A few seconds later, Penny's voice rings a tentative 'Jane...?' up the stairs.

It's not me... it'll never be me – and yet I follow the sound of the voice towards the stairs.

Penny is standing on the bottom step and, across from her, next to the front door is the tomato-coloured man from the photo. His skin is more of a normal colour today, though he's brawny, with a bread-bin chest and a polo shirt with horizontal stripes that's far too tight.

I edge down the stairs until I'm only a little behind Penny.

'This is my husband, Chris,' Penny says. 'Chris, this is... Jane.'

She holds out both hands to present me, as if I'm an elaborate cake being wheeled out for Paul Hollywood to scoff. Chris's forehead dissolves into a deep scowl of disapproval.

'It's Hope,' I say. 'I'm called Hope.'

'The miracle happened.'

Penny is proud and delighted but her husband has the face of a man who's just had a prostate exam.

'Who's Jane?'

There's another voice in the hall, someone I hadn't noticed at first. He's standing around the corner, next to the photographs away from which I was shooed by Penny. It only takes one look for me to know this is Chris's son. They share the same bloated faces and too-tight fashion choices.

'This is Kyle,' Penny says. 'He's Chris's son… I suppose you could say he's your stepbrother.'

Kyle and I stare at one another and I'm not sure which of us is more put off by this idea. He is roughly my age, with flat gelled hair and bum fluff on his chin. I used to know lads like him when I was in my younger days and would spend Friday and Saturday nights in the pubs of Elwood and Macklebury. He's the sort I can easily imagine giving someone a good kicking down an alley at three in the morning. The sort who'd slur 'you up for it?' to some girl at kicking-out time.

Penny's not done. 'Jane's my stolen daughter,' she says. 'I've told you about this.'

Kyle nods along, although he doesn't seem convinced. Penny said quite specifically that he was *Chris's* son – and, seeing as we're around the same age, it seems safe to assume they were in different relationships back when Jane was taken.

There is a long, long silence as the four of us weigh up one another. There is such hostility from the men that I can feel it poisoning the atmosphere.

It's Chris who eventually speaks. 'We haven't got anything here,' he says.

There's another pause before I realise he's talking to me. 'What do you mean?' I ask.

He shrugs at me: 'If it's money you're after, then we haven't got any.'

'Why would I be after money?'

Another shrug: 'Everyone's after something.'

'I'm not.'

'Sure you're not. I'm surprised it took this long for someone to turn up, saying they're her.'

We stare at one another and I feel something burning in me that I've not felt in a long time. The injustice and the fire.

'I never *said* I was Jane,' I reply.

Chris looks to Penny, who has cowered into the corner on the stairs and is suddenly quiet. A painted smile is on her face as she stares wide-eyed and almost manically at her husband. When he gets nothing from her, Chris turns back to me.

'Who are you then?'

'My name's Hope. I already said that.'

He's confused, looking between Penny and me until she eventually offers an almost apologetic: 'Look at her ear…'

I shiver under the attention as I feel both Chris and Kyle's gazes fix on the side of my head. I have no idea how to respond.

'What d'yer do?' Chris's tone is harsh as he moves on from looking at my ear to looking at my face.

'How do you mean?'

'For a job.'

'I work for a non-profit that tries to help young people get into the arts.'

Chris is rolling his eyes before I've finished the sentence. He glances towards his son and I can feel another set of eyes rolling. 'Oh, right,' Chris says. 'That lot.'

'What lot?'

'Do-gooders. Never done a day's work in their lives. Betcha end up on all those protests, don't ya?'

He shares another look with Kyle that makes it clear they both think it's not a real job. I could argue – and it wouldn't be the first time in my life – but I'm watching Penny's fixed smile and know this isn't the time to get in between whatever's going on with her and her husband. It's not as if I'd change his mind.

'You got a fella?'

It's Kyle who does the asking this time. I turn from him to his dad and then Penny, wondering if either of them might tell him to mind his own business. There's an undercurrent of stirring about it. The sly smirk on his face already tells me there's no answer I could give that would be the right one.

'I'm not sure that's any of your business,' I say.

Kyle shrugs dismissively, although the sneer remains. 'Suit yourself.' He nods towards my necklace. 'That looks expensive.'

I cup the pendant with my hand, again self-conscious but in a different way this time.

It's now that Penny – finally – speaks up. 'There's no need to grill her now,' she says. 'I'm sure we all have things we want to ask…'

She looks to me hopefully and I can see the desire to know within her. That anticipation of wondering whether I have children that could be unknown grandchildren for her. She is already all in on me being Jane and the idea of doubt isn't something she's entertaining.

I realise we're both standing with our arms folded, a mirror of one another. As I untuck mine, she does the same with hers.

The four of us continue to stand awkwardly across the mix of stairs and hallway, each seemingly looking to one another to decide what comes next.

Perhaps predictably, it is Chris who breaks the impasse. He looks towards Penny. 'Why are you home?' he asks. The ever-present edge remains, as if he's only ever a wrong response away from fury.

'I got out early,' Penny says.

'Is he still paying you?'

There's a second of hesitation before Penny responds: 'I'm going to make up the hours later in the week.'

That gets a curt nod before Chris turns to take in Kyle. 'I guess that solves one problem,' he says. 'We're meeting Nick at the Legion in forty-five minutes. We can all go together.'

Nobody moves and then I suddenly realise that Penny, Chris and Kyle are all looking to me. He means the three of them are going to the Legion – wherever it might be – and that it's time for me to leave.

Chris steps to the side, away from the front door, signalling that he's not joking.

'Can you give me five minutes?'

It's Penny who speaks. Her voice is shaky and cautious, as if she's not sure what sort of reply she'll get. She's looking to Chris, who is deliberately avoiding eye contact. After a stand-off of a few seconds, he makes a point of looking at his watch and then nods Kyle towards the stairs.

'Five minutes,' he says.

I come down the rest of the stairs to let the two men pass me on their way up. Their footsteps boom through the house and then there's the sound of two doors banging closed. After a wardrobe or cupboard door is slammed, there is finally peace.

Penny takes a breath. The enthusiasm of before is gone – and the effortless skill she showed in dealing with multiple things at the pub has dissipated to nothing. She seems shattered.

'He's not always like that,' she says. Her voice is quiet, not wanting to be overheard. 'He's worried that you might be something you're not. He's only looking out for me but I know it comes across a bit more aggressive than he means.' She tails off and sighs before adding: 'He's a good man.'

I know what I should say – except that I don't know her, or him.

Penny isn't done: 'Your dad came off his motorbike about twenty years ago. I was always going on at him about that thing but he said it was his escape. He'd spend hours polishing things, or buying new parts to fix. He'd go up and do a bike tour of the

Highlands every summer. He'd stop in guest houses or B&Bs and then head on to the next place. It started the year after you were taken and he'd go by himself for a week or ten days. We both had our own ways of dealing with it. His was his bike. I got the call one day to say that they'd found his bike in the middle of the carriageway somewhere north of Inverness. They thought he'd hit a deer, something like that. There was blood but no animal. He, um… well… you know…'

She tails off again but the picture is clear. Everything has come out in one go, as if this is her one opportunity to let me know.

'What was yours?' I ask.

'My what?'

'You said you both had ways of dealing with things…?'

Penny gives a small smile but there's no humour in it. 'I got fit,' she says.

I follow her gaze across to the wall and the photographs. There's one of her running through a field in a pair of short shorts, speckles of mud splashed across her legs.

'I finished twelfth in the national cross-country championships for over-forties,' she says.

'That's impressive.'

Penny glances away and focuses on a spot of the carpet. 'Gave myself an eating disorder. Got a bit carried away…'

She gives a nervy laugh and neither of us have any idea what to say next. It's such a small window into her world – but I can picture it now. Her with an obsessive training and dieting regime; him out on his motorbike through every free moment. A couple growing endlessly apart after the child was taken until, perhaps inevitably, one tragedy followed the first.

Her bottom lip bobs and I want to hold her tight and tell her that it will all be okay. I *want* to, except that I don't. She's convinced I'm someone that I might not be – and where would the fairness be if I'm not? When I decided to come to Lower Woolton I was thinking about me – but I'm not the only person involved in this.

Penny nods upstairs: 'I remarried eight years ago. I'm Penny Morse now…'

It could be a simple statement of fact – except it isn't.

'You don't have to justify anything to me,' I say.

'I'd rather stay and talk everything through with you but Chris has plans and—'

She's interrupted by a loud thump from upstairs, as if something heavy has been dropped. Penny jumps and then puts a foot on the next step up from her, ready to take the unsubtlest of hints.

'Can I take your number?' she asks. 'Perhaps we can arrange a proper chat another time?'

Penny takes out her phone, ready to take the details and so I tell her the number out loud and she enters it. She taps a few things and then, a second later, my phone buzzes. I open it to see a message from her number, with the selfie of us attached.

'You've got mine now,' she says. 'Let's stay in contact. See what we can—'

The loudest bump yet echoes down the stairs and Penny winces. It's so all-encompassing that it feels as if the roof could come down. We each take a second to settle before Penny takes another step upwards.

'I've got to go,' she says. 'I'm really sorry.'

I pick up my shoes from the rack and hastily put them on, before I reach for the door and open it.

'I'm *really* sorry,' Penny repeats.

There is one more bang and I don't wait to see the aftermath. By the time the shouting starts, I'm already two doors away, trying to figure out everything that's just happened.

SEVENTEEN

When I get back to the pub car park, there are four or five cars queueing on the road outside, waiting to dive on any newly free spot in the rammed lot. As I get into my car, a man in a Volvo points a thumb towards the road and mouths the word: 'Leaving?' When I nod, he gives a thumbs up and I don't think I've ever seen a grown adult be more relieved.

I follow the roads without any aid from the Maps app on my phone. Getting lost wouldn't be the worst of outcomes as it feels as if I can think better in the middle of nowhere. Regardless of what I believe, Penny is certain I'm her daughter. Given that, and that she hasn't seen her daughter in more than thirty years, it is very odd that she hurried me out the door.

My phone weighs heavily in the cup holder next to the handbrake. Penny's message with the photo of us sits on it with no response. I could pull over and send something back, asking if she's all right and – perhaps – wondering if she wants to meet again.

Narrow lanes turn into slightly wider ones. There is barely any traffic on the road at this time on a Sunday and it feels as if the world has shrunk so that it's only me who's in it.

It's as I drive past the first signpost for Macklebury that I think of Stephen. I need to ask what he thinks and know he is honest enough not to say what I might want to hear.

It's as I'm thinking of him that my phone starts to ring. It's connected to the car's Bluetooth and Stephen's name appears on the central console, almost as if I've willed him to be there.

I press the button to answer and am expecting some sort of cheery 'hello' – except that his tone is sullen and direct. 'You home?'

'I will be soon,' I say.

He coughs and there's an uncommon gruffness to him. 'How soon?'

There's something else in his voice, too, a nervousness perhaps.

'Half an hour?'

There's a silence now in which I can hear him breathing through the speaker. He sounds a little out of breath, as if he's been out jogging – which I one hundred per cent know he won't have been. Exercise, especially in public, is not Stephen's thing.

'What's up?' I ask.

There's a breathy pause which tells me something's wrong – and then his voice again.

'I'll be at yours,' he says. And then, more quietly. Pleading: 'I need you.'

EIGHTEEN

When it comes to driving, I am not the sort of person who speeds. The trembling uncertainty of Stephen's 'I need you' gives me such chills that I find myself pushing seventy on the straighter parts of the journey home, even though the limit is sixty. It might not sound like much but, for me, this is as extreme as I get.

By the time I pull onto my driveway, my heart is racing with adrenaline from the drive. I let myself into the house and call Stephen's name. He has a key and knows the alarm code, and I find him in the kitchen. He's sitting at the counter with the fingers of one hand looped around a steaming mug of tea. His other hand is holding a bag of frozen peas to the side of his face. When he pulls it away, there is a purply-red welt across a cheek that's so swollen, it's as if he's holding a golf ball in the side of his mouth.

I step across to him and crouch to get a closer look. 'What happened?' I ask.

'My date never showed. I waited for a bit, sent a message, and then, when I was walking back to the car, these two guys appeared out of nowhere.'

'Did they…?'

Stephen returns the peas to the side of his face and puts down his mug. He sounds exhausted.

'I think one of them hit me,' he says. 'I didn't see it because they were off to the side. I guess it was a sucker punch. Next thing I know, I'm on the floor and this guy is going through my pockets. They took my wallet. My phone was left – but the screen is cracked.'

I rest a hand on his shoulder, wanting to hug him but unsure if it might cause more pain.

'Bloody hell, Steve…'

'They gave me a bit of a kicking. Called me a fag and a poof. Few other things…'

I step back and stare at him. I suppose I'm wondering if there's some sort of weird joke mixed up in this, even though I know there isn't.

'This is like something from the eighties,' I say.

'I know.'

Neither of us speak for a few moments. Stephen's eye is twitching and he's slumped in a way he would never usually sit.

'Was the whole date a set-up?' I ask.

Stephen winces and cracks his jaw from side to side. 'I have no idea. I never got a reply to my text asking where he was. It might have been.' He puts down the peas and gently touches his cheek, which causes him to grimace. 'How bad does it look?'

'You're not going to be Britain's Next Top Model.'

He cracks a smile but then it instantly disappears as the pain kicks in.

'Have you taken anything?' I ask.

'Couple of paracetamol and half a cup of tea so far.'

'Careful with that tea. Don't want you getting hooked.'

There's another hint of a smile that quickly shrinks and then he bats a hand in my direction. 'Stop making me laugh.'

'I'm not the one considering hot railing PG Tips.'

'Neither am I!'

He lets out a small chuckle and then settles back onto the stool as I slot in alongside him and rest a hand on his knee.

'Have you called the police?'

The lack of an answer *is* the answer.

Stephen picks up the peas again and presses the bag to the side of his face. 'You hear from the old-timers about how this used to be their lives. They'd go places in pairs in case there was some group of lads around the next corner waiting to give them a hiding. They never called the police – because there was a chance they'd get another smack off them.'

I squeeze his knee softly. 'I don't think it's like that now.'

He removes the peas from his face and twists so that I can get an even closer look at his bruises. 'Isn't it?'

'Steve—'

'I'm not going to the police. Don't ask again.'

He returns the peas to his cheek and angles himself away. We never argue and his slightly raised voice is about as cross as we might ever get with one another.

I ask if he wants anything to eat but he doesn't, so I end up getting a can of Coke from the fridge for myself. We sit quietly at the counter for a while and I watch as his eyes wander to the article that's been there more or less ever since it came through my door.

'How was your day?'

He asks as if he knows, even though he can't.

I don't feel ready to let go the issue of him taking the assault to the police, except I know it'll lead to him storming out if I mention it again.

'I drove to Lower Woolton,' I say.

He nods, again as if he knew. 'I thought you might.'

'I saw Penny Craven. Spoke to her. She's Penny Morse now.'

Stephen lifts himself off the stool and crosses to the fridge, where he squeezes the peas back into the freezer compartment underneath. When he returns to the stools, he turns to face me and it's as if the disagreement never happened. 'What was she like?'

'Really good at her job. Friendly. She's convinced I'm her daughter.'

Stephen bites his lip, angles away a fraction, and then says it anyway. 'Maybe you are…?'

It's such a simple, logical thing to say. The thing that's niggling the edge of my thoughts anyway. It sounds brutal out loud.

Perhaps it's my lack of reply but Stephen follows up his first question with another: 'Do you think your mum… Barbara…?'

He tails off but it's the other half of the same question which is scratching away at me. If Penny is my biological mother, then what does that make the people who brought me up?

'I don't know what I think,' I say.

'You can get home DNA test kits nowadays. I think it's saliva in a tub that you send off to a lab. Either that, or hairs. You could find out once and for all.'

'It's so complicated.'

'I honestly think it's just saliva in a tub—'

'Not the test!'

Stephen gives a little smile, letting me know he was joking.

'I read an article a while back,' I begin. 'It said home DNA kits were causing chaos because of the price. Lots of people can afford them now, so they're being used more often. Men were checking the paternity of their kids. There would be trouble if a kid turned out to be someone else's – but, even if not, it would also be bad because a wife would want to know why he was checking. In the end, it wasn't about DNA, it was about neither person trusting the other.'

Stephen gives himself a moment to take this in. 'Are you saying you'd rather not know?' he asks.

'I'm saying there doesn't seem like there are many good outcomes. What's the best that can happen?'

'You'll know the truth…'

I'm close to telling Stephen that the truth is what worries me. A DNA test might give an answer but what then? If everything Mum says is true, then I've destroyed her faith in me by questioning it. If Penny is right, then everything from the past three decades is tainted. I don't think there's a winner.

I take out my phone and select the photo Penny took of us both, before passing it across to Stephen. He holds it at arm's length and then brings it closer to his swollen face, before handing me back the phone. He takes a breath and half turns away.

'You can say it,' I tell him.

'You have the same eyes,' he replies.

'I know.'

'What colour are your mum's?' He coughs and then corrects himself. Or, perhaps, he makes it worse. 'Barbara's eyes?'

'Brown,' I reply. 'Like Dad's.'

Stephen starts to say something else but I hear his jaw crack and then he grunts slightly, before rubbing his hand against his cheek.

'You might need the hospital,' I say.

A shake of the head: 'They need the beds for actual sick people. This just needs resting.'

'You might've broken your jaw.'

'It looks worse than it is. Remember when I fell down those steps in town? That hurt way more.'

He's talking about the time he got a new job. We went out to celebrate, got tipsy on sparkling wine, and then he fell down the steps outside the pub and had to start work with a pair of black eyes. The memory of that evening at A&E and the marks on his face now bring me back to the furious bumps from upstairs at Penny's house.

'There's something else about Penny,' I say.

'What?'

'She seems scared of her husband. When it was just the two of us, she was so excited to talk. She thinks I'm her daughter and, whether that's true or not, Jane was taken thirty-odd years ago. You'd want to talk, wouldn't you? Except she basically threw me out of the house because her husband didn't want me there.'

'Perhaps he was being protective of her? He doesn't know who you are.'

'That's what she said when I was leaving.'

Stephen takes another moment to consider this. 'Did anything else seem wrong?'

'I don't know. Maybe. I keep thinking about her, wondering if there's something I can do.'

'Like what?'

I sigh and stare down towards the article. The thing that started all this. 'I wish I knew.'

NINETEEN

I sleep in the next morning, not by design, more through exhaustion. By the time I come to, a slim sliver of light is beaming through a crack in the curtains, sending a crescent of yellow across the empty pillow on the other side of my bed.

After a trip to the bathroom, I edge open the door to the spare room, fully expecting to see Stephen sprawled half under the covers, half on top. He's always been the most extraordinary of sleepers, able to bunk down on a spot regardless of light, noise or anything else. I've seen him sleep in a single seat at an airport, in the luggage rack of a train, curled up like a cat at the bottom of a bookcase and many, many times in the corner of a booth at a pub.

He's not in bed now, though. I had already re-tidied the crates in the corner, while Stephen has remade the bed. Everything is as neat as it ever gets.

I head downstairs, into the kitchen, where Stephen is sitting at the counter with a mug of milky coffee. He's wearing only his pants from yesterday – which, accidentally or not, shows off a series of yellowy-brown bruises around his chest.

'They look sore,' I say.

He shrugs a little, as if to repeat that they look worse than they feel. The swelling around his face has gone down, although the colour has come through on the bruises. Instead of the purple, it has lightened and spread into something more of an olive green with a blackened centre.

'I've called in sick to work,' he says.

'I'm not surprised. You'd scare the kids.'

It comes out harsher than I meant but Stephen's a primary school teacher and he takes it in good faith with a gentle smile.

'I didn't think looking like a beaten-up boxer would be a good look,' he says.

I pour myself a coffee from the pot Stephen's made and then we sit together at the counter, as we did yesterday afternoon. The living room would be more comfortable but this has become our spot over the years. It's hard to explain why but we discuss everything and anything while sitting with a coffee or a tea and staring out towards the trees at the back of the house. It's only when other people are around that I tend to host them in the living room. It feels like this place in this kitchen is for only Stephen and me.

'What are you going to do?' I ask.

'I cancelled my bank cards and have registered my driving licence as stolen. The bank said I'll be refunded any money that's taken out or spent on those cards, so I guess the only thing I've really lost is the cash. There was only thirty or forty quid, so it's not that bad.'

'I meant about the blokes who did it. If they get away with beating up and robbing you, they might think it's fine to do it to someone else.'

Stephen is silent for a moment. He has a sip of his coffee and then returns the mug to the counter before sighing.

'I know…'

We've known each other for long enough for me to see that something has changed in him overnight. We can joke with one another, put on brave faces, but in the darkness of the night, alone in a bed, it's hard to escape the voice of truth whispering in an ear.

'We have to go to the police,' I tell him. 'If not for you, then for any future or past victims.'

Stephen slumps lower on his stool, his back curved, shoulders hunched. 'Okay.'

'This morning.'

He nods slowly. 'Let me drink this and have a bagel and then we'll go.'

I place a hand on his knee and rest my forehead on his shoulder. I listen to him breathe, slowly and steadily.

'This is the right thing to do,' I say.

He takes my hand from his knee and places it on his chest, letting me feel his heart beat. 'I thought they might kill me.'

There's a crack in his voice. A moment of truth and clarity in among the way we usually talk to one another. I don't reply because that isn't what he wants. I keep my hand where he placed it and listen to the steady thump.

'We'll get through whatever this is,' he says.

I almost tell him that his bruises will heal – but then I realise it's not himself that he's talking about.

The police station is a modern-looking single-storey building on the edge of a trading estate. It sits somewhere in between Elwood, Macklebury and Stoneridge. With none of those places big enough to sustain their own police station, it seems that someone decided this was the next best option.

A friendly man in uniform at the front desk takes our details. After a short wait, he leads us through to a room with a sofa against one wall, with a separate armchair opposite. There's a television on the wall and posters of various children's TV characters placed at regular intervals. The man tells us that someone will be with us soon and then he closes the door, leaving Stephen and me alone.

It's Stephen who speaks first. 'Aren't police stations supposed to be grey?' he says. 'I thought the furniture was bolted to the floor?'

I'm not sure if I was expecting the sort of gulag he was, but I also didn't picture this.

'Did we accidentally walk into an IKEA showroom?' he adds.

'Do IKEAs have police officers at the front?' I say.

'They probably should. Have you ever been to one of their cafés? I've seen prison breaks on the news that are calmer.' He takes a breath and then adds: 'This is like the time-out room at school, where we send the kids who won't calm down.'

It's not long until there's a knock on the door and then a man in uniform appears. He's a little younger than us, bright-eyed with a hint of stubble that he's missed with the razor. He introduces himself as PC Harrison and then asks if we want anything.

'We've got tea and coffee,' he says. 'Made by the machine but it could be worse. I saw a packet of Hobnobs around earlier if you fancy that.'

Stephen says that a tea would be great and then the constable disappears back out the door, leaving us alone once more.

'You and men in uniform…' I say.

'What?!'

'"I'd *love* a tea with one sugar, please",' I say, mocking Stephen's voice. 'You almost told him he was sweet enough.'

'I did not.'

'Close enough. I'm surprised you didn't say you'd love to go Hobnobbing with him.'

Stephen snorts. 'Is that a euphemism?'

'Might as well be.'

PC Harrison is back a few minutes later. He puts a plastic cup with Stephen's tea onto the table, plus a plate with three biscuits. 'I found the Hobnobs,' he says cheerily – and it's all I can do to stop myself laughing. The constable pulls out a pad and says he's going to take some notes – then he asks Stephen to talk him through everything that happened the day before.

I know much of the story but any thoughts that the attack might have been a coincidence seem ridiculous when Stephen lays it out. He met a man through his dating app and they went through the usual process of swapping messages that turned increasingly flirty. They swapped details and agreed to meet. The other person didn't show up, or reply to messages asking where he was. When Stephen returned to his car, he was set upon by two strangers.

The officer notes everything down, with times and places – and he gives Stephen an email address where he can send screenshots from his communication. For the first time, I have a look at the other man's profile, although it's largely unremarkable. Stephen suggests the photos attached could be fake and neither the officer nor myself disagree.

I watch as Stephen withdraws into himself the more he talks. Like someone on a consumer show who knows they've been scammed and is riddled with embarrassment and shame when they have to admit it. I can see why he didn't want to come and know I'd have been the same. It doesn't matter how kind the police officer might be, the indignity remains.

The officer admits that the app companies aren't necessarily easy to deal with in terms of tracking down the other party – but says he'll pass it up the chain and see what comes.

After that, PC Harrison asks Stephen if they can go through to a different area, where someone can take photographs of the injuries. Stephen says this is fine and then we're led through a series of corridors until he is directed into a room by himself. While Stephen is having his injuries documented, the constable takes me through more corridors back towards the reception area, where we sit together.

He stares down at the notebook in his hand and gives me a closed-lip smile.

'Have you heard of this happening to anyone else?' I ask.

There's a shake of the head. 'Not around here. Anecdotally from other districts – bigger cities, that sort of thing.' He must see something in my face because he offers a kind smile. 'Your friend did the right thing in reporting it,' he says. 'There might be others who come forward. I'll go into the archives and see if there's anything outstanding.'

'What happens with old cases that are never solved?'

'Broadly speaking, they're left open. There's a database and new evidence could come in that sheds new light on something.'

I realise he's dumbing this down, that he's talking about Stephen, except it could apply with Penny, too.

'What happens if it's *really* old?' I ask. 'Like, thirty years.'

The officer's eyebrows dip for a moment, as if he's wondering if I'm trying to catch him out somehow. He glances towards the counter but then answers anyway.

'There's a cold case division – but it's very unlikely what happened to your friend could be linked to something from that far back.'

'But you do you ever solve cases that are really old? Not just this…'

PC Harrison presses back in his chair, perhaps aware that we're having different conversations. 'Not me personally – but other divisions might. It's rare for something that old.'

'What happens if someone committed a crime thirty years ago but they're quite old now? Frail, maybe?'

The constable shuffles awkwardly. 'I don't know what to tell you,' he says. 'That's all a bit above me.' He pushes himself up so that he's standing. 'I'm just going to check on Stephen. He shouldn't be long.'

He makes a quick exit, for which I can't blame him. In everything with Jane Craven, plus Penny and Mum, I've framed it by the effect on me – except it's deeper than that. Whoever stole Jane all those years ago committed a crime and there's presumably an open file on it somewhere. There'd be a criminal record and a punishment involved for whoever it was. Someone could – perhaps *would* – go to prison.

I picture Mum burning those documents and pretending everything is fine. It takes me back to the conversation with Stephen, wondering if knowing is worse than not.

The dark thoughts are interrupted as Stephen breezes his way back through a pair of double doors, with PC Harrison at his side. The constable says he'll be in contact and then he leaves us, as Stephen and I head back into the car park.

'It was the right thing to come,' Stephen says.

'I'm proud of you. Hopefully you'll stop it happening to someone else.'

Stephen doesn't reply, but then we don't pay one another too many compliments, so it isn't a surprise. We're almost at the car when I speak next.

'Did he sound confident that they'd find the men who did it?'

Stephen rests against the driver's door. 'He talked about checking security cameras in the area. I think it'll probably be the last I'll hear of it. It'll end up in a big pile of unsolved crimes.'

'Like Jane Craven,' I say.

Stephen opens his mouth but then closes it again – and then we both get into the car.

TWENTY

Stephen drops me off at my house, before saying he's going to drive himself back to his own flat. He needs a change of clothes, if nothing else, and we leave it there. Outside of things for Creators' Club, we've never been people who plan too much. He'll turn up at mine, or vice versa, and we take it from there.

I let myself in and turn off the alarm, before deciding against it and heading back out again. I give a wave to Mr Bonner, who's in his window, and then get into my own car. Being with Stephen at the police station has clarified one thing: this isn't going away. I can't spend the rest of my life avoiding Mum, or trying to pretend that Penny doesn't exist.

It's an uneventful drive through the country lanes until I arrive outside Mum's house in Elwood. I let myself in, and call out that it's me, before she calls me through to the living room. There's some solace that, after everything from the barbecue the other night, she's now back in her chair with a television presenter shouting quiz questions at her at full volume. She makes her usual motion to stand and it's as if the other night never happened when I offer the inevitable invisible mug-to-mouth sign.

I make us both tea in the kitchen, while staring out the back window towards the barbecue off to the side. The faded green cover is back over the top once more, as it had been ever since Dad died, up until the night before last. The metal brush scraper he used to use to clean it is resting against the fence, with a series of black specks on the ground underneath.

I only realise I've been staring when the kettle finishes boiling. I make two cups of tea, knowing full well I won't be drinking mine, and then head back into the living room. The television is muted now, with subtitles flashing across the bottom of the screen.

'I didn't expect to see you on a Monday,' Mum says chirpily. This is another part of our routine that's repeated on a loop. I can come on literally any day of the week and she'll say she didn't expect to see me on that particular day. We're creatures of habit and this is our comfort blanket.

Or, it used to be.

'Stephen was attacked,' I say.

She gasps at the news. '*Your* Stephen?'

'I wouldn't call him mine – but yes.'

Mum puts a hand over her mouth and is so shocked, she lowers her legs from the rest and puts them on the ground. 'No! What happened?'

I give her a brief explanation and Mum shows the expected levels of surprise and outrage. Stephen might be my best friend but nobody loves him like Mum does. When we first started hanging around, she'd tell him – to his face – that it was a shame he was gay because he'd make the perfect husband for me.

Times have changed, and so has society. I doubt she'd say that now but there was a sort of compliment hidden among her clumsy way of expressing it. Stephen was never offended but he does use it as something with which to tease me now and again. He'll say that Mum will always love him more than me.

She asks if he's going to be all right and seems satisfied that he's been to the police with it. She calls him a 'poor dear' and asks if I think he'd like her to make some soup for him. I tell her no, although I do make a mental note that when I had shingles last year, she never offered to make *me* soup.

I think about texting Stephen to tell him about the soup thing. I'll be waiting for him to come back and say that Mum *still* loves him more than me. For a few minutes, in among the chaos, it's nice to have things feel normal.

Except they're not normal.

Mum moves on, asking if I want something to eat, or if I might prefer to go out for lunch or brunch. One of her friends went to some fish place that she calls 'a right bargain'. In a pure stream of consciousness, she moves on to tell me about a new place she saw in the paper. She thinks she might have had a voucher come through the door. She's pointing me towards a drawer in which it might be contained, except that I don't move.

'I went to Lower Woolton,' I say, forcing the words. 'I met Penny Craven. She's called Penny Morse now.'

Mum stares at me for what feels like a long time. Her mouth is open slightly and I can't read what she's thinking. A car beeps its horn somewhere out the front of the house but Mum doesn't flinch, or turn towards the sound. There's a second beep, then a longer third until a screech of tyre on road. That sense of the big square, small square is back. Believing something I don't believe at all.

'Why?' she asks eventually. Her voice is quiet and husky.

'Why do you think?'

It's as if she's ageing in front of me. I suddenly notice the liver spots pocked around her eyes and the intersecting lines from her mouth.

And then, unsure of what to do next, I simply ask the biggest question of them all: 'Was I stolen?'

Mum continues to stare and then she pushes herself up a little more rigidly. She crosses her knees, winces, and uncrosses them. Then she stares off towards the corner of the room, avoiding any possible eye contact. 'Of course you weren't.'

I'm ready for the answer. 'Dad bought a car from that area just before Jane was kidnapped,' I say. 'It's a place called Higher Woolton that merges into Lower Woolton. I saw the receipt in his scrapbook and there's a date on it. He bought a Talbot car that I never knew he had. I went to where the garage used to be. I saw how close it is to the newsagent where Jane was stolen.'

Mum is silent and still staring at a spot in the corner of the room. I stand and move around so that she's looking at me instead.

'Coincidence,' Mum says firmly. 'I didn't know that's where your father bought that car.'

'It's miles away, Mum. It's not like he saw an ad for a second-hand car in the newsagent's. He went a couple of hours out of his way. He was literally in the same area that Jane disappeared from at more or less the same time.'

'You're *my* daughter.'

There's something different about the way she says this. A defiance as opposed to a denial.

'Mum…'

She cradles her head in her hands and scratches so hard at her scalp that flakes fall onto her dark skirt. By the time she looks up and takes a breath, I already know what's about to come. Perhaps a part of me always knew?

'I should have told you,' she says.

And then she does.

TWENTY-ONE

I return to the seat as Mum focuses back on the corner. It doesn't feel as if this is the kind of conversation she'll get through if she has to look at me. She stumbles over a series of words, trying to find a way to begin.

'I couldn't have children,' she says. 'I know I told you that I couldn't have children *after* you but I never could.'

The room is cold as if we're outside. Now she's started talking, I want her to stop so that we can go back to a point where none of this had to be said.

'Your father and I wanted to adopt but it wasn't as simple as that. He had a conviction for drink-driving and—'

'What? Are you joking?'

There's a sad shake of the head. She catches my eye momentarily, knowing what it means to me of all people, then she glances away again. 'It was different times, not like it is now where everyone knows it's a bad thing.'

'It was *always* a bad thing, Mum.'

'I know. *He* knew. It's not an excuse, I'm just trying to explain what it was. He regretted that his entire life. We never told you because it didn't feel as if it mattered. He got his punishment and that was the end. Then, when you got a bit older and, well… you know, with your leg, it never would have been right.'

Even with everything else, this new revelation leaves me floored. 'I can't believe I never knew this.'

Mum twitches her arm. Not quite a shrug but almost. 'Would you have wanted to know? You adored your father. Would you *really* have wanted to think differently of him?'

I don't answer because she's probably right. I was always a daddy's girl and we would often go off to do our own thing at weekends while Mum was left behind. He bought me my first pair of hiking boots and we'd end up trekking up some hill before coming home to find that Mum was making bacon sandwiches, as if we were conquering heroes rather than weekend ramblers.

It's been a long time since I've hiked up anything and even the thought of it brings back the smell of drying mud in a neighbour's car on the drive home, the mist of the windows, the football commentary on the radio. It was never about the hiking.

It feels so close. If I were to close my eyes, I think I'd be able to see that car and to smell the mud.

I don't get a chance because Mum is still speaking.

'There was a girl from the area,' she says. 'Your dad got chatting to her boyfriend in the pub one night. She was pregnant but didn't want to raise the baby. Your father and I talked about it and we thought, maybe…?'

I stare at her but she doesn't finish the sentence. 'Thought what?'

'I know it doesn't feel like it was that long ago but it was a different time. There was no internet then. Everything felt further apart.'

I wait but she still doesn't say it, and so I do. 'Are you saying you bought me in a pub…?'

It doesn't sound real, even when it's me who's said it out loud.

Mum bites her bottom lip and takes a breath. This can't be true.

'It wasn't like that,' she says quietly.

'What was it like?' I snap the reply, not meaning to.

'We really wanted a child. We thought we could give someone a good life, that we'd be good parents. It seemed like the best thing for everyone.'

'So you bought me in a pub?'

'No. That makes it sound seedy and awful. Nicky never had the resources to raise a child – and she didn't want to anyway. It felt like it would make everyone happier. You *weren't* stolen.'

'I *wasn't* stolen but I *was* bought?'

Mum won't look at me. Her bottom lip is trembling as she resolutely stares at the wall.

I stare at her but she doesn't add anything – and so I do. 'Why did you lie?'

My question hangs for a few seconds. There's only one answer and Mum eventually gives it: 'What else were we supposed to do?'

She's right – and yet it feels as if she's so, so wrong. As if nobody could ever be more wrong.

'And we didn't really lie,' she adds. 'We just never said anything.'

'You told me my ear was damaged when you gave birth to me. You said that two nights ago! How is that anything other than a lie?'

She bows her head a tiny amount, acknowledging the point.

There's a moment that's hard to describe. A resigned sorrow that's more about the way she angles her head. Among what has apparently been a lifetime of lies, this feels like the truth.

'Who's Nicky?' I ask.

Mum blinks and breathes out. 'That was the surrogate,' she says. 'She introduced herself as "Nikki with two-Ks". It's why I remember the name so well. I'd never known anyone spell their name like that. She lived in Stoneridge and we only met one time. She was only about seventeen or eighteen and everything else was done through her boyfriend. None of us ever spoke again after the swap.'

The word 'swap' sticks and clings to the air. A dirty word in a dirty business. They swapped money for a child. *For me.*

Unexpectedly, and utterly out of character, Mum springs up from her chair. She moves quicker than I've seen her since Dad died. She stomps a little past me towards the cabinet where Dad used to keep all the manuals for various appliances. He never read any of them, preferring to tinker around with items until he figured something out himself. If not that, then burned himself, cut himself, or broke the brand new purchase. Either way, he *did* keep the manuals.

Mum opens the drawer and reaches in, before passing across a ripped shred from a brown envelope. It's tatty and rigid, a little like the article that came through my door, though not as fragile.

'What's this?' I ask.

Mum doesn't reply at first. She shuffles across to retake her seat, while I look down at what she's given me. On the back, in red ink, is my dad's handwriting. It reads a simple 'Nikki', which is followed by a phone number. It's a landline, with just six numbers and no area code, the way I remember them being when I was a kid. My friends and I each had one another's house phone numbers and would usually have to go through a parent to be able to speak to each other.

Dad had a sheet of paper taped to the wall by the phone that listed the numbers for his friends, or the businesses he might want to call. We never needed an area code because we never called anyone from outside the area. Mum's right about one thing: the world felt so much smaller then.

'I don't know why I kept it,' Mum says.

'*Where* did you keep it?'

'Around. In drawers, that sort of thing. I'd forget about it and then it'd show up somewhere or another. I could never bring myself to throw it away.'

I remember the smouldering papers from Saturday night, wondering if this was one thing too far of which Mum decided she couldn't rid herself. And if this is what she kept, then what did she burn?'

'Were you ever going to tell me?'

Mum is quiet and, for a while, I don't think an answer is going to come. I already know it anyway and then, quietly, reluctantly, it's there.

'No,' she says. 'Especially not after your father died.'

I give myself a moment to let it sink in. 'What changed?' I ask.

She makes no eye contact and instead stares at a spot on the floor. Her voice sounds frail. 'Because your father's not around to explain any of this. To try to make you understand what things were like and why we did it. I don't want your memories of him to be poisoned by whatever this is.'

I wish I didn't understand but I do. I came here thinking I'd been stolen and now I'm being told I was bought instead. I can't fathom whether one is better than the other. I don't think it is. Everything feels awful.

Mum isn't done yet. 'Nikki didn't want to give up the child,' she says.

'You mean me?'

She doesn't acknowledge this. 'Nikki changed her mind. She was so attached to the baby that—'

'*I'm* the baby!'

Mum falters and stops. She blinks and takes a breath, before picking up as if I haven't spoken: 'She was so attached that she didn't want to give up the baby. Your father and I could hardly go to the police and say that Nikki and her husband had taken our money. We didn't know what was going to happen. We didn't care about the money. We wanted the baby. We wanted… *you*.'

'What happened?'

She doesn't acknowledge the question at first. She swirls a hand in the air. 'I think he was called Bobby or Robbie,' she says. 'Something like that.'

'Who?'

'The husband or the boyfriend. It was always him we'd talk to. We all went back and forth, mainly over the phone.' She nods towards the envelope scrap in my hand. 'Your father would ring more or less every night. Sometimes they'd answer, sometimes not. We thought they'd ask for more money but they didn't. It wasn't some sort of blackmail or bribery. Robbie said that Nikki had grown attached and didn't want to give you up. We might have accepted that, even with the money, but he'd say things like they couldn't afford to get you nappies. He said they couldn't afford your food, or that you'd grown out of something really quickly. There was always something else. We were so worried but had no idea what to do. We kept saying we'd visit. I thought I might be able to talk them round – but they wouldn't have that. In the end, after about six months, they finally handed you over to us. That was the last your father and I ever heard from them.'

I slip deeper into the armchair and rub my eyes. It feels like far too much to be taking in – and that would be true without everything else from the past few days.

'What did you tell people?'

'When?'

'About the baby that appeared from nowhere!'

She rubs her own eyes and then stops midway through, as if realising she's mirrored me. 'We said it was a surprise birth, that I didn't realise I was pregnant. That you were a big baby.' She stops a moment. Blinks. Breathes. 'If anyone was unsure, then they didn't say anything. That sort of thing felt more common then...'

I picture the happy neighbours and friends, with whom I grew up. How they'd all been sold the same lie.

'I can't believe I'm only finding this out now.'

Mum still won't look at me. 'It was out of love,' she says.

'It's been thirty-four years, Mum.'

'Because of love. The moment we set eyes on you, that was it. Your father loved you in a way he could never love me.'

There's a lump in my throat now as I picture the sea of black at his funeral. People talked a lot about love that day.

I stand and tug at the shortened thread of hair that curls around my ear. The moment of feeling my scalp being pulled, the millisecond where it actually hurt, is something I want to repeat over and over.

Mum looks up from her chair, finally taking me in properly. 'It was out of love,' she repeats. 'All of it.'

I pause where I am but only for a second. Mum motions to stand but that's enough for me as I hurry into the hall – and then out to the car.

TWENTY-TWO

I remember reading an article a while back about how people shouldn't be judged for laughing at the most inopportune time. It was predominantly related to children being told off but then moved on to saying how some people deal with trauma by nervously laughing their way through it. There was an interview with a woman who couldn't stop giggling the entire way through her dad's funeral, which led to a massive fall-out in her family. I've never forgotten the line where she said she couldn't explain what was going on – which only infuriated the rest of her family more.

I'm driving back through the country roads, with the radio on silent, as I realise I'm laughing at the fact I've gone from having one mother to potentially having three. It's obscene and ridiculous – and yet I have no basis for being able to cope with it. There's Penny in Lower Woolton, who's convinced I'm her stolen Jane. There's someone named Nikki who either lives, or lived, twenty minutes away, who Mum says is my biological mother that sold me. Then there's… Mum. The person who raised me. The one I visit every two to three days. With texts and the like, I've been in contact with her more or less every day of my life. Even now, after the conversation we've just had, it's impossible to think of her as anything other than 'Mum'.

Since opening that envelope, for every answer I've received, it has given me more questions. Did Nikki steal and then sell me? Did my mother or father snatch a baby after all? Is Penny simply a stranger who had a daughter with a damaged ear?

And who put the article through my door to trigger all this?

I continue driving along the road and pass a crossroads that signals Macklebury in one direction, Elwood in another, and Stoneridge in the other. It seems extraordinary that my parents bought a baby, bought *me*, from someone who lived so close. Who might still live such a short distance away.

My phone rings as I drive, with 'Mum' flashing onto the central console. There were times around Dad's death that she'd call me immediately after I left her house and we would talk for the entire time it took me to get home. The speakers in the car would make it sound like her pauses and breaths were echoing around me.

I reject the call and continue driving, except that she tries again a few seconds later. When her name flashes onto the console a third time, I pull onto the verge and put the car into park. I almost press to answer, wondering what else she'll say apart from, presumably, 'sorry' – which is something I don't want to hear. That feels like a word that's used if a person accidentally bumps into someone, or drops something. It's not big enough to cover what she did.

The call rings off and the screen doesn't flash a fourth time. The road is empty and everything is quiet. Up ahead is another crossroads with a signpost that signals the way to Stoneridge. It's a village that's smaller than either Elwood, where I grew up, or Macklebury, where I live. The sort of postcard place that exists only in Britain.

I leave the car idling on the verge and delve into my bag until I find the envelope scrap that Mum gave me. Nikki's phone number only has six digits and I have the vaguest recollection that my parents' used to be the same. I try dialling it with the local area code and then a guesswork of numbers to go in front. Everything I try comes up with a series of beeps and then a woman's voice telling me that the number has not been recognised. It happens over and over to the point that I tell her, out loud, that *she* has not been recognised, even though I'm fully aware she's automated.

I think I'm losing my mind.

I turn off the phone and then ease the car into drive before starting back on the road. It's a whim, a stupid one at that, but instead of heading towards home, I take the turn for Stoneridge and keep driving until I reach the centre.

The sky is blue and there is a scant smattering of people ambling along the largely empty high street. One of the nearby shops has a piece of paper in the window, on which someone has scrawled 'customer parking ONLY' in thick red letters. It feels like things such as parking and kids having a beer in the park might be the sorts of low-level issues that give locals something to anguish about in between pandemics and referendums.

I get out of the car, not entirely sure what I'm planning to do, and then head along the street. There's an Italian restaurant that has chairs and tables blocking much of the pavement, then a couple of banks, a hairdresser, some charity shops, a bakery and a WH Smith. After that, at the end of the stunted street, there's a pointy obelisk that's been dumped in the middle of a green. I don't know why it's there but I can easily imagine some sort of festival taking place around it every summer.

It's all very cosy and familiar.

I end up in the Black Horse pub. It's a mix of outdated slum and something straight out of a guidebook for tourists. There are stone walls, low beams and a fireplace, plus large pump handles that line the bar. It doesn't feel like the sort of place that would be doing two-for-one Tequila Sunrises on a Friday night, let alone a Monday afternoon.

The guy behind the bar clocks me as I walk in and gives a nod of acknowledgement as I approach.

'What can I getcha?' he asks.

I only realise what I'm going to ask as it comes out. 'This might sound a bit weird but I was wondering if you know someone around here called Nikki?'

I tail off as his eyes narrow. He pouts a lip. 'Don't know any bloke named Nicky…?'

'It's a woman. She spells her name with two Ks. Maybe Nicola, or Nicole? Something like that…?'

He starts shaking his head slowly. 'Not in here, love.'

'Do you know anywhere else I can ask?'

The man pushes himself away from the bar and stands taller. At first I think he's going to tell me to get lost but then he calls into the back. Moments later, a woman appears and he asks her if she knows someone called 'Nikki with two Ks'. When she shakes her head, she turns to me and then pokes a thumb towards the outside.

'Try Via's,' she says. 'It's a café a few doors down. They know everyone in there.'

I thank them both and then hang awkwardly before the man snorts a laugh and tells me I don't have to buy anything. 'All part of the service,' he adds. 'I always say we're fifty per cent tourist information in here.'

Outside, and I start to walk back the way I came. Deep down, I know how ridiculous this is. I'm asking about a person who *might* have lived here more than thirty years ago – when all I have to go on is a name that's spelled in a slightly unconventional way. My only reference point is that people around here don't really move – and, if they do, it's not far. I shifted from one town to another that's a short distance down the road. Of the people with whom I went to school, I would guess there are a single-figure amount who've moved further. Some disappear off to university but many return. It's a pull that's hard to explain to anyone who never grew up in a community like this.

Via's is the sort of café that exists on every high street in the country. There are huge windows at the front and a smattering of tables that spill out onto the pavement. The menu board inside lists various teas and coffees, plus breakfast items, smoothies and bowls. There's a small group of women with pushchairs at the back, all talking over one another as coffee cups clink and babies babble.

A twenty-something freckled girl with red hair is behind the counter and I catch her rolling her eyes as one of the women says much too loudly that her husband is up for some promotion. The waitress then takes me in with a sideways glance, before continuing to clean the espresso machine pipes, until I step up to the counter.

'Vegetable paninis are on special today,' she says, with all the enthusiasm of a doctor explaining to a patient that they have cancer. 'Also, any coffee is a pound if you order food.'

The cynicism makes her instantly likeable.

'I came from the pub,' I say. 'I was looking for a woman called Nikki and they said it might be better to ask in here.'

The young woman's brow creases a little as she takes me in properly. 'Nicky?'

'With two Ks. It might be short for Nicola, or Nicole. She'd be in her early fifties…'

'Is she a customer here?'

'I have no idea – but I think she lives locally.'

It's a bit of a stretch, although the server seems to be considering it seriously as she takes a couple of seconds to mull it over. 'I don't know everyone's names,' she says. 'Even the locals. If you've got a photo, or something like that, I can have a look…?'

'I wish I did…'

She smiles with a degree of friendliness – and it's probably that which has me ordering a latte from her, even though it's the afternoon and I know it won't help me sleep. She says she'll bring it over and then I head to a seat in the window where I sit and look out towards the largely empty street. I listen to the sound of the coffee machine popping and half think about telling this stranger that my mother today told me I'd been bought from someone who lived in this village. It feels like something that's both intimate and should only be shared with the closest of friends – and yet something I could only tell to someone who doesn't know me at all.

A minute or so later and the server brings across the drink and places it in front of me. There's a small, square biscuit on the side and a heart shaped into the froth.

'I'm sorry I can't help,' she says – and it feels as if she means it. I thank her and then sit by myself, fighting the urge to turn on my phone before eventually giving in.

I'm expecting a list of missed calls, perhaps even voicemails, but nothing comes through. It leaves me both sad that Mum stopped calling and glad that she did. It feels like those duelling halves cannot be reconciled. A part of me never wants to talk to her again, while another wants to curl up to her on the sofa and let her tell me everything is going to be all right.

It's as I'm deleting emails that my phone begins to ring. It's not Mum, it's an 07 number from someone not in my contacts list. I realise most people ignore these sorts of call – but Stephen has a habit of losing his phone and then calling from whatever the new number is. It happens roughly once every six months, so I press to answer and give a quizzical 'hello?'.

There's a man's cough on the other end. It's gruff and something beyond a simple throat-clearing. 'That Hope?' he asks.

'Who's calling?'

'Kyle.'

He says this with an assurance that I should know who that is. I try to remember if it might be one of the parents from Creators' Club, except nobody comes to mind.

The pause must make it clear I have no idea who he is because, after an empty couple of seconds, he adds: 'Your brother.'

It takes me another moment to realise he's Penny's stepson. He's the scowling thirty-something who was leaning on a wall in the hallway as his father interrogated me. I never gave him my number, so he must have either got it from Penny, or perhaps overheard me giving it to her.

'What do you want?' I ask.

'Just thought I'd check in, seeing as we're related and all that…'

Even from the short amount of time I spent with him, I know that Kyle is not the type to check in on another person unless he's after something. It's also quite the assumption that we're 'related'.

I don't reply and so he keeps going.

'I looked you up,' he adds.

I feel the hair rising on my arm. Of course he did.

'What did you see?' I reply.

'You know what I saw.'

'Remind me.'

He gives a little snort. It's only a noise, not even a word, but I can hear the cockiness within it. The confidence of a bully. I know what he's going to say, although it's still a shock to hear it out loud.

'I know about the money.'

TWENTY-THREE

I suppose I knew deep down that it wouldn't be long before someone brought up 'the money'. I couldn't hide it, even if I wanted to. Kyle has presumably typed my name into Google – and it is there as the second link, behind some American lecturer's LinkedIn page.

'What about it?' I reply, trying to sound assertive.

There's a pause, which goes on for so long that I eventually realise Kyle has hung up. I stare at the screen wondering if he did it by accident and whether he's about to call back. When he doesn't, I'm left thinking that he hung up on purpose. That he didn't have any questions, it was that he wanted *me* to know that *he* knew.

I put the phone on the table, wishing I hadn't turned it back on. As if she knows something is not quite right, the server drifts back a few moments later and asks if there's anything she can do. She's probably checking that the coffee is fine, although she does linger for a second or two after I tell her that I'm good.

Stoneridge feels like a wasted journey. It is a small community but it would still be the longest of long shots to hope that somebody can be found three decades on, based off a first name alone. I finish the coffee, leave some money underneath the saucer, and then offer a cheery wave to the waitress before heading back to my car.

In the time it takes me to make that short walk and get into the car, I've missed a new call from Mum. She could leave a voicemail, except that she never does. Even in the days of physical answer machines, with their tapes and audible clicks, she would slam down the phone the moment she heard anything other than a live voice. It was like she'd been given an electric shock through the phone cord.

I start driving and am barely past the Stoneridge sign when Mum calls again. I think of the phone call I missed from her when Dad died. I was out with Stephen, doing terribly at a pub quiz, and everyone's phones were supposed to be off. Mine wasn't, obviously, but it was on silent. I only realised she'd called fifty minutes after I missed it. I went outside, which is when she told me I had to get to the hospital as soon as possible. I didn't need to ask why or what for, because I could hear it in her voice.

Not long afterwards, I reorganised the settings so that she was a priority contact and her calls would always get through. I vowed I would never miss another one of her calls – and yet here I am deliberately skipping a bunch of them.

The call rings off – but then the car console almost immediately lights up with another name. I've never been so popular when it comes to phone calls – except it's not Mum or Kyle this time, it's Mr Bonner.

I answer and he says my name hesitantly, as if not quite sure he's called the right person.

'It's Hope,' I tell him.

'Are you going to be home soon?'

'Maybe twenty minutes or so.'

'There's someone sitting on your doorstep.'

The hairs on my arms stand up. 'Who?'

'The red-jacket woman from the other day. She's been out there for about forty minutes. I went across and asked who she was but all she'd say is that she was waiting for you. I asked if she was one of your friends but she wouldn't say that either.'

'Did you ask her name?'

'She wouldn't give it. Do you want me to call the police?'

I tell him no and he says he'll keep an eye out through his window until I get home. He hangs up and I keep driving with a new urgency. I still don't know who put the article through my door.

I've only gone another couple of miles when the low-fuel light begins to flash. In any usual situation, I would pull into the petrol station close to home – but I don't want to stop before finding out who's on my doorstep.

I see the woman before I pull onto my driveway. Her red jacket stands out against the greying backdrop of the sky and the cream brickwork as she leans against the front of my house. Technically, I suppose she's trespassing. She checks something that might be a watch and then looks both ways along the street before noticing my car approaching. I slow, indicate, and then take the turn onto the drive.

We eye one another through the windscreen as I edge fully off the pavement and then pull on the handbrake. Out of the car and we stand half a dozen paces apart staring across to one another. She's younger than me but probably not by much. At a guess, I'd say she is thirty – although it's hard to judge because she looks as if she might have slept under a bush last night. Her dark hair is unwashed, with matted strands hanging around her ears. There's a smudge of dirt across her right cheek and her left eye is slightly swollen. It's not quite black but it's not far off.

There's a large backpack at her feet; the sort of thing that people drag off to festivals every summer and then leave behind because they're too big to lug around while hungover at the end.

Her arms are folded across herself as we continue to take in one another.

'Hope…'

She says my name as a definitive, not a question.

'Yes…?'

Her eyes dart sideways and she coughs a little, before quickly covering her mouth a fraction too late. 'I'm Stella,' she says. 'I think I'm your sister.'

TWENTY-FOUR

Stella pauses for breath but any reply I might have is stuck in my throat.

'Well, sort of sister,' she adds. 'Not really but kind of.'

'What do you mean?'

'It's a bit of a long story.' She nods towards the front door and hugs herself a little tighter. 'I was wondering if I could come in…?'

I glance next door and spy Mr Bonner standing at his front window, almost contorting himself in order to be able to see as far sideways as he can. I give him a small wave, letting him know that everything's fine, even though I'm not sure that it is. The glare from the glass makes it hard to see for certain but I think he nods at me – and then he's gone.

'It's cold out here…'

When I turn back to her, Stella is shivering – which isn't a surprise. She has the red jacket but it's thin and more like something to protect against a light breeze, as opposed to an actual chill. She's skinny in the way that someone with an eating disorder might be, with angular cheekbones and a gaunt, hollowed look to her eyes.

She glances towards the door again and I start fishing in my bag for the keys.

'How long have you been out here?' I ask.

'Maybe an hour…'

I step around her and unlock the door, then head inside and tap in the alarm code, before holding the door open for her. It's instinct as I start taking off my coat and shoes. Stella does the same, probably to be polite in the way I was at Penny's place. Her sleeve gets caught as she removes the jacket – and it's impossible not to notice the splodge of interlinked brown-purple bruises that dot her arm. As soon as she realises I've seen them, she rolls down the sleeve of her top and then crosses her arms over her front once more.

I lead her through to the kitchen and she carries her backpack with her, seemingly not keen to let it out of her sight. She places it in the corner as I pick up the newspaper cutting from the table, and then hold it up.

'Was this you?' I ask.

Stella glances away and chews the corner of her lip, answering without actually doing it. 'It's such a long story,' she says.

'I'm not in a rush.'

We stand across from each other for a couple of seconds. The next thing, we've slipped onto the stools where Stephen and I would usually sit when we're putting the world to rights.

The newspaper cutting is back on the counter and Stella takes a deep breath while staring towards it. She says nothing, as if expecting me to start but then, eventually, it comes.

'I was going out with this guy,' she says hesitantly. 'He's called Wayne and used to get drunk all the time. Things… happened. It went on for a while but it was basically always out of hand.'

Stella scratches the arm and the bruises, which is covered by her sleeve. When she realises she's doing it, she stops.

'I walked out in the end. I should've gone sooner but it wasn't that simple…' She swirls a hand around. 'Y'know what I mean…?'

She blinks as if she expects me to tell her that I *do* know. I'm not ignorant of abusive relationships, which is what she seems to be hinting at, but I can't pretend I actually *know*. I want to say something but don't know what and, in the end, she continues unprompted.

'I moved back in with my mum. Embarrassing, isn't it? Almost thirty and living in the room you had as a kid. I didn't want to be there.'

She snorts and holds up her hands as if to indicate my house. It almost makes me feel defensive, as if I should have to justify *not* being back at my parents' home, or feel guilty that I've not been in an abusive relationship.

'I left really quickly, which meant a lot of my stuff was at Wayne's house. I crammed some of it into my bag but had to leave clothes, shoes, all sorts. I'd left without telling him and didn't want to go back but I also didn't have any money to replace everything. I was trying to figure out what to do when I remembered some of my old things had been kept in this cupboard at the top of the stairs in Mum's house. It was mainly stuff I had as a teenager – a few clothes, some other bits and pieces.' She stops and smiles for the first time, tugging at her top. 'I don't know about you but I had awful taste when I was that age.'

If I wasn't waiting for her to get to the point, then I'd likely be smiling too. I narrowly missed the shell-suit generation – except that I somehow ended up with one anyway and thought the light purple and bright turquoise get-up was the greatest thing ever.

When I don't join in, Stella sucks in her already gaunt cheeks and glances towards the article once more. I immediately feel bad, as if I've booted a puppy.

'I went into that cupboard and started hunting around. There was a box of my old clothes and I was going through everything, seeing what might fit and trying to figure out if it was any good. Anything that meant I didn't have to go back to Wayne's.' She pokes a thumb towards the hallway. 'That jacket came right from the box. I used to wear it to school when I was about fifteen.'

Stella stops and tucks a strand of hair behind her ear, before taking a breath. 'Can I have some water, or something?'

She shivers and it's as if it starts somewhere around her chin and then works its way down until her entire body is trembling. I ask if she wants a tea instead and then I fill the kettle before flicking it on. Stella stares longingly across the kitchen towards it and I watch her gaze shift sideways as she takes in everything else. It's as if she's seeing all these things for the first time – even though it's simple items like a fridge, a toaster and a blender.

'Everything's so clean here,' she says.

That *does* make me laugh – partly because I see every smudge and blemish and also because I essentially never clean. It's Stephen who'll pick up a cloth and start absent-mindedly dusting and wiping. He says he finds cleaning kitchens therapeutic and, in his own words, 'zen'. A choice of word for which I laughed at him for a full five minutes.

I hang around close to the kettle until it clicks itself off. Stella asks for a little milk in her tea and then I'm back with her at the table. She has a sip from the steaming mug and takes a breath.

She sounds hesitant when she next speaks. 'There was all sorts in that cupboard. It's not like that…'

Stella points towards a cabinet in the corner of my kitchen, in which all the plates, cups and pans are kept. It comes up to my waist, with a set of double doors at the front. An IKEA special.

'The one at Mum's house is huge. Cupboard might be the wrong word. She lives in this old council-built home and it's almost a small room that's at the top of her stairs. I think there used to be a boiler or water tank in there that was removed. After it was gone, she used the space to stuff inside anything she didn't want to throw out. As well as my old stuff, there was a big bag of wire coat-hangers, a Christmas tree that hadn't been up in at least twenty years, suitcases covered in dust, an old Casio keyboard, with half the keys missing. Junk, basically. But there was a box in the corner that was dusty and had some sort of writing about bananas on the side. I assumed it was from a supermarket, or fruit shop.'

I picture the box from Mum's attic that had seemingly been emptied.

'I don't know why I looked inside,' Stella continues. 'There were newspapers in there. Whole ones – plus little snippets that had been cut out.'

I follow her gaze, again, to the one that now sits on my table. 'Was that in there?' I ask.

Stella nods slowly. 'It wasn't only that. There was paper out of a notebook with names and amounts of money written next to them. There was a baby weight. There was a handwritten contract, with signatures at the bottom and a date at the top.'

She pauses to sip her tea and every microsecond she isn't speaking leaves me on edge.

'The date was about seven years before I was born. I couldn't figure it out at first but maybe I just didn't want to believe it. I realised the names were of potential parents. The money was what they paid – and the baby weight related to what had been sold.'

I stare at her as she cradles the mug.

'I don't understand. You think your mum *sold* her baby – but you gave me a clipping about a baby that had been stolen…'

I say I don't understand but, deep down, I think I do. I just need to hear it.

Stella gulps. 'It took me a while to figure out but it was there in the clippings and the documents. There wasn't just one set of parents named on those pages, there were two. Mum gave birth to one baby – but she sold two…'

TWENTY-FIVE

Stella is trembling and tea spills over the top of her mug onto her hand. She gasps and drops the cup, sending it crashing to the floor, where it explodes in a shower of ceramic and brown liquid.

'I'm so sorry!'

Stella reaches towards the ground but I tell her I'll deal with it as I head to the cupboard under the sink and grab the dustpan, brush and a cloth. I mop up the liquid and then sweep the shards of mug into the pan, before depositing everything into the bin. It's only when I'm done that I realise Stella is sucking on the skin at the base of her thumb. I ask if it's okay and she holds it up to show a red mark that arcs across the joint of where her thumb meets the rest of her hand.

'It's fine,' she says.

I go to the freezer anyway and pull out a blue ice pack, which I wrap in a tea towel and hand across to her. Stella takes it and presses it to her hand.

'Sorry about the mug.'

'Don't worry. I got it for Christmas last year from a friend. He thought he was being funny.'

Stella has no idea what I'm talking about, so I cross to the bin and pick out the largest unbroken shard, which I hold up for her to see. Written on the side, in red capital letters, is 'Stephen is the best'.

Stella stares blankly at the mug.

'Stephen's my friend,' I say. 'He also got me a shirt to sleep in that says, "Stephen's great in bed".'

She doesn't see the humour and I find myself sheepishly returning the shattered mug part to the bin. I suppose it's one of those things that is funnier in the context of friends. I wish Stephen was here.

The atmosphere has changed now. The shattering of the mug has left me less on edge.

When I sit down, Stella continues: 'There were two sets of names in the pages in the box. At first I thought Mum might've had twins and sold both babies. But there was the cutting you now have – and I couldn't figure out why she'd have a newspaper article about a random kidnapped child from thirty years ago. It's not like it was a kid who lived in the same town as us. I ended up showing those things to Mum and asking her what it meant. I think I knew anyway. I thought she'd try to hide it, or pretend the pages weren't hers, but she didn't. It was like she wanted me to finally know.'

She motions to pick up the mug that's no longer there and so I push mine across towards her. I've not sipped from it – and she doesn't seem to mind that it isn't hers. She clasps it and sips, then turns towards the back of the house. Whoever was putting on the party now sounds like they're chainsawing through a tree.

'What's your mum's name?' I ask.

Stella's flickers back into the kitchen and puts down the drink. She sighs the reply: 'Nicola… but everyone calls her Nikki.'

I try to keep a straight face, even though I'm not sure if it matters that I already know the name. If Stella notices anything change from me, then she doesn't show it as she continues.

'Mum said that she got pregnant when she was a teenager, way before me. She had no family and didn't think she could look after the baby. Her boyfriend reckoned he could find someone to buy it. She said she wanted to give the child up for adoption – but I guess…' She tails off momentarily before picking up the thought again. 'I guess she went along with it. I don't know what happened, or what changed – and she didn't want to talk about details. I think she was embarrassed but she'd been drinking and…'

Another sigh. Stella tugs at her hair once more and makes sure she's not looking anywhere near me. 'Mum has a history with drink. Sometimes she's good with it, sometimes not. She said her boyfriend ended up agreeing a sale with two couples, not one. Except she only had one baby…'

It's so surreal to hear this out loud. Stella speaks as if this is something normal, like someone was having an eBay clear-out.

This time, she does seem to see something in me, because she quickly adds: 'I didn't just sit there and say it was fine. I told her I couldn't believe what she'd done, that it was disgusting, that *she* was. That she'd denied me a brother or sister, that she'd stolen someone else's child and *sold* it. She kept saying it wasn't her, that it was him, but I couldn't face her. I didn't want to hear any more.'

She stops for a breath and it feels as if everything just said came out in one go.

There is a moment of respite and then: 'I walked out and I've not seen her since.'

Stella sounds distraught now, as if this has been sitting with her and building.

'How long ago was that?' I ask.

Stella turns away and scratches at the marks on her arm. 'C– couple of weeks? I've been staying with friends. Few nights here, few nights there. I'd sleep on the sofa, the floor, or wherever. At my last place there was a three-year-old and a dog. The three-year-old would wake up at four every morning – and I'm allergic to dogs. Not only that, I didn't want Wayne to catch up to where I was staying, so I had to move on.'

The manic energy of before has fallen out of her now. She's slumped and staring at the counter.

'How did you find me?' I ask.

'Barbara and Ged Taylor were two of the names on Mum's pad. There was a funeral notice online about Ged Taylor dying and it named his wife, Barbara, and their daughter, Hope. I couldn't believe you all only lived a few miles away. There was a picture of you – and a picture of the stolen baby – and… well…'

Her gaze flicks to my ear and then quickly away again. She mutters a soft 'sorry' and we sit in an uncomfortable silence for a short while. It doesn't feel as if either of us know what to say.

'I was lucky about your parents' names,' she says, speaking quietly. 'I looked for the other baby. My *actual* sister. The one Mum had. I couldn't find anything connected to the names on her pad. It was a really common name – John and Jenny Smith – and there were too many matches to narrow it down. I wonder if they gave fake names, or if they moved right after getting the baby. I don't know. Then I found you and I suppose I figured it was something.' She stops and then quickly adds: 'I didn't mean it like that. I was happy to see the names, to know that you might be close.'

She squirms a little on the stool, hugging her arms across her front – and, from nowhere, I feel an urge to reach out and let her know that it's all right. It sounds as if we're both dealing with betrayals from parents.

'Why send an anonymous clipping? Why didn't you just tell me?' I ask.

Stella twists and stares at me now and I can see the desperation of her wanting me to understand.

'We don't know each other. Imagine if I came up to you on the street and said we were sisters, or that you might have been snatched. Or that your mum and dad might've bought you. You'd never have believed me. I put the article through your door because I thought you might look into it and ask around. Maybe even ask your mum…?'

There's a question there that I don't answer. Not yet, anyway. I feel exhausted and don't know what to say or do. It's not only that there's a lot to take in, it's the speed at which everything has happened.

We sit for a few moments more and then Stella pushes herself up and crosses to her bag, which she picks up. As she strains downwards, I notice a line of bruises on her neck that I hadn't seen before.

'Are you leaving?' I ask.

She blinks up with surprise. 'I figured that was everything. I wanted to leave you a few days with the cutting but you know as much as me now.'

I nod towards the mug on the counter. 'You should finish your tea. Well, my tea…'

She looks between the mug and me. 'I don't really drink tea. I didn't want to say no…'

There's the slimmest of smiles on her face, which I realise I'm mirroring. It was Stephen who got me back into hot drinks because cups of tea are his heroin. I ended up drinking teas and coffees with him more for socialising than anything else.

'Where are you going to go?' I ask.

Stella tugs at her unwashed hair again. 'Not home to Mum, if that's what you mean.'

She sounds affronted and I suddenly see the depth of disgust within her. Those conflicting feelings I'm having for my mother are what she's having for hers.

'That's not what I meant,' I reply. 'You said you were with friends but that you moved on. I didn't know what that meant for you.'

I almost say that it looks as if she's been sleeping rough but stop myself.

'There's a hostel,' she says. 'I've got enough money for the next few nights.'

'What about after that?'

Stella hoists her bag onto her back and doesn't answer.

'Do you want to stay over?' I ask this so quickly that I surprise myself. The words seem to come automatically. 'I've got a spare room. There's a shower and...'

Stella pauses in the door, her back turned to me. Since moving into the house, I have only ever lived by myself – even though Stephen stays over semi-regularly. I almost want to retract the offer as instantly as I made it.

'We're sisters,' I say. 'Not really but kind of...'

Stella turns and a hint of a smile is on her face as I've copied her phrase.

'Are you sure?' she asks.

'I wouldn't have offered otherwise.'

'Maybe just tonight.'

TWENTY-SIX

TUESDAY

Stella's bag is packed and resting against the front door when I get downstairs the next morning. She is already in the kitchen and the bitter smell of coffee clings to the air. She's sitting in the same stool as the day before. When she turns and sees me, she shrinks into herself slightly, tightly clasping a mug.

'I didn't know if this was okay,' she says. 'I didn't want to wake you and—'

'Did you find the good stuff?' She frowns a little and so I add: 'There's expensive coffee on top of the fridge and cheaper stuff in the cupboard by the machine.'

'I used the stuff by the machine.'

She sounds nervous and embarrassed, perhaps not realising that I'm joking. There's coffee in the jug underneath the machine and I fill a mug for myself before sitting with her.

'How did you sleep?' I ask.

She shrugs and I realise I've turned into a mother. If she slept anything like I did, then it involved a lot of thoughts and not much sleeping.

Stella took a shower last night and her hair is now dry. Without the grease and grime, it's a lighter shade of brown than I thought. The smudges of dirt have gone from her face and everything about her seems brighter than the previous evening. She's wearing jeans with a hole in the knees and the same long-sleeved top as yesterday.

'I think I'd like to meet Nikki,' I say. She doesn't respond to this, not at first anyway, and so I add an unnecessary: 'I'd like to meet your mum.'

'Is that really what you want?'

'Wouldn't you?'

Stella squints towards me: 'But she stole you. She *sold* you.'

'That's why I want to meet her.'

Stella breathes in and holds it. She closes her eyes for a second and then reopens them. 'Are you going to call the police…?'

I almost answer immediately but then realise I don't know what to say. In everything that's been going through my head overnight, the police hadn't been in my thoughts. I wonder if this is why Stella has been so nervous – not because this is all so crazy but because she's worried about the consequences.

'I don't think so,' I say. 'But there's so much I'd like to ask her.'

'She could go to prison. We don't get on but she's still my mum.'

I think of my own mother, sitting by herself at home with those photos and memories of Dad. With all the unanswered calls. She hasn't tried to contact me since I dodged her yesterday. The act of buying me was surely illegal in itself. It wouldn't only be Nikki in trouble.

Even that thought seems insane.

It's suddenly real.

Things have been building ever since the article came through my door. The thought that it couldn't be possible, then an inkling – a fear – that it might be… and now that it is. There are still so many questions and it feels that if I stop for too long, I'll end up having to try to figure out who I am and what it all means.

Contacting the police would mean leaving those questions to be asked and answered by somebody else. I'm not sure what that would leave me with.

'I don't think I want either of our mums to go to prison…'

Stella opens her mouth and then closes it. I'm not sure why but it's as if I know that she was going to say that my mum *isn't* my mum. Or, perhaps that's the main thought that's kept me up and I don't know how to deal with it?

'Do you really want to talk to Mum?'

'Yes.'

Stella reaches across to the counter and picks up the pad and pen that has been sitting there, largely unused, since I moved in. She scribbles in the corner to get the ink going and then starts to write. When she's done, she slides the paper across to me. On it is written the name 'Nikki' and then an address, with 'Stoneridge' at the bottom. I don't know the village well enough to know how close it is to the centre and where I was barely a day ago.

Stella puts down the pen and looks up to me. 'Do you know where Stoneridge is?' she asks.

I almost say that I was there yesterday. 'I grew up in Elwood,' I say. 'Went to school there, got my first job there, opened my first bank account there. Everyone in Elwood knows where Stoneridge is.'

She nods as if she knows this already. 'Are you going to visit her?'

'Yes.'

'Today?'

'Yes.'

We sit silently for a few moments, each sipping our drinks. There's something about her presence that's comforting. It's difficult to explain but I think it's because we're going through a similar thing at the same time.

'Do you want to come?' I ask.

'To see my own mum?'

'I thought it could be different if we're together…?'

She holds the mug close to her mouth, seemingly thinking it over. 'I don't think I want to see her,' she says. 'Maybe another day but not today.'

Stella finishes her drink and then puts the mug down a little too forcefully, something for which she immediately – and unnecessarily – apologises.

'What are you going to do with the day?' I ask.

'Sort out a place at the hostel. After that, there's a temp agency I've been talking with.' She holds up her hands. 'I don't have a job. It's been difficult because I've been living in so many different places.'

She looks away as she says this and I wonder if she's actually been living rough since leaving her mum's house; whether the 'friends' she spoke of yesterday actually exist. There was a definite vagueness with what she was saying. She reaches for her phone and holds it up. It's not new. It's a Samsung from a few years ago with a scratched cover and case that easily fits in her palm.

'I had to change my phone,' she says. 'Wayne was texting and calling all day and night, but he doesn't know this number.'

'Where's the hostel?'

'On the outskirts of Elwood. I was looking at the buses and there's one at ten-thirty, then another every hour.'

'Tell the agency you live here.'

She doesn't react at first and it feels as if I've again surprised both of us. The bruises at the base of Stella's neck have faded a little overnight, although she's still rubbing the ones that I know are on her arm.

'For pay cheque reasons?' she asks.

'Just stay. That room is empty and it's got to be better than a hostel.'

Stella doesn't react, other than to take a breath through her nose. There's another buzzing sound from the back of the house and her gaze flickers towards the windows and away again.

I want to tell her that it's as much for me as her. That it feels as if she's the only person I can talk to about everything that's going on. We're not sisters as such… except we sort of are because we're united in betrayal by our respective mothers.

'I don't want to impose,' she says.

'You wouldn't be.'

'But we don't know each other…'

'I don't mind if you don't mind.'

Stella's eyes glance towards the front of the house and, for a moment, I wonder if she's about to pick up her bag and go. I'm as surprised as anyone that I don't want her to do this. That I want her to stay.

'I'm going to get dressed and then I'm going to go out,' I say. 'It would be great if you were here when I get back, so we can talk to you about what your mum says.'

She nods along. 'I don't want to be in the way.'

'Have you seen this house? I'm the only one who lives here!'

I know what she's going to say a moment before she does. Her shoulders loosen and she stands a tiny bit taller.

'Only if you're sure,' she says. 'And not for long. Maybe a day or two.' She stops and then adds: 'Can I have your Wi-Fi password? It'll make everything easier. The internet at Mum's house was terrible. She's always going on about how slow it is on BT and…' Stella stops herself, perhaps because of the mention and thought of her mother. I'm not sure.

I dig through the drawers until I find the letter with the password and then leave her to it, before heading upstairs to shower and change. By the time I get back downstairs, Stella's backpack has been moved from the front door and is now resting in the corner of the kitchen once more.

As I enter the kitchen, Stella speaks softly, almost as if it's to herself. 'Mum's not usually a good drunk,' she says. 'Sometimes she finds everything hilarious, other times she throws things, or shouts and cries. If you get her on a good day, she might tell you whatever you want to know. If you don't…' – she looks away – 'you're best leaving her.'

Despite the gentle tone, there's something ominous in Stella's voice. I wonder if the bruises came from her ex-boyfriend, or her mother – or somewhere else entirely. Whether there are more hidden away, as well as those on her neck and arms.

'Does anyone know you're here?' I ask.

'Like who?'

'Your ex-boyfriend.'

'Wayne…' Stella says his name with a half-sigh and it's almost wistful. It's difficult to know what that means. If we knew each other better, I'd ask. 'He doesn't know,' she adds. 'Nobody does, except you.'

'You're safe here.'

I've made a big jump in logic but Stella doesn't tell me I'm wrong.

'Your neighbour knows,' she says.

'I'll talk to him. It's not as if he's going to know loads of people to tell anyway.'

'He was watching me from his window.'

'He's protective over me. Don't worry about it.'

Stella finally seems to take this. She looks up with an accepting smile: 'I'll be here when you get back,' she says.

I give her the spare key that's usually left attached to the fridge by a magnet – and then grab my stuff before heading outside. It feels strange to lock the front door, knowing there's somebody inside. I've lived by myself for a fair while and that brings a routine with it, such as setting the alarm. I consider going back to explain the code and how it works – except that there seems little point. If she leaves and comes back, I figure the house will be fine without the alarm. This area of Macklebury is hardly a crime hotspot and the alarm system was already installed when I moved in.

I have one foot over the fence to next door when Mr Bonner's door opens. He was clearly waiting for me and his face is etched with concern as he steps outside. That instantly fills me with regret at not knocking on his door the day before.

'You all right, love?' he asks. 'You look exhausted.'

He doesn't mean it as an insult – and I suppose it's true.

'Everything's fine,' I reply, attempting to sound chipper. 'That girl in the red jacket is a relative. She's called Stella. Feel free to say hello if you see her around. She might be staying for a few nights.'

One of Mr Bonner's eyes twitches and I wonder if this means that he somehow knows everything isn't quite as straightforward as I'm making out. If he does, then he doesn't let on. 'As long as you're safe,' he says.

We stand awkwardly and I don't know what else to say, so I turn and head back to the car. I've unlocked it and got into the driver's seat, while Mr Bonner hasn't moved. He gives a small wave from the fence and continues to watch as I back out onto the road.

As soon as I start driving forwards, the low-fuel light reminds me that I ignored it yesterday in my rush to get home. I turn away from the road that will lead me to Stoneridge and Nikki's house, instead heading to the petrol station that sits a little outside the town's boundary, on the way to the main road.

It's only as I'm fiddling with the pay-at-the-pump card reader that I realise I'm being watched.

I look through the gap between two pumps to see Angel standing next to her own car. It is, somewhat predictably, a pink Mini with eyelashes attached to the headlights. From memory, there's a sticker in the back window along the lines of 'Don't piss off this bee-yatch'.

I'd almost forgotten about the scratch along the side of my car – but it's clear and obvious as I round the vehicle to get to the pump itself. I still think she did it.

I turn away, focusing back on the card reader, except that my ex's girlfriend isn't ready to let this pass.

Suddenly, she's a few steps away, eyeing the side of my car. 'What happened to the car?' she asks.

I ignore her momentarily but the smugness of the question makes me tingle with annoyance. When I look back to her, she has one hand on her hip and nods towards the slashes along the side of my car.

'Did you do it?' I ask.

It's only four words – but that's seemingly enough for Angel to march around the petrol pump until we're side by side.

'What did you say?'

'I asked if you keyed my car.'

'Don't you *dare* get in my face.'

I turn away and pick up the nozzle, before putting it into my car and holding down the handle to start the flow.

'I'm not in the mood for this, Angel.'

'You think you're better than me, don't you?' she hisses.

I consider saying 'yes', solely because I know how much this will annoy her. Instead, I bite my tongue and focus on gripping the handle of the fuel pump.

Angel takes a small step to the side, putting herself back into my eyeline. We're only a step away from one another, with the hose of the pump separating us.

'You ignoring me?'

'I asked if you keyed my car. If you say it wasn't you, then fair enough.'

'I told you it wasn't me.'

'You didn't actually, you—'

Angel doesn't wait for me to finish. She lunges forward and snatches at my arm. I wince away involuntarily as she steps back, too. There's a second where she seems shocked at what she's done, while I'm confused. There's a gash in my forearm from where her lengthy, sharp nail broke the skin. There's a hint of blood as I stop pumping and hold my arm up for her to see.

'Why'd you do that?'

The mark doesn't hurt, although there's a steady dribble of blood. If it wasn't for everything else, I'd probably be more angry. This run-in with Angel seems so tame in comparison to what I've found out in the last couple of days.

I can see Angel's indecision, not sure if she wants to argue, or back away. She was trying to grab me for some reason, not scratch me.

Angel takes a couple of steps back, checking over her shoulder as she does. 'Just stay away from him,' she says.

'*I* broke up with Aki,' I say. 'If I had any interest in us being together, I wouldn't have done that.'

'I know your game.'

'You don't.'

She continues to eye me before disappearing back through the gap between the pumps. The engine of her pink monstrosity roars and then, seconds later, she surges off the forecourt.

TWENTY-SEVEN

I park in the centre of Stoneridge, close to Via's café from the other day, and then check Google Maps to see where I should go next.

There are soft scabs on my arm now – Angel's handiwork – but I do what I've spent all this time attempting to do: ignore her. I've got bigger problems anyway.

Nikki's house is on the very edge of Stoneridge – and, as I follow the route on foot, it quickly becomes clear that there is a separate part of this village that's almost part of another place, perhaps another world. Away from the postcard High Street and Britain in Bloom signs, there's a housing estate over the river and up a hill. From the High Street, it's a glowing emerald mound of hillock and trees, except, hidden behind is a sprawl of red-brick two-storey flats.

There's no way they've been built in this spot by accident and I can picture planning meetings where social housing had been demanded. Council busybodies worried about their house prices would have zoned a secluded spot well away from the village's picturesque ideal. Those social houses *could* be built – with the proviso that nobody actually had to look at them.

The two-storey row of flats immediately behind the trees is ugly and blocky: all right angles and dirt-coated guttering. The hum of somebody's god-awful music is being drowned out by someone else's god-awful revving of an engine. A giant phallus has been graffitied on a garage door and then 'cock' written underneath, just in case it's not clear what it is. I keep walking and it's a world away from my own cosy existence a few miles along the road.

It's another couple of minutes until I arrive at a row of squat terraced houses. They all share the same mucky double-glazing, plus tiny patches of land at the front, most of which have cars parked across.

And then I'm there.

I tell myself it's only a front door. I've opened the one that leads into my house thousands of times. I've knocked on them, or rung their doorbells over and over. Except there's hardly ever been a time when I was not sure what to expect from the other side.

Nikki's front door used to be white. There's a card stuck to the inside of the glass that reads 'NO PAPERS' and then a smaller one next to it with 'NO SOLICITORS'. At first, I figure it's somewhat specific but then I realise she probably means 'no soliciting'. Or, perhaps, I was right the first time.

There's no doorbell, so I knock hard on the glass and then wait. I eye the scab on my arm as I'm again very aware of my heartbeat. It's as if it's counting the moments that the door goes unanswered.

A minute passes, or at least that's how it feels. There's no answer and no movement and so I knock a second time. This brings an almost instant reaction as a woman growls a grumpy: 'I'm not buying anything!' from inside.

I call back to say that I'm not selling anything and then there's an even grouchier moan and sigh before I hear the sound of someone shuffling ever closer.

The door is wrenched open a fraction, locking in place with the length of the chain. A face appears in the gap – and there's an instant similarity to Stella. The woman has greasy long hair that's clumped around her ears and gaunt cheeks, as if she could really do with a good meal.

'I'll call the police,' she says.

I don't get a chance to reply because, as she's speaking, I see her focus in on my ear. Her eyes go wide and, in an instant, as she finishes the word 'police', the door is slammed in my face.

The wham of impact fizzes through the air and I feel the rush of air against my face. There are no footsteps on the other side of the door – and, even though I can't see her, I sense Nikki on the other side, within touching distance.

I crouch and sit on the step – which is harder than it would once have been, given my leg. I open the outside flap of the letterbox and then push through to nudge the inner one.

'Nikki…?'

There's a pause for a moment and then a slight brush of movement that's close but out of sight.

'It wasn't me,' Nikki says. There's a croak to her voice.

'What wasn't you?'

She doesn't answer the question, instead asking if the police are with me.

'You know they're not,' I reply. 'Look out your window if you want to check.'

There's a long sigh, a silence, and then: 'I always knew you'd find me one day. Didn't know how old you'd be but I knew.' A pause. 'Did Stella give you my address?'

I don't answer that. When Nikki says her daughter's name, she sounds sorrowful, as if she's lost something. Perhaps she has?

'Can I come in?'

My question goes unanswered at first. I figure that's a reply in itself – probably the predictable one – but then, eventually, there's another trundling movement out of sight and the door clicks.

I pull myself up and then push on the door handle, which gives and opens inwards. I edge into a darkened hallway, squinting through the gloom to where Nikki is sitting on the bottom step of the stairs.

'Stella found you, didn't she?' Nikki already knows the answer and adds: 'The daughter who doesn't want to know me.'

I close the door behind me and then we remain where we are: me standing, her sitting. I have so many questions and yet none of them want to come out.

Nikki looks shattered in more sense than one. Exhausted through a lack of sleep, hungover, perhaps – but also broken. Her bony shoulders are slumped as her head hangs low to her knees.

'What did Stella tell you?' she asks.

'That she found some cuttings and some papers. I know I was stolen. I know I was sold.'

I should be angry. I *want* to be furious – except I feel something else that's difficult to quantify. Perhaps a sense of sorrow that any of this had to happen? A sense that at least three families were never what they should have been and, from now, will never be the same.

I thought I might end up shouting at Nikki but, instead, I'm not sure I feel anything at all for her.

After a while, she sighs again and pulls herself up using the banister. She edges around the hall, keeping a distance from me and then pressing on towards the doorway at the far end. I follow her through into a kitchen that looks like it was fitted in the seventies or eighties and hasn't been touched since. There are grimy checked Formica counters; plus cheap, patchy lino on the floor. The hob of the oven is coated with black, burned overspill and there are brown patches on almost all the walls.

'You want a tea?'

I stop eyeing the kitchen as I realise Nikki is watching me. She's standing by the sink, with the kettle underneath the taps.

'No.'

She fills it and then plonks it on its stand before flipping it on. When she next takes me in, she follows my stare towards the open back door.

'Cat flap doesn't work,' she says. 'No way for the cat to get in unless I leave it open.'

I don't reply to that as I try to find the words to ask the questions I actually want answered.

Nikki is watching me through oily strands of hair that are plastered across her face. She pushes them away, back behind her ear.

'What did Stella tell you?'

'Doesn't matter. I want to hear it from you. You owe me that.'

Nikki pushes herself up onto her tiptoes momentarily but then hunches back down and gives a small, accepting nod.

'Do you really want to know?'

'I think I've waited long enough.'

In truth, it's only been a few days but it feels a lot longer.

Another sigh. 'You might not believe me but none of it was my idea. I wasn't in a great place. I was young and addicted and…'

She doesn't finish the sentence but she does cross the kitchen, open a drawer and pull out a blister pack of tablets. She pops two into her hand and swallows them dry. She stands still for a second and glances towards me, perhaps hoping I've left.

'I was pregnant but I couldn't cope,' she says. 'Robbie – my boyfriend – said he thought we could get some money from the baby. I said no but…'

Nikki shrugs and fully turns away, facing the kettle and waiting for it to finish. When she next speaks, her voice is low and husky, like someone with the flu.

'I didn't *want* to sell my baby.'

'But you did.'

'Robbie did… but yes. Except it wasn't so simple. There was a time, early on, when there was a blip on the scan and I thought it might be twins. The woman at the hospital wasn't sure. She said she didn't know but Robbie became convinced there was going to be two babies, even though the hospital later said there was definitely only one.'

The kettle flicks itself off and Nikki stands still for a few moments before drifting across the kitchen to pour the water into a mug. She plops in a teabag and squishes it with a spoon before pulling the bag back out and dumping it in the sink on top of at least half a dozen others. She fills the mug with too much milk and then scoops in a full tablespoon of sugar. After that, she gives her drink the most cursory of stirs.

It's an abomination.

'Robbie kept talking about double the money,' she says. 'I said there was only one baby but what I didn't realise was that he'd already made some sort of agreement with two different couples. He met one guy in a pub and another was related to someone he knew on a building site.'

She shrugs and holds up her hands as if to say, 'What is he like?'. The sort of thing someone might do if their partner stayed out late one night. I don't think it's meant to minimise what happened but, at the same time, I want to shake her and say that this is my life.

'Robbie had been collecting expenses. That's how he used to talk about everything. He wouldn't say they were paying us, he'd say they were covering our expenses. He'd say we needed money for the car, so we could get to the hospital; or something to cover groceries to keep me healthy. Whatever he could think of. I honestly didn't know at first – but I found his book and saw that he'd been collecting from two sets of people. He'd been stringing them along, promising them both a baby – except there was only ever going to be one. He said he'd deal with it and then, a bit later, that he'd found a way to make everyone happy. I should've asked him what he meant but I was almost due by then and I suppose…'

The sentence ends and the gist is clear. I'm surprised at how believable I find it. I have no idea who Robbie is, or what he looks like, but I can picture a person realising he's on to a good thing money-wise – and then wondering how he can double the income. When Mum told me she and Dad were strung along for a while after the birth, I can picture Robbie's panic as he tried to figure out a solution. How he came to a horrifying idea and then saw it as the only way out of the dilemma into which he'd dropped himself.

Nikki is staring at her tea: 'I didn't want to do it.'

'But you went along. You recognised me – so you must have known about the baby's ear. You *knew* Robbie had stolen a baby and then sold it.'

She rocks backwards a moment. Blinks. Then gives the gentlest of nods. 'You don't know what he was like…'

There's something lingering in her words that means any anger that might have been bubbling stays stuck within.

'I always felt guilty,' she says. 'It's not like it could be undone – then it was too late.'

'Where's Robbie now?'

I find myself looking back towards the hall, as if he might be there.

'Fell off some scaffolding about ten years ago. Think he had something up with his liver anyway. We weren't together at the time. We broke up not long after everything happened with… well… you know.'

I'm still looking towards the hall, not wanting to believe it. If Robbie was still around, at least there would be someone on whom I could take out my anger. Someone who definitely deserves it.

'Why did you keep his documents and the clippings?' I ask.

A shrug. 'Couldn't quite let go. I used to read that article now and then. I don't know why.'

'Can I see them?'

Nikki puts down her drink and gulps away a sigh. She shakes her head. 'I got rid of everything after Stella found them. It went out with last week's rubbish.'

I wonder if she knows that Stella kept the article. Whether it matters. I think of Mum's own barbecue and wonder what she burned when she was still trying to pretend this wasn't happening.

Nikki has seemingly moved on. When she next speaks, it's with a new-found speed, as if the words can't come quickly enough.

'I always wanted a daughter,' she says, 'especially after I had to give mine away. Stella came along seven years after and she was perfect. All I ever wanted.' She looks up and catches my eye. 'She's not Robbie's.'

I almost ask who the father is but then realise it doesn't matter. The chances of me knowing the person are almost zero anyway.

'I've blown it,' Nikki adds. 'She doesn't ever want to see me again – not after all this. Not after she found out what I did. She won't answer my calls and I think she's changed her number.'

She peeps across towards me, wondering if I'm looking at her. When she realises I am, she glances away once more.

'Are you expecting me to feel sorry for you?'

A shake of the head. 'No…' She takes a breath and then dumps her grim-looking tea into the sink, where it belongs. 'I'll never know my grandchild now – and who else is there?' She holds up her hands to indicate the house and her isolation.

I almost miss it in among the self-pity. Almost move on.

'Stella's pregnant…?'

It's the first real acknowledgement that I've spent any time with Nikki's daughter, although she doesn't react to this. I suppose it's obvious given that I'm here.

Nikki nods.

'How far along?' I ask.

'Few months.'

I picture Stella with all her bruises and the story of how she escaped her drunken boyfriend. How she might have been sleeping rough since leaving this house – all because she was so disgusted with her mother. How it feels as if she sacrificed so much to tell me something I would never have found out otherwise.

'What happened to the other child you sold? Your own baby?'

Nikki looks up and blinks at me, as if this is a question she hadn't expected. 'I don't know.'

'Nobody ever made contact?'

'Why would they? It's taken this long for you to find me.' There's an edge to this but she bites her lip and then continues more softly. 'I never forgot her. Robbie always said she went to a good place. Some couple with plenty of money. He said they moved not long after. Even if I wanted to look, I didn't know where to start. It wouldn't have been right anyway.' She looks down to her feet and then back up to me. 'This isn't fair on anyone.'

She's right – except that it doesn't sound good coming from her.

'You're not going to the police, are you…?' Nikki's fully watching me now, hands tucked into the opposite armpits as she holds herself. 'I wouldn't blame you,' she adds.

That's both Nikki and Stella who've asked whether I'm going to take this to the police and, for the first time, I'm wondering if perhaps I should.

Except I look around at the kitchen with all its clutter and mess. Then there's the tatty carpet in the hallway, the cat flap that doesn't open and the crack in the window ahead of me and I wonder what good it would do. Nikki has to be in her early fifties – but she looks seventy. She's been on the planet for half a century and has almost nothing to show for it.

Everything – all of this – feels so utterly pointless.

'I don't think so,' I say.

She nods again, solemnly and almost as a thank you. 'Do you hate me?'

'I don't know you.'

I take a small step away from her, suddenly wanting to leave. I figure I know as much as I'm going to.

Nikki must notice because she moves towards me. 'Were you brought up right?' she asks. 'I mean did your mum and dad look after you properly? They didn't hit you or owt?'

It comes out as a jumble of words but there's desperation in her voice. It feels as if I could break her with a lie to say I had a traumatic childhood. Her gaze flickers to the mark on my arm from where Angel grabbed me with her nails.

'They were good to me,' I say.

She settles back, leaning on the edge of the sink. 'I was always so worried, wondering what sort of people they might be when they knew you were stolen.'

I've already taken a couple more steps towards the hallway and her words almost wash over me a second time. It takes a moment to sink in.

'Are you saying they knew…?'

'Who knew?'

'Are you saying Mum and Dad *knew* I was stolen?'

A blink. 'Whose idea do you think it was to do the kidnapping?'

TWENTY-EIGHT

I've been sitting in my car, in the centre of Stoneridge, for at least fifteen minutes. There's hardly anyone in the village today but the sun is now out and it's singeing through my windscreen. If Mum was here, she'd be talking about how I'll get burned without cream, no matter that it's still cold outside.

Could she have known?

It's incredible that it feels like I'm trusting the word of a stranger over the person who brought me up – but only one of those people has lied to me for thirty-odd years. Mum said she and Dad had been strung along for a while after the birth, because Nikki didn't want to give up her baby. Nikki says her boyfriend had arranged to sell two – and that my parents both knew that. Once it was clear there was only one baby – and that Robbie handed Nikki's child to the other couple – that's when another idea was hatched for how to get a second.

I want to say that I don't trust Nikki, except I believe the other things she said. She also wasn't the person standing over a barbecue on a cold night burning documents.

The car clock ticks around to a little after noon and I turn the key to start the engine. From nowhere, I'm suddenly clear about what to do next.

I drive out of Stoneridge and follow the road back to Macklebury, passing the petrol station where Angel took a chunk out of my arm. I can hear Macklebury Primary School before I see it. The high-pitched howl of children chimes loud above everything as I pull in at the opposite side of the road from the railings that ring the school.

It's lunchtime and, because it's not raining, all the children are in the playground. I lock the car and then cross the road, standing and peering through the prison bars towards the tarmac below. Kids are roaring back and forth, all screeching at the same time. There's a camera on a pole above my head and another across the playground, sitting above the main doors. The security is a far cry from when I was a child. Back then, adults would happily march across the field at the back as a shortcut from their houses to the shops. Nobody would think any differently of it but, now, the police would be called.

With that context, I realise how dodgy it looks with me being here. I quickly scan the playground through the rails until I spot Stephen standing next to another adult near the front doors. I start waving, hoping to catch his eye – although I only succeed in attracting the attention of a group of young girls, who start waving back.

As everything is beginning to look *really* shady – Stephen finally glances up from his conversation and realises what's happening. He mutters something to his colleague and then strides across the playground until he's standing on the other side of the railings from me.

'I'm going to have to call the police,' he says. 'Can't have strangers coming up to the gates and grooming kids by waving at them.'

I roll my eyes at him. The blackening around his eye has turned into more of a yellow. I nod towards the injuries. 'Get beaten up by a six-year-old again, did you?'

'She was seven *actually* – and she wants to be a boxer when she grows up.'

I laugh and he turns his back so that he's facing the children, while I can talk into his ear. This isn't our first rodeo.

'Things have moved quickly,' I tell him. 'The person who put that cutting through my door was called Stella. She found out her mum and her mum's old boyfriend snatched Jane and sold her to my parents.'

It seems easier talking – and thinking – about 'Jane' as if she's another person.

He turns and takes me in, eyebrow raised. 'What?'

'I'm serious. That's all happened in the last day. I've just visited the woman who sold me.'

Stephen's eyes widen as he tries to figure out if this is some sort of elaborate joke. In many ways, I don't blame him. I've barely absorbed it myself.

'You *visited* the woman who stole you?'

'Sort of. She said it was her boyfriend from the time.'

Stephen starts patting his pockets. 'I can get someone to cover this afternoon and we'll go to the police. If not, then I'm done at four anyway.'

He doesn't wait for a reply, instead taking a couple of steps away from the railings. It feels as if everyone's first thought is the police – except mine.

I call Stephen's name and he stops moving, then turns back to me. 'I don't want the police,' I say.

'Are you joking?'

He starts patting his pockets once more.

'Stop!'

Stephen halts what he's doing and takes a step back towards me.

'She seemed kinda pathetic,' I add. 'It was more than thirty years ago and she's in her fifties. If she's arrested, and she confesses, what's the point? It's not going to be undone. Or, if she doesn't confess, there's a trial and publicity and my whole life gets torn apart... again. Then Mum might get in trouble and Penny has to relive everything...'

He looks as if he's about to say something and so I add a quick: 'I don't want that.'

Before Stephen can reply, a boy runs up to him and starts talking about how another boy is throwing rocks. Stephen gives an exasperated sigh and tells me to wait, before heading off to the furthest corner of the playground, where he gives a group of sheepish-looking boys a talking-to.

It never seems right when Stephen's being an authority figure. He's the guy who bought me the 'Stephen's great in bed' shirt and has slept next to my toilet on more than one occasion. That's when he doesn't trust himself to get from a bed to the bathroom after we've shared a few bottles.

He returns to the railings after a couple of minutes, shaking his head. 'It wasn't rocks,' he says. 'One kid was lobbing handfuls of dust at another kid and…' He shakes his head again and then turns to me properly. 'What *do* you want to do?'

I almost tell him that I have no idea how to punish the child – but then I realise he's following up from me saying I didn't want the police involved.

'I don't know,' I reply. 'Nikki reckons that Mum and Dad knew all along.'

'They *knew* you were stolen?'

'That's what she said. I don't even know who I should be calling "Mum" any more.'

He turns and stares across the playground, possibly taking everything in but maybe unsure of what to say next. 'Why would you believe her?' he asks.

It's the question that's been niggling at me the entire drive here.

'Who can I believe?' I reply. 'I caught Mum burning things on the barbecue the other night. At absolute best, she lied for three decades about where I came from.'

'But this Nikki stole – and sold – a baby! Why would she tell you the truth?'

That's the other half of the same question I was asking myself – except I could only come up with one conclusion.

'Isn't the opposite true?' I reply. 'Why *would* she lie? It could get her in trouble. She could be arrested, fined, jailed – whatever. What benefit does she get from telling the truth? To me of all people.'

Stephen has started to say something and then stops himself. It's the question for which I don't have an answer – and he seemingly doesn't either.

A whistle blasts from the far side of the playground and the cacophony of screaming stops almost in an instant. It must be such a power trip for the person with the whistle. Children start slowly moving towards the doors of the school as Stephen twists on the spot.

'How did the other woman find out?' he asks. 'The one who put the cutting through your door.'

'Stella. She found the clipping in her mum's cupboard. I asked why she didn't just tell me but she said I wouldn't have believed her. I think she's right. She ended up having a big argument with her mum and I let her stay at mine last night.'

Stephen goggles at this, as if he can't believe what he's hearing. 'You let a stranger *sleep* in your house?'

There's something about the way he says this that sets something burning in my stomach. There's a level truth in what he's saying but it's as if we're no longer equals and that I need telling off.

'It's not that simple,' I say, trying to remain level-headed. 'She's not a stranger.'

'When did you first meet her?'

'That's not the point. You didn't see her. She was skinny and dirty – and carrying more or less everything she owns on her back. There are bruises on her arms and neck. I think she's been sleeping rough and her mum says she's pregnant.'

Stephen continues to stare, which makes his point known clearly enough.

'Don't look at me like that,' I say.

'Like what?'

'Like I'm one of your kids you're about to stick on the naughty step.'

He glances over his shoulder towards where the final few children are disappearing back into the school. His colleague is holding open the door while staring across the playground towards us.

'Stella could be anyone,' he says.

'I wouldn't know any of this if it wasn't for her.'

'I know – but *why* has she done all this? You're saying she fell out with her mum, blew up her life, and for what?'

'To do the right thing.'

Stephen clamps his lips closed, not saying what he wants to. I know him too well. The way he's standing rigid and his fists are clenched belies his annoyance. He really does want to tell me off as if I'm a kid throwing sand.

'You don't know her,' I say.

'Neither do you.'

The other teacher from across the playground shouts Stephen's name – except he calls 'Mr Evans'.

Stephen turns between the school and me, while taking another step away from the railings. 'Just be careful,' he says.

'Like you?'

I nod at his darkened eye and regret it the moment I've done it. He was mugged and is back teaching primary school children barely two days later. We've never argued, not really, and yet here we are.

We stare at each other and I know I should apologise. It's as if he's waiting for it. A simple word or two and this will all be behind us.

A second passes. Two. Three.

Then he turns and takes a couple of steps towards the school. I could call him back and make it right, except that I don't. His strides become longer, his pace faster – and then, as I'm ready to call out to him, it's too late because he's through the doors and out of sight.

TWENTY-NINE

I spend more time sitting in my car, this time at the end of Mum's street. I know she isn't in because her drive is empty and it's a Tuesday afternoon. She's in a reading group with some women she met on Facebook and they meet in a local Costa every week to discuss whatever one of them has chosen. She tends to go for mysteries and is not happy if someone in her group picks a book that, in her words, 'is all lovey-dovey'.

As all that flitters through my mind, I realise how deeply I still think of her as 'Mum'. Despite everything, her routine is embedded within me. It's impossible to think of her as anything other than my mother.

Except she bought me.

And Nikki says it was the idea of her and Dad to steal me.

I have no idea how I'm supposed to reconcile all those things into seeing her as one person.

I find Penny's name on my phone and consider calling to let her know everything I've discovered. I would, except I'm not sure I'm ready to say it all out loud to her quite yet. There's also the issue of her stepson's unwanted call telling me that he knew about my money, which, somehow, I'd almost forgotten.

After locking the car, I walk quickly along the street and then let myself into Mum's house. I call for her but there's no reply – and nobody is sitting in her chair in the living room. I let myself out through the back door, towards where there are still blackened scraps around the wheels of the barbecue. With the way she hosed it down, I wonder if these are new. If there are still things she's trying to hide.

Back inside and I find myself staring at the family photos once again. The caravan parks and seasides. The donkey rides, summer fetes, wildlife and water parks. Alton Towers. Edinburgh.

I'm so happy in all of them – but, more than me, so is Dad. Pride is carved into his face as he beams next to me, Mum, or – if we could get someone to take the photo – both of us.

You adored your father. Would you really *have wanted to think differently of him?*

Does the present destroy the past? Like a person finding out their husband or wife has been having an affair. Does knowing the truth destroy everything good that went before? Perhaps Mum is right? Perhaps I'd have been better never knowing.

I'm lost in that as the door clicks, which is immediately followed by Mum huffing and muttering under her breath. She passes the door to the living room without noticing me and continues along the hall, out of sight, until she's in the kitchen. I go towards the door the leads directly into the kitchen from the living room and stand in the frame while gently saying her name. I'm trying not to make her jump but she spins, screams and grabs her chest.

'Hope! Goodness me! Are you trying to give me a heart attack?'

There's a moment where I'm ten again, hiding behind the door of Mum's wardrobe and leaping out to make her jump. Dad always found it hilarious when I'd tell him about it.

Back in the kitchen, Mum straightens her top and then reaches for the shopping bag that's next to her foot. I didn't notice her drop it but a box of own-brand Corn Flakes now sits on its side on the floor. She picks up her shopping and puts the items on the counter, as if everything is normal.

I wish I was that ten-year-old again; full of innocence and wonder. When I thought my parents knew everything and were capable of nothing but good.

Mum reaches for the cupboard door to start putting things away when she thinks better of it.

'I'm glad you're here,' she says.

She's so small before me and I'd swear she's shrunk an inch or three since Dad died. A part of me wants her to put her arms around me and say everything is fine.

It's not the biggest part, though.

'I know, Mum.'

She cranes her neck backwards a fraction. 'Know what?'

'At first you lied about where I came from – then you said there was a surrogate that you paid.'

A frown creases her face. Mum's always been the sort that would say whatever needed to be said and then consider it done for. After everything she told me before, she would never have wanted it to be brought up again.

'Hope, I—'

'I was stolen, Mum. I'm Jane Craven. I found Nikki – and she told me all about everything you knew.'

Mum's features don't move, not at first. She stares at me open-mouthed and then her eye starts to twitch.

'Knew what?'

'Nikki sold two babies – except she only gave birth to one. The second one – *me* – was stolen. She said you and Dad had the idea.'

Her eye continues to twitch, as if it wants to jump away from her face. Her mouth bobs and the reply is croaked and hardly there. 'That's not true. I never knew.'

'Did Dad?'

'No. We were told by her boyfriend that Nikki had her baby but was reconsidering giving it up. That's why there was a delay in everything.' She gulps and then speaks a little more quietly. 'Are you saying… that you were… *kidnapped*…?'

She says the final word so reluctantly that it almost doesn't make it out of her lips.

I don't know how to reply but, when she takes a step towards me with an outstretched arm, I step away, back into the living room.

'I've not been sleeping,' she says.

As soon as she says this, I notice the deepened dark creases around her eyes. She once told me that it wasn't the same sleeping in an empty bed as it was sleeping alongside Dad. Now, it looks as if she hasn't slept in months.

'I don't know how to make this better,' she adds.

That part of me still wants to comfort her – except that it remains in the minority.

'You're my daughter and—'

'I'm not. I never was.'

Mum stops and there are tears in her eyes now.

'I didn't *know*.'

I look past her, towards the barbecue in the back garden. 'I don't believe you.'

THIRTY

I park on my drive and am surprised to find that I'm anxious to see Stella. It feels like I've spent the day burning bridges and, somehow, despite not knowing her a day ago, I'm now desperate to have a connection.

It's perhaps because I'm lost in thinking about my day that, when I get out of the car, I don't immediately notice the woman marching towards me. She's already shouted my name and jabbed a finger in my face when I realise that it's Oliver's mother. With everything that's been happening, my commitments at Creators' Club have been somewhat forgotten.

I can't remember her name but the ferocious glint in her eyes is unforgettable. There are at least two rings on each of her fingers and so much fake gold jangling around her neck that it's a surprise she doesn't have a hunchback.

I bat away her finger but she pokes it towards me once more. 'Who do you think you are?'

'What are you on about?'

'We don't need your charity.'

'What char—'

'I know your sort – thinking you're better than everyone else. Thinking you're some sort of saint.'

'I have no idea what you're talking about.'

Oliver's mother pushes herself up on the heels of her shoes, which is actually impressive considering they're a good couple of inches high. This makes her momentarily taller than me and it's only as she does this that I realise what she's talking about.

'I'm *lending* Oliver the art supplies,' I say. It feels like such a long time ago that I gave him the pad and pencils.

His mother isn't fooled. 'Who lends *paper?*'

'It was more the pencils.'

She takes a half-step away and digs into her enormous bag before she pulls out the tin of pencils I gave her son a few days ago. She spins them towards me, where the tin bounces off my midriff and lands on the ground with a metallic clatter.

'Keep them,' she says. 'I'm perfectly capable of raising my own son without *you* sticking your nose in.'

'I didn't mean—'

'I know what you meant. You think you're special just because you got lucky.'

She wafts a hand up and down, indicating my body as a whole. I almost wish I didn't know what she was talking about this time – except that I do.

'I'm not sure why you think I got lucky.'

'Easy for you to say when you're lording it over us peasants. That's the problem with this country: too many do-gooders.'

She spits the words as if doing good, or attempting to, is a bad thing. The venom with which she speaks makes me take a step back, towards the house and the safety of inside.

'Stay away from my son.'

'I'm just trying to—'

'I don't care what you're trying to do. If you don't—' She takes a step towards me, hand raised as if she might be about to throw a punch.

Before she can do anything more, the front door opens behind me and then, from nowhere, Stella is at my side. I might be many things – but I know I'm not the sort of person who can intimidate anyone. I'm not tall or broad, let alone particularly athletic. Unless I've had a good few hours to come up with something, I'm not smart with words.

Yet there's something about Stella that's hard to label. Oliver's mother feels it too because the moment Stella appears at my side, she takes a step back. Her confidence ebbs away in front of me and it's almost as if she shrinks.

'Is there a problem?'

Stella isn't talking to me but she isn't really talking to Oliver's mother, either. It's more of a declaration; like the biggest bloke in a pub cracking a bottle over the bar and asking if anyone has a subject they wish to discuss.

Oliver's mum quickly glances to me, although her focus is almost instantly back on Stella before she decides this isn't a battle she wants after all.

She backs away towards the edge of the drive and then, when she's at a safe distance, offers a sharp 'I'm not done with you', before hastily retreating along the street.

Stella and I stand united for a moment before she crouches and picks up the tin of pencils from the ground and hands it to me.

'What was that all about?'

I take the tin from her. 'Long story. Basically, I was trying to help out her son and she didn't take it too well.'

We turn together and head into the warmth of the house. As soon as the front door is closed, I notice that Stella's bag is still packed and resting against the wall close to the door. She's wearing a turtle-neck with tight jeans. Her jacket hangs on the peg, her boots underneath.

'You're not leaving, are you?' I ask.

She doesn't answer and the two of us move through to the kitchen, as if we're old friends who do this all the time. We take our spots on the stools from the night before. The article that started all this still sits on the table between us.

'I've been looking for jobs,' she says. 'I'd forgotten how hard it is. I need to sort out my CV but I don't have a computer and it's a nightmare on my phone. I was thinking about going to the library but I'm not a member here and I didn't know if it would be easy to sign up without ID and a local address.' She nods through to the hallway. 'I'm ready to go but I wanted to say goodbye and I suppose was curious about…'

'I did visit your mum,' I tell her.

'What did she say?'

'A lot of what you told me and of what I'd figured out. She talked about the two babies that her boyfriend sold. She said I was stolen… that I was sold…'

It never gets easier to say out loud. Never feels more real.

Stella is quiet at first and then she gives a solemn: 'I'm sorry…' She is trying to make eye contact but I can't quite face her because the lump in my throat is growing. 'If you want to go to the police, I'll tell them everything I know…'

The police are there again as an option and I'm starting to wonder if I'm the one who's wrong for consistently failing to see that as a choice.

'I don't want the attention,' I say. 'There'll be police and media – and then people on the street. I don't want any of that.'

Stella nods and I hope it's the last time she brings it up. 'So what now?'

'I have no idea.' I place a hand on the article. 'I'm going to have to tell Penny… just not today.'

She nods again and then clears her throat slightly before changing the subject. 'I contacted the council today about temporary housing. They said—'

'Your mum told me you're pregnant.'

Stella stops herself and then, perhaps without realising, she touches her belly.

'How far along are you?' I ask.

She stares past me towards the window at the back of the kitchen. 'Around six weeks.' She bites her lip and then adds: 'I don't know if I want it. I don't want the dad around and it's not like it was planned.'

'Is it that guy, Wayne, who you talked about? The guy you left?'

There's a nod of reluctance, as if Stella wishes she'd never told me that.

'You've got bruises,' I say. 'Are they from him?'

It's Stella's moment to turn away from an uncomfortable question. She twists to face the front door and her bag. I wonder if I've gone too far and that she'll up and leave.

'Yes,' she breathes.

'Stay here if you want,' I reply. 'That spare room isn't going anywhere. Wayne doesn't know you're here. He doesn't know I exist.'

'It's just—'

'I *want* you here. You've done so much that you didn't have to.'

Stella continues to stare out towards her bag and Stephen's words run through my mind that I don't know who she is. He's right and yet it feels as if he's wrong.

'You don't have to do this for me,' she says.

'I want to.'

Stella slumps forward a little, running her hands through her hair. 'The reason I stopped staying with friends wasn't just outstaying a welcome. It's because Wayne came round and… he threw a few things and did a lot of shouting. The police got called – so he left. He would never have gone to Mum's house and made a scene – he was too scared of her – but, after I left hers, I guess he decided it was fine to track me down.'

'When did you last see him?'

'At my friend's place about a week ago.' She stops and then adds: 'He doesn't know I'm pregnant. He won't take it well if he finds out.'

'How come?'

'At first, he'll insist we have to get married for the sake of the baby. When I tell him that's definitely not happening, he'll decide that, if he can't raise the baby, then nobody – least of all me – will.'

There's a chill in the room now. Stella's bruises are covered but we both know they're there. They've done well to last the week or so since she last saw her ex-boyfriend.

'He doesn't know you're here, though…?'

Stella shrugs. 'I don't know how he could – but he's clever when he wants to be.'

'That settles it then. Stay here. You'll be safe.'

She takes a breath and then, finally, she begins to nod. 'Okay.'

THIRTY-ONE

WEDNESDAY

It's strange how quickly things fit into place. Stella does us both cheese on toast that night, while I do some work for Creators' Club on my laptop in the living room. After that, we watch a movie together, as if we're pre-teen sisters being shut up by our parents. I even manage to take in most of the movie, while blocking out the rest of what's been going on. I had spent a large part of the day believing that I'd never think of anything other than what my mother did, yet, by the evening, I somehow managed to switch it off for an hour or so.

I'm back in the living room the following morning, typing out an email to try to arrange a Creators' Club expert for next month, when Stella comes in. Her hair is wet and she's dressed in clean clothes for the first time since she turned up on the doorstep.

'I didn't know which shampoo to use,' she says. 'One looked expensive and I thought—'

'Use whatever you want. There's nothing in that bathroom that's *that* expensive.'

'The water pressure is really good. You should see it at Mum's place – it's just a dribble.'

She smiles and I return it. There are shorter sleeves on her top today and the bruises are fully on show. They've faded since I first saw them and are now more of a mottled yellowy-green. Stella notices me looking at them.

'I bruise easily,' she says. 'I always have. I used to go to school with bumps and marks all over my legs and thighs because I'd knock into cupboard handles and things like that. The teachers once asked if I was being abused at home…'

She lets that hang, almost cryptically.

'My friend was recently assaulted,' I tell her. 'He'd gone on a date and someone jumped him. We went to the police and they said—'

'I'm not going to the police.'

I almost reply – but there's been a lot of talk about the police in the past few days and I'm quite the hypocrite when it comes to advising others.

Stella slips onto the opposite end of the sofa and starts combing her hair with her fingers. If there was any awkwardness from the talk of police, then she has moved instantly past it. She nods towards my laptop: 'Is this your job?'

'I work for a non-profit,' I say. 'We run creative classes for kids on Saturdays and Wednesdays – and then through the summer holidays.'

'What does that mean?'

I allow myself a little smile. 'We get young people writing, or painting, or making things,' I say. 'That sort of thing. At school, it's all maths, science and English. The core subjects. That's fine – but not all kids are good with school. They want to create things.' A pause. 'I know I did…'

She nods, although I'm not sure she quite understands why any of this is needed. I've had these conversations with other people – sometimes senior local politicians – who don't appear to believe this is a 'real' job, or that any of this is necessary.

'Does your boss let you work from home?' Stella asks.

'I'm sort of my own boss. I founded the organisation and put the initial funding in. When I'm not planning the week-to-week sessions, a decent amount of my time is spent applying for various grants. Because there are children involved, there's a lot of forms and paperwork.'

Not that I've had much time to work this week.

Stella continues to nod, although there's a blankness to her stare and it doesn't feel as if she's listening.

'Did I tell you there are only two slices of bread left,' she says. It's an abrupt switch of direction and takes me a couple of seconds to absorb. 'I was going to have toast but didn't want to finish the loaf.'

'Eat whatever you want,' I say. 'There's a pad in the kitchen by the fridge. Write down anything you finish and I'll get more whenever I'm next out.'

Stella has a way of nodding that makes it seem more like an act of confusion than acceptance. It always feels as if there's something she wants to say that isn't quite ready to come out.

She wriggles on the sofa and squeezes a phone out of her pocket, like toothpaste from a tube. 'I've got some emails from the job agency to follow up,' she says.

'Anything exciting?'

'Requests for more information. Nothing yet.' She pauses and it again feels like there's something unsaid.

'Is there something you want to tell me?' I ask.

She rolls her tongue around her mouth, considering it, and then: 'Is it worth it?'

'Is *what* worth it?'

She holds up her hands, indicating the house; indicating everything, I suppose. 'I almost didn't put that cutting through your door. I thought about forgetting it. Not forgetting what Mum did – but I didn't know if you'd want to know. I tried to think about me and whether *I'd* want my life blown up.'

We look to one another and, at first, I'm not sure what to say. 'Would you?' I ask.

Stella makes gentle humming sound to herself. 'I don't think I know the answer to that.'

'But you blew your own life up for me. You walked out of your mum's, even though you're pregnant.'

Stella bows her head a little and then glances away. I don't blame her for avoiding that subject.

'Have you thought about your name?' she asks.

'What do you mean?'

'If you're the girl from the article, then you're called Jane.'

She's right – and I suppose it's obvious. I don't know what legal implications there are. I have a birth certificate that I used to get a passport and driving licence. I have no idea where that certificate came from. Whether it's another apparent fraud on behalf of my parents. It wasn't one of the things I thought to ask when I was with Mum.

Except Jane will have a birth certificate.

'I don't feel like a Jane,' I say.

'How would you know what being a Jane felt like?' She laughs gently. 'Perhaps what you thought was feeling like a Hope was always feeling like a Jane?'

It feels like far too deep a thing to be thinking about and it's not even one of the bigger issues I have. I'm avoiding everything for now but, sooner or later, I'm going to have to face the issue of who and what 'Mum' actually means to me.

Perhaps sensing this, Stella lets the issue drop… except fate is in charge here. As soon as there's a silence, the sound of the doorbell echoes through the house. Stella looks to me but I'm staring past her towards the front of the house.

I can't explain how – but I already know who's there. I stand and move across the living room, into the hallway. I get there a moment before the doorbell sounds a second time.

I unlock and open the door, then take a step back.

'Hi,' I say.

And then the world changes again.

THIRTY-TWO

Penny stares across the threshold towards me. 'Hi,' she says in return – and, for the first time in my life, I'm looking at someone other than Mum, who I think could actually have that moniker.

'Can I come in?' Penny nods past me towards the house and I realise that I haven't moved. 'I wanted to see you,' she adds. 'I've been thinking about you almost non-stop since Sunday.'

It's difficult to believe that it's three days since we last saw one another – and yet, in the scheme of things, there are so many things that are harder to believe.

I step back, allowing Penny inside, where she proceeds to take off her shoes without any sort of prompting. As she's doing that, Stella emerges from the living room and stands at the side until Penny looks up and notices her.

There are a few seconds of awkwardness until I realise that I'm the only one who knows for sure who everyone is. Stella might know Penny's name – but I don't think I'm ready for full revelations yet.

'This is one of my friends,' I say, nodding towards Stella.

Penny angles her head as a greeting, although her attention is solely for me and she doesn't introduce herself.

I turn to Stella. 'Can you give us a few minutes?'

She doesn't take the hint at first, so I indicate the stairs and then she moves hesitantly towards them, pauses for a moment, and then continues her way up. There's another brief hiatus and then she disappears around the corner towards the spare room.

Penny is looking around the hall and through to the kitchen. I remember hers, with the rows of photographs and memories in the hall. For some reason, it's only now I realise the mirroring in that there are photos on the wall of my hall, too.

'You've made a nice life,' she says. 'This is a nice house. You've got a nice car.'

I manage to stop myself wincing at the repeated use of the word 'nice'. I know she means it as a compliment but she doesn't yet know what I had to go through to get this. 'Nice' often feels slightly backhanded in any case. Not 'good' or 'great'; not 'lovely' or 'tasteful' – just 'nice'. Acceptable. The bare minimum.

Penny steps across towards the photos and cranes over them.

'Is this your husband?' she asks.

Even with everything going on, it's impossible not to laugh. 'That's my friend, Stephen,' I say. 'We're definitely *not* married. We went on a road trip around the US a few years ago.'

The picture shows Stephen and me standing underneath the famous 'Welcome To Fabulous Las Vegas' sign. What it doesn't show is the twenty-minute queue of people in which we stood as the temperature reached forty Celsius.

Penny's eyes flicker towards the stairs. 'Oh, is she your, um…?'

'No,' I say.

There's another awkward moment and then I lead Penny through to the kitchen. I quickly scoop up the article from the counter, without really knowing why – other than that I don't want her to see it. I slip it into a drawer and then reach for the kettle. It feels as if every major conversation I've had in the past few days has been taken over tea. I suppose, if anything, it proves that I'm British.

Penny has hers with three sugars, which shows there's something I haven't inherited from her. As I make our drinks, she spends her time taking in the kitchen, before crossing to the back window and looking out towards the garden.

'It's such a nice house,' she repeats. 'I'm so proud of you.'

She means well, I know that, but it makes me cringe. We're strangers and, regardless of whatever blood we might share, if we do, there is no easy way to get past that. I'm not even sure I want her to be here – except she's taken that decision out of my hands. I suppose she's decided that I'm her daughter and that's that.

Penny sits on the stool that's usually mine and I have to fight the urge to tell her. Everything feels wrong.

'We've got so much catching up to do,' she says cheerily. 'I want to know everything about you.'

'I, um…'

'I've been thinking about stuff, like whether you were in something like the Brownies, or the Girl Guides? Or girls are allowed in the Scouts now, aren't they? I did the Brownies when I was a girl and always thought my daughter might be into it too…?'

It's not the conversation I thought we'd be having. I could tell her everything that Nikki told me about the two babies she sold. About her boyfriend and my parents… but then I might've misjudged all this. Now the initial shock has gone, perhaps that doesn't matter to her and all she wants to do is talk to the daughter she never had.

That would be fine – if we didn't feel like such strangers.

'I wasn't in the Brownies, the Guides or the Scouts,' I say.

I feel bad for shutting her down and she momentarily bites her bottom lip, as if disappointed.

'Kyle called me,' I say.

She blinks at me and then stares for a second. '*My* Kyle?'

'Yes. I didn't give him my number…'

More staring. 'I didn't either,' she replies. 'I guess…' Penny tails off and then turns away. 'He said something to me about money. He'd been looking for you on the internet. He and his dad were worried about me, I think. All that stuff they said to you…'

She doesn't apologise outright but it's in her voice. At the mention of her husband, Penny glances towards the front door, as if he might be there.

'There was an article about you being in a critical condition,' she says. 'Something about a collision – and then Kyle showed me a second one about the payout…' She stops and then spins and grasps my hands in hers so quickly that I don't get a chance to pull away, even if I wanted to.

'That's not why I'm here,' she says. 'I didn't go looking.'

It's not as if I'm called Sarah Jones, or something where there might be thousands of hits on Google. If people look for me, they find me – and then, worse, they find out *about* me.

I can always tell when a person has looked me up. There's a sort of knowing in their eyes. I'm not famous but I would imagine it's like a well-known actor being on a regular street and seeing people's heads turn as they wonder if it's truly the person they believe it to be.

Some people are honest after they've looked me up – and will ask whatever questions they have. Others will stare and mutter to whomever they're alongside.

My experience of that is why I believe Penny when she says she didn't go out of her way to look me up.

'I was hit by a delivery van,' I say. 'It belonged to a supermarket, with all the logos on the side and everything. I had the green man and was crossing the road but the driver switched off, I guess. He could never explain why he didn't stop. Everything was on camera.'

I lift my leg and roll up my trousers until the full residual limb and prosthetic leg is on show. I watch as Penny's eyes almost yo-yo out of her head, like a cartoon. My leg ends a little below my knee and slots into the padded cup of the prosthetic. That curves down towards a metal pylon, which connects to the moulded foot – that she can't see properly as it's within my sock.

It can be a shock for people mainly because, when I'm wearing trousers, there's more or less no difference between me and anyone else.

Penny doesn't speak, perhaps because she can't.

'I was in physio for a long time,' I say. 'I had to relearn how to walk. How to balance. Lots of things.'

She stares from my leg back up towards my face. 'But we walked back to my house together. You took your shoes off when you came in. We went up the stairs. We went *down* the stairs…'

She seems amazed that I'm capable of these things – which isn't uncommon when people find out for the first time that I'm an amputee. There was a time when it might have upset me that people thought I wasn't capable of being 'normal', as much as I hate that word, but I suppose I'm past that.

'I'm pretty good at getting on with things,' I say. 'I still go to physio regularly but I don't *need* it any longer. I can even run a little bit.'

Penny reaches forward and hovers her hand close to the cup of my prosthetic. I nod and she touches it before removing her hand.

'I was awarded just over a million by the supermarket's insurance company,' I say. 'There were other expenses on top. We settled out of court and the actual amount was never announced – except that someone tipped off the paper to say it was "seven figures".'

'Wow…'

I don't know if she's referring to the amount of money or the fact any of it happened.

'There was a time when they didn't think I'd walk. My solicitor said we'd get more if it went to court but I didn't want that. The money's not meant to be some sort of lottery win. It's because there are a lot of things I'll never be able to do again.'

I roll back down my trouser leg as Penny continues to goggle. 'I promise I'm not here because I found out about the money,' she says. 'I wanted to see you because I'd not heard anything since Sunday.'

'How did you know where I lived?'

'You're on the electoral roll and that's online. I suppose I *did* look you up a bit… but not for anything bad.'

I can sense that she wants to add something like: 'You do believe me, don't you?' – except that she stops herself. In any case, I do believe her.

There's a few seconds in which she continues looking towards my leg and then Penny looks up. 'This is all *her* fault,' she says out of nothing.

'Whose?'

'That *witch* who stole you. Who raised you. You would have never been in a position to lose your leg if you hadn't been taken.'

I hold up a hand to stop her. Penny has gone from zero to a hundred in an instant and there is a curdling nugget of underlying fire and fury that I can't deal with.

Penny takes the hint and cuts herself off before she can get more angry.

'Not now,' I say, as calmly as I can. I tap my leg gently. 'I'm okay with this. I wouldn't have chosen it but it's who I am. I used some of the money to start a club that teaches the arts to kids – and that would never have happened otherwise.'

Penny doesn't acknowledge this, although I suspect it's because she's still quietly seething.

'How did you cope after Jane was taken?' I ask.

It takes Penny a few seconds to acknowledge me. A few more to actually answer. 'I didn't,' she says. 'Not for a long while. There was a time where it didn't feel as if I had anything to live for but I had support from someone who knew how it felt. Then, in the end, I guess it was Chris who helped me to come out the other end.'

Her voice is raw and, as bad as it sounds, I'm not sure I want to know the full truth. I don't think I can handle it.

I want to ask about Chris and can't get from my mind the power he seemed to have over her when he talked to her in the hallway. I'd be almost certain that he doesn't know she's here.

The opportunity to ask anything further doesn't come – because the doorbell rings. As I'm on the stool where Stephen usually sits, I have a clear view through the hall towards the rippled glass of the front door.

I know who's here – and it's the worst person it could be given the circumstances. The one who could turn an awkward situation into something outright hostile.

I don't move – even when the bell sounds a second time.

Penny is watching me, perhaps wondering if I've somehow managed to not hear the door. I hope the person on the other side will go away – but then there's the scratching of a key in the lock and the handle begins to turn.

THIRTY-THREE

Mum bustles in through the front door and then closes it behind her. She mutters something I don't catch and then looks up to see me watching her from the kitchen stool. She mouths an 'oh' and then starts fussing in her bag before properly latching the door behind her.

'I saw your car at the front but nobody was answering,' she says. 'I wanted to make sure you were safe. After everything from the other day, I didn't want to—'

She doesn't finish the sentence because Penny stands and moves sideways until both women are facing one another like some sort of stand-off in a Western. There could be sand and dust between them, pistols in holsters: except they're at opposite ends of my hallway.

Without any of us needing to speak, the two of them intrinsically appear to know the identity of the other.

It's Penny who speaks first. 'You're the woman who stole my daughter…'

I move quickly, shuffling around Penny until I'm standing between the two women.

'No,' Mum says.

'I left *my* daughter in the back of my car and now, thirty years later, she's *your* daughter.'

She's shouting, on her tiptoes, arms flailing as Mum shakes her head. 'It's not like that.'

Because things aren't bad enough, Stella suddenly appears on the stairs. She makes her way halfway down and then stands and looks upon the scene below. I feel frozen as all these elements of my life suddenly converge.

Mum looks to Stella and then to me, seemingly not sure of the identity of the newcomer. Then she focuses on me.

'You *know* I didn't steal you. You must *know*.'

'Mum…'

As soon as I say the word, I feel Penny bristling behind me. When I turn, I half expect her to be directly behind, breathing on my neck, except she hasn't moved.

Mum isn't done: 'If you were stolen, then I didn't know.'

Penny replies before I can. 'What do you mean, *"if"*?'

I twist between the two women, unsure what to do. Mum wants some sort of confirmation that I believe her, except I can't give her that, even if I wanted. The words are stuck in my throat.

'I think you should go,' I say. 'We can talk another time. Not today and not now.'

Mum slumps in front of me, her knees buckling as she uses the door handle to hold herself up. 'Hope…'

Penny gets in first again: 'She's called Jane!'

I hold up both hands, willing them to stop and, perhaps surprisingly, they do.

'Can you go?' I'm talking to Mum but with a big part of me unsure if I still think of her like that.

Mum pulls herself up until she's standing straighter again. She looks so old in front of me. So frail. My body is fighting with itself. I want to comfort her but I want her to leave.

Mum ignores Penny and continues to speak to me: 'I'm still the person who raised you. I didn't *know*. Tell her.'

I can sense Penny ready to say something but I get in first as I turn to face Penny. 'She didn't steal me,' I say.

'But she *knew*. She *knew* and she raised you anyway.'

I turn from Penny back to Mum and I can see the desperation within Mum that she wants me to believe this key part isn't true.

The truth is that I don't know. Someone is lying. It could be Nikki, or it could be the woman who raised me as her own. One of them is someone I barely know and the other is a person who I *thought* I knew but who lied to me my entire life.

I'm looking towards Mum and the front door again. 'Can you go?'

'But—'

'I don't think I can see you right now.'

It's this that finally breaks her. Mum's face doesn't fall and she shows no outward emotion. There's something in her eyes, though. A sadness that feels as if it reaches all the way through to her soul. Her fingers grip the door handle tighter, her knuckles whiten, and then she pulls the door inwards and steps around it.

'She was *never* yours!'

Penny's words boom around the hallway. I want to tell her to shut up – but it's already too late. Mum pauses for a fraction of a second before crossing the threshold until she's outside. She closes the door without another word and then her silhouette shrinks in the rippled glass until, eventually, it's just a dot. Moments later, there's the sound of an engine – and then she's gone.

I stare at the door, wondering if I should go after her but knowing I won't. I close my eyes, hoping that, when I open them, everything will have gone away.

When I open them, everything is as it was.

'Sorry…'

Penny speaks softly from behind me – and, even though she sounds as if she means it, I don't think she does.

'Perhaps I should go, too…'

I think Penny might want me to try to talk her out of this – except that I can't.

There's a moment of silence and then Penny steps around me and starts putting on her shoes at the front door.

'Maybe I shouldn't have come,' she says.

'I didn't mind seeing you… but this was all a bit… much.'

She doesn't acknowledge this, instead focusing on putting on her second shoe. When she's done, we stand a metre or so apart, neither of us making the first move to hug, or anything similar.

'Can we stay in contact?' she asks. 'Not talk every day if that's not what you want but… I don't know. I'd like to know you're safe.'

'We can do that.'

Penny holds up her phone momentarily but then lowers it. She looks between me and the door that's directly behind her. 'I didn't mean for that to be an argument,' she says. 'It's just difficult.'

'I know.'

'Maybe we can try this again another day?'

'Maybe…'

She hovers in the doorway, much like Mum did a couple of minutes before. There's so much to say and yet none of it feels as if it should come anytime soon.

Penny offers another apology and then lets herself out. I watch her silhouette disappear, too – and then there's the sound of another engine.

Stella has been watching all this from the stairs, on which she's now sitting. She offers a small smile.

'You okay?' she asks.

'It feels like everyone's lying to me. Mum says she didn't know I was stolen but yours says she did.'

Stella nods at this. 'Mine can tell lies,' she says.

'But how many has she told that's lasted thirty years?'

And, for that, Stella does not have an answer.

THIRTY-FOUR

It's such a relief that it's Wednesday. Creators' Club has gone from something that's enjoyable, but still my job, to being the one thing that isn't related to the rest of my imploding life.

I arrived early to the community centre to start laying things out and, within a few minutes, I realised that I'd not been thinking about Mum, Penny or Nikki.

It's fifteen minutes until I'm ready to welcome the children when the doors open anyway. Stephen strides in with a smile on his face. We haven't spoken since our argument and I wondered if he'd come.

It only takes one stupid invented word for me to know that everything is going to be okay.

'Trenim!' he shouts, the word echoing across the largely empty hall.

The excitement that flows through me is as if he's just told me he's won the lottery on his wedding day, which was also my birthday – and we're both in the sunny Bahamas with cocktails.

'You're joking,' I reply.

Stephen gets his phone from his pocket and jabs at the screen, before handing it across. The photo shows a woman pushing a shopping trolley while wearing jeans, a denim shirt and a denim jacket.

'I can't believe this happened,' I say.

Trenim is a stupid game that we began on our road trip around the United States. If either of us spotted someone wearing two items of denim, we had to shout 'DD' before the other. A double denim spot was worth one point – but an elusive *triple* denim – the trenim – was a full ten points.

Neither of us has kept score in years, and a full trenim has been much harder to find in the UK, but the game has never died.

'This has got to be worth a meal out or something,' Stephen says. 'I was happily walking along the aisles of Tesco when, BAM!, it's the Holy Grail right in front of me. The Loch Ness Monster for the Instagram generation. Big Foot for TikTokkers.'

'This is world-class trenim,' I reply.

Stephen puts his phone away and then places his arm around my shoulder. He pulls me in so that my face is resting on his shoulder and then angles himself so that he can whisper in my ear. 'Sorry about yesterday,' he says. 'It had been a long morning and—'

'You don't have to apologise. I'm sorry.'

He steps away and I notice that the bruising around his face has faded so that it's almost the same colour as his skin. If I didn't know it was there, I wouldn't necessarily have noticed.

'Have you heard anything from the police?' I ask.

'Like what?'

'Maybe they found the person who did it?'

He shakes his head. 'I doubt I'll hear from them again. It'll be one of those things. I'm a crime statistic now.'

I want to tell him that he's wrong – except I can't know that. The police were great with me after I was hit by the supermarket van but these are different circumstances.

'I think I want to forget about it,' he adds. 'Just one of those things. A lesson to learn about safety, I guess.' He pauses, then adds: 'What about you and your mum? Or *mums*?'

I grin at him and it's fantastic to really feel it. To be friends again. 'I think I want to forget about it.'

He smiles back to me and there's a large part of the world that's right again.

'Hard to forget a mum, though…?'

'They met earlier…'

Stephen's eyes go wide and I fill him in on what happened at the house, which he christens 'the brawl in the hall'. If anyone else joked about it, it'd feel wrong – but it's okay for him.

'What are you going to do now?' Stephen asks.

'I have no idea. Life goes on and it doesn't change who I am.'

'Doesn't stop you being annoying, then?'

I give him a nudge with my elbow, at which he laughs.

We're distracted by the door sounding again. The poet I arranged is here and we make our introductions before I open the doors for the children to enter.

Newcomers only tend to come at weekends and it's a regular crowd tonight, where everyone knows what they want to get into.

I watch the poet for a while. She reads a funny verse about a rabbit who wanted to learn to fly and, within seconds, she has the kids eating out of her hand. When she's done, she asks them to write the final part of the poem – and then everyone separates off to do their bit.

Oliver isn't here tonight – and it's the first session he's missed that I can remember. The painting station is still going strongly – but it doesn't quite feel the same without him looking to me for reassurance.

The evening flies by, in the way all the club sessions seem to. At the end, I have to remind everyone that there's no session this coming Saturday, because it's one of the weekends where our hall has a prior booking. It happens a few times a year, usually when the council needs the larger space for one of its own projects.

After everyone has gone, Stephen and I are clearing away when he offers a quiet: 'No Oliver…?'

'I had a run-in with his mum,' I say. 'She came to the house and started shouting.'

'About the gifts you gave him?'

'The things I *loaned* him… but yes. She told me to mind my own business.'

He has a knowing *I-told-you-so* look on his face, although he doesn't say it. 'Sounds like you're making lots of friends at the moment.' He points towards the scratch on my arm. 'Where did that come from?'

'Aki's new girlfriend. I ran into her at the petrol station. I don't think I told you – but someone keyed my car the other day and I asked her about it. She denied everything and ended up scratching me with her nails.' I pause. 'I don't think she meant it.'

This onslaught of information takes Stephen by surprise. 'Someone keyed your car? You're not having much luck, are you?'

'Am I really this unlikeable?'

He smirks: 'I didn't want to be the one who said it…'

We finish packing away the equipment and then Stephen helps me carry the tables across to the back corner. We're used to the routine by now. Although there are cleaners on the weekend, everything is down to us on Wednesday nights.

It's as we're finishing that it feels as if something changes. Stephen is walking slowly towards the doors, almost scuffing his feet in a way that isn't like him. We're at the doors and I'm about to set the alarm when he says it.

'Have you got a minute?' he asks.

'Of course.'

He nods towards the doors and so I finish locking up before we head outside. Stephen settles onto the top step and I slot in at his side. It's a chilly evening and we're close together, using one another for warmth.

'After everything with your leg, did you ever meet the driver who did it?' he asks.

It's a question out of the blue. Stephen and I became friends after what happened and, even though we've talked about various aspects, something like this has never come up.

He rubs his temples with his thumb and middle finger as he rocks forward slightly.

'Why?' I ask.

'I don't know how you deal with the anger.' He holds up his hand to indicate his slightly blackened eye and then clenches his fists. 'I can put up with the bruises but it's the anger. I've never felt like this before. Sometimes I just want to hit something.'

I look down towards his still clenched fists. He's talking through clenched teeth and I've never seen or heard him like this. He rarely shows any anger, let alone something that might approach violence.

'The guy in the van was banned from driving,' I say. 'I didn't need to be in court for that because they had the CCTV. There were doctor reports, plus he pleaded guilty. The criminal part was all straightforward – but his insurance company were digging in their heels over compensation. There was a time when it looked like that might go to court. I thought I'd have to face him but that ended up being settled about a week before we had a date. It was another week after that when I got a note from my solicitor. The driver had contacted him through his own solicitor, asking if we could meet. He wanted to apologise in person but said he'd understand if I said no.'

'What did you say?'

'I thought about it over a weekend. I was going to say "no" because I didn't see what good it would do. I'd just lost my leg and it was hard to imagine what the world would be like. I had a temporary prosthetic that didn't really fit – and I couldn't walk in it at that time. I could barely stand properly. The physio all came later. I was living with Mum and Dad, sleeping in their living room and generally not doing anything other than watching TV and feeling miserable. A part of me wanted to meet the driver just to tell him how he'd wrecked my life. I was angry, too.'

My chest feels tight. It's been a long time since I thought about this, let alone said any of it out loud.

'What did you do about the anger?'

'It was Dad who helped…'

I close my eyes and can picture him sitting with me in the garden on the most beautiful of days. The cloudless blue of the sky, the smell of summer in the air. The warmth of the sun on my arms and face.

'What did he do?' Stephen asks.

'I was sitting in this scratchy, old wheelchair. I was miserable and Dad dragged himself across a deckchair and sat next to me. He started telling a story about how, when he was around my age, he was working on a building site. The guy who drove the forklifts was off sick and there was nobody in the yard trained. Dad's boss told him to do it, even though he'd never learned how to drive one. He wasn't insured and had no idea what to do – but he needed the work and so did as he was told. Course, being Dad, he was trying to show off for a couple of the other guys but ended up accidentally putting it in reverse when he thought he was going forward.'

I stop to catch a breath and open my eyes to see Stephen staring, hanging on the words. I can hear Dad's voice in my mind, with his measured delivery that always felt as if he was a word or two away from turning something into a joke.

'Dad reversed into some guy who was busy sweeping up behind him. The bloke went under the wheels and he broke both legs. Dad's boss did his best to cover it up. The guy with the broken legs was paid off so that he didn't go to tribunal, the papers, or anything like that. Anyway, the reason Dad said all that was because he was trying to tell me that accidents happen. He ended up becoming friends with the man he ran over. They'd go to football together.'

Stephen gives himself a few seconds to take all this in. The street is still, the moon white and bright. A breeze flitters around the buildings and I tuck myself in closer to Stephen's shoulder.

'So you ended up meeting the driver?' he asks.

'Just once. It was at a café on the side of a roundabout out by the main road. A Little Chef, or something like that. I got there first with Dad and we were sitting at the edge of a booth. I was the watching the door, waiting, and the second I saw him come in, I knew that I forgave him. He was this broken shell. His face was pale and his clothes were hanging off, as if he'd not eaten since what happened. I remember the way his hair was patchy, as if he'd been pulling out clumps. He sat opposite me in the booth and spent about ten minutes saying how sorry he was and that he wished he could change it. He said he'd rather he lost his own leg. I listened and then, at the end, I told him I forgave him – and he must have cried for about five minutes straight. Dad ended up putting his arm around the guy.'

I take a moment, blinking away the hints of wetness more because of the memory of my father than anything else. Then I realise that I'm still thinking of him as *my* father. I can't see a time when I'll ever think of him as anything else.

'I didn't know any of that,' Stephen says.

I can't reply at first but the words come eventually. 'That's how I dealt with my anger,' I say. 'I don't know what else to tell you – but there are people you can talk to. Professionals.'

Stephen bows his head and I know what's coming before he says it. 'I don't think that's for me.'

I take his hand and interlock my fingers with his. 'You're better than any of them,' I say.

He squeezes my fingers with his. 'I don't know what I'd do if I saw any of them on the street…'

'Call the police.'

Stephen doesn't reply to this and, as he withdraws his hand, there's a second in which it feels as if something has changed. A moment later and he sits up straighter and clears his throat.

'Can I say something else to you?'

'Of course.'

'It was just a thought. Don't get mad, but if you were stolen and then sold, then that woman you met in Stoneridge made good money from that…'

'Nikki.'

'Right. Her and her boyfriend. Except why would they stop there?'

'What do you mean?'

'You said she had one baby but arranged to sell two. They made twice the amount of money. But why stop at two? They had hit upon this mad, barely believable, scheme and got away with it. But if you ever watch those true-crime documentaries, people never just stop. They're addicted to the money. They learn from whatever they do first time and then find a way to hone whatever they're up to.'

It takes me a couple of seconds to absorb what he's said. 'Are you saying they might've stolen more than one child?'

Stephen presses back onto the step and stretches his arms high. 'I don't know. It was just a thought.'

Everything stops for a moment, as if the world is waiting for the cogs in my brain to turn.

At first I think I'm going to keep it to myself… but then I can't. 'How much?' I ask, talking to myself more than Stephen.

'How much what?'

'How much did they pay for me?'

Then I realise there's something else that niggles. In the kitchen, there was something Penny said that I skipped over at the time. Something that now feels important.

Stephen must see it in me because he asks: 'What else?'

'Probably nothing,' I tell him. 'But I think I need to make a phone call.'

THIRTY-FIVE

To save me walking, Stephen drops me home from Creators' Club and then I sit in my car on the drive with my phone in my lap. This call feels like something I don't want Stella to overhear, whether purposefully or not.

It's late but not crazily so. I think ten is the unofficial cut-off for unscheduled phone calls and there's a good forty minutes until then.

I press the button to call and then listen as the phone rings a few times before going to the automated voicemail. I almost leave a message, except I'm not sure what to say and so hang up instead.

When I get out of the car, I notice a movement from the front of next door.

Mr Bonner steps out into the gloom, dressed in slippers, fleecy lounge wear and a cap.

'Chilly one tonight, isn't it?' he says.

I step across towards the fence, so that we're standing a few paces apart. 'I've lost all track of days and weather,' I reply.

'It's good to be busy.' He smiles a little but doesn't step away, instead nodding towards my house. 'All okay?'

'As far as I know. Has it been quiet while I've been out?'

A nod. 'Not a peep, love.' He shuffles and then adds: 'I wait up for you on Wednesdays. I know you have your club and don't like to head up until I've seen you get in safely.'

Something surges in my chest. A skipped heartbeat, perhaps, and I suddenly find myself blinking away another tear.

'You don't have to do that,' I say.

'I know, love. That's not going to stop me doing it, though.'

I don't have a way of replying to that, certainly not one that isn't going to leave me a sobbing mess. Sitting on the steps with Stephen and thinking of Dad has left me close to the edge – and Mr Bonner's stand-in parenting is almost too much.

'Thank you,' I manage.

Before either of us can say more, my phone starts to ring. I check the screen and give a quick apology to my neighbour before hastily climbing back into my car and closing the door. Mr Bonner's going to wonder why I can't take the call in my own house but I don't have time to deal with that now.

When I press the button to answer, I first think I've missed the call – except there is someone there. The woman's voice is a husky whisper.

'It's Penny,' she says. 'I missed your call.'

I almost ask if she's okay, because the muffled lack of an echo makes it sound like she's hiding in a cupboard.

'It was so good to see your name on the screen,' she adds. 'I keep thinking about earlier. I didn't want to cause a scene, I just wanted a chat. Things got the better of me and I didn't know how to say sorry properly.'

There's emotion in her croaky tone and she sounds close to tears, too. It must be the evening for it.

'I understand,' I tell her. 'It's been hard for everyone.'

'I thought you might not want to talk to me again. I've been so worried. It's been going around my head ever since I left. I was so desperate to get answers for everything that went on before that I'd forgotten about the now. I was hoping you'd call, or text, because I wanted to say that perhaps I can put all that to one side. Get to know you as you are now and not worry about everything from all those years back.'

There's a gentle sob to her voice and I feel the lump forming in my throat too. This isn't the conversation I planned. It's such an enormous offer. Perhaps not to forgive sins of the past but to forget. After everything Penny has been through, this doesn't feel like something I can deny her... even if I wanted to.

'I think that would be good,' I say carefully. 'Perhaps we can meet somewhere next week? Maybe a café, or something like that? Once it's all sunk in a bit?'

Penny lets out a low breath of relief that I can almost feel.

'I'll wait to hear from you,' she says – and it's nearly a plea.

We go quiet and I almost start to say goodbye before I realise that it was me who first called – and that it wasn't to talk about this.

'You said something earlier,' I tell her. 'I didn't catch it properly at the time but I've been thinking about it. I asked how you got through everything and you said that you got support from someone who knew how it felt. I was wondering who else could have known how it felt?'

There's a shuffling from the other end of the line and, when Penny next speaks, she sounds a little unsure of herself. 'Oh... I suppose there's no reason for you to know. Gosh, it was so long ago. Another lifetime...'

She tails off and then says something that makes the hairs on the back of my neck stand up.

'You weren't the only child stolen from our area.'

THIRTY-SIX

Penny keeps talking, which is a good job because I have no words.

'There was a little boy,' she says. 'He disappeared from Higher Woolton about a year before you were taken. He was only four months old and taken right from his crib in a back garden. I became friends with his mum because she was the only one who understood.'

'There was someone else...?'

Penny replies instantly, the name burned into her mind. 'William Fletcher,' she says. 'His mum was called Emma. I suppose we weren't really friends in any traditional sense. We'd sit and have a cup of tea at each other's house, sometimes for hours, and we'd hardly ever talk. There wasn't anything to say – but that wasn't the point. I can't speak for her but, for me, it was enough to be around her. There was something comforting about it. I don't think I'd have got through the first year if it wasn't for her. I think—'

Penny cuts herself off and there's a muffled sound of a bang.

A moment later and she's back. 'I have to go,' she says quickly. 'It's late and—'

There's another stifled bump and I offer a quick 'look after yourself' before the call drops. I might be wrong but I picture Penny hiding in a bathroom, or a wardrobe, hastily calling me back away from Chris's accusing stare. I think of the way Mum and Dad empowered me to let me think I could do anything with my life. When the worst happened, they helped me pick up the pieces and find something new. Dad came to the first Creators'

Club session and stood in the corner watching. It's a contrast to Penny, who – through no fault of her own – is cowed and possibly scared of her husband. Two different lives. I don't know what to do that could help her.

I get out of the car and lock it before letting myself into the house. There's a faint sound of voices from the living room, so I head through to where Stella is sitting bare-footed on the sofa, watching some sort of reality show on TV. There's something disjointed about seeing somebody else so comfortable in my house and surroundings. It isn't her fault, of course – I'm the one who asked her to stay – but, when Stella picks up the remote control and mutes the TV, I feel a strange sense of ownership.

'How was everything?' she asks.

'Good.'

I sit in the armchair and there's a moment of awkwardness between us. When I asked her to stay, I suppose I'd forgotten that we're still strangers and not related in any real way.

'I thought of something earlier,' Stella says. 'It's a bit stupid…'

'What?'

'Just that you know how banks are always asking for a mother's maiden name? It's one of their security questions and I was wondering which you'd give now.'

She sounds upbeat, as if this is a joke. I don't think she means anything by it but there's nothing funny in what she's saying.

I don't reply and Stella winces a little. 'Sorry,' she adds.

'It's fine.'

'It popped into my head. Mum's maiden name is Crowley and I needed that for a form. I thought about you when I was filling it in.'

'Okay.'

I'm thinking of William Fletcher and how I need to look him up.

Stella smiles uncomfortably and then looks back to the TV, even though she doesn't unmute it.

'I'm going up to bed,' I say.

I stand and Stella looks up to me with surprise. 'Oh... um... sorry about that. I didn't mean anything by it. You don't have to—'

'It's not you,' I say. 'But it's been a long day.'

She nods. 'Well, um, g'night, I guess...'

I'm halfway up the stairs when the sound returns to the TV – and, for a reason I can't explain, I wish I was on my own.

THIRTY-SEVEN

I'm awake early the next morning. The prosthetist said it isn't physically possible but, sometimes, when I've had a bad day, I wake up the next morning and my residual limb throbs. The physio told me it might be a mental thing – and, though he didn't mean it unkindly, it wasn't the sort of advice that helped.

It's throbbing now.

I pop a couple of paracetamol tablets from my bedside table and then pull myself onto the side of the bed before rolling the padding part of my prosthetic onto my leg. When I first got it, there was a tortuous process to try to attach the prosthetic. The prosthetist showed me how everything went together and, in theory, there wasn't too much to it. It would still take me almost ten minutes to get everything to a point where I felt safe to stand on it, though. If the padding felt a little too loose, or tight, I'd start again.

Now, I have everything down to a minute at the absolute most. Often, it can take seconds if I'm on a roll.

I use the handrail to get myself downstairs and then head through to the empty kitchen, before setting the coffee machine running. I could have looked for details on William Fletcher last night but forgot to take up my laptop. I tried my phone but it was difficult to find anything – and the pop-ups made the whole process too much of a chore.

On the laptop, I search for '"William Fletcher"+missing+"Higher Woolton".' There is a handful of hits from archived news stories, as well as the similar sorts of articles about unsolved mysteries, much like the ones in which I first found details of Jane Craven.

William Fletcher was left in his crib in the back garden on a warm spring day. His mother went into the house for 'a minute at most' to fill up his bottle. When she returned to the garden, the cot was empty. The garden backed onto a narrow lane where there were no other houses. Its only purpose was to serve as a way for homeowners and tenants to quickly access the backs of their properties. There was no through way and nothing else there. When William's mother checked the alley, there was no sign of anyone in the area. Her neighbours saw no strange cars or people in the vicinity – and it was as if William disappeared into thin air.

The dates listed in the articles are a little vague and sometimes contradictory but the details tie into what Penny told me: that it happened around a year before Jane disappeared.

I look for other disappearances from Higher or Lower Woolton and the surrounding area from the same time. I try various combinations of places and years but, as best I can tell, it was only the two children who were taken: William and Jane.

William and… me.

A four-month-old and a six-month-old.

One of the articles has an interview with William's mother, Emma. It was done a little over six years ago as part of a newspaper feature about unsolved 'cold' cases. In the photos, there's one of her cradling an old black and white photograph of her baby. There's a deadness in her stare. Thirty years of pain summed up in a single snapshot that says as much as needs to be said. A little like Penny, she never had another child. She only had one – and it was taken from her.

I search for Emma Fletcher along with Higher Woolton, which brings up a few more hits.

Emma died around a year after the cold cases article. There's a small obituary that mentions brief details and then a second, slightly longer piece, about the funeral. A neighbour told the paper that Emma died of a broken heart that never healed.

I jump at the sound of footsteps on the stairs and it takes me a moment to remember that I'm no longer the only person in the house. I close my laptop lid just as Stella emerges in the kitchen. She bats away a yawn as she heads to the sink and retrieves a mug.

'There are clean ones in the cupboard,' I tell her.

She wipes away sleepy tears with her sleeve and then gets herself a clean mug, before filling it with water and then leaning against the counter as she fights another yawn. In the couple of days since we first met, her appearance has changed almost completely. I suppose a few showers will do that – but it goes beyond the immediate. Whatever marks were on her neck have now largely gone and she's wearing a vest that shows off skin that almost seems to be glowing.

'I slept so well,' she says. 'That bed in your spare room is magic.'

'My friend Stephen says the same whenever he's in there… although a lot of that is probably because he only usually stays over if he's had too much to drink.'

Stella doesn't react to that.

'How's the job-hunting going?' I ask.

'Waiting on a few call backs. I filled in so many forms yesterday.'

For the first time since we met, there's something in the way Stella says this that leaves me feeling as if it is a clear lie. It might be the way she scratches her top lip as she speaks, or the borderline dismissive tone. It feels like a waitress at a restaurant wishing people a good evening at the end of a meal, when it's clear she couldn't care less.

I'm not sure what to make of it.

'Has your mum been in contact?' I ask.

The question takes Stella by surprise. Her fingers grip her mug slightly tighter before she breezes over it. 'Not for a week or more.'

'Do you think I was the only one?'

Stella's brow creases as she turns to take me in. 'The only what?'

'Nikki told me that Robbie saw taking a baby as a way to make money. So why stop at one? Maybe there was a second child taken after me? Or, maybe, *I* was the second? Or the third?'

Stella's nose twitches a little, as if there's a bad smell in the room. 'Why would you think that?'

'My friend mentioned it and I think he might have a point. Your mum made it sound as if it was all Robbie – and that it was about the money. So why would he stop at one if it was so lucrative?'

'It would be a big risk.'

'But it was a risk anyway. If he got away with it, which he did – and he made money, which he did – why would it have only happened once?'

Stella seems stumped by this and I don't blame her. The fact this is seemingly a normal topic of conversation would have been extraordinary a week ago, except this is apparently the new normal.

'When you found the article, was there anything else in there about another child?' I ask.

Stella answers quickly with an 'I don't think so' – and then adds: 'Has something happened…?'

I tell her it hasn't, although I can feel the invisible tug back to my laptop and the articles about William.

Stella moves on quickly as she changes the subject. 'I have a job interview,' she says. 'I didn't know whether to say anything in case it doesn't come off.'

It's a quick change from what she said a few moments before, although I don't necessarily blame her for that.

'That's brilliant!' I say.

She smiles slightly and angles away from me, like a nervous schoolgirl around a boy she likes. 'I don't want to impose on you too long,' she says. 'I'm hoping it all comes off and I'll be able to sort out a room somewhere.'

'You don't have to.'

'I want to.' She twists on the spot and then adds: 'Did you go straight to sleep last night?'

'More or less. Why?'

She winces a little, turning towards the front of the house.

'After I went up to bed, I pulled the curtains and I thought I saw… something.'

'What?'

She takes a breath and rubs her head. 'Maybe… I don't know.' A pause. 'It might have been the shadows but I thought it was… *Wayne*…'

I don't immediately recognise the name but then I realise she's talking about her ex-boyfriend. The one who gave her the bruises. The reason she changed her phone number and was at her mother's house in the first place.

'Are you sure?' I ask.

Stella shrugs and is avoiding all eye contact now. 'No. I don't know. There was someone.'

'How could he have found you? Nobody knows you're here…?'

Without meaning to, I state that as a question. Stella shakes her head. 'I haven't told anyone except one person at the job centre and a couple at various agencies. None of them would know Wayne.' She pauses again. 'You don't know what he's like, though. He's clever. He's found me before. I don't know how he does it.'

She stares past me towards the front door. As I follow her gaze, I half expect there to be a shadow through the rippled glass – except there isn't.

'You're safe here,' I say.

Stella nods, although she doesn't reply – which leaves me really hoping I'm right.

THIRTY-EIGHT

Stephen is on lunch duty in the school playground again. Ahead of him, there is the usual chaos of screaming kids running in all directions and the noise is so high-pitched that it feels as if my ears are bleeding.

He stands close to the railings, with me on the other side. I'm trying not to shout, while also wanting him to hear me. 'I don't know how you do this every day,' I say.

'Be friends with you?'

'I mean the screaming!'

He doesn't turn all the way around to face me but I see the hint of a smile on his face. 'I have heard you're a screamer,' he says, devilishly.

'I'm trying to be serious.'

He rolls his eyes a little and faces me properly. 'I thought you were joking when you said you wanted me to help you break into the house of the woman who stole you?'

'I wouldn't call it a break-in.'

'I think the police might.'

'It's more of a *get* in.'

'Knock and ask her then.' I raise my eyebrows towards him and Stephen continues talking as if I'm one of his naughty students. 'What if you're caught?'

'What if I am? Do you think she's going to call the police after everything that's happened? Imagine what would happen if I *did* get caught and then told the police why I was in Nikki's house in the first place.'

Stephen twists back towards the playground, which is his way of conceding I have a point.

'What about your leg?' he asks.

'What about it?'

'I love you – and you're many things – but you're hardly light on your feet.'

He makes a quick glance sideways, letting me know this is meant with affection.

'I'm like a ballerina when you're not around.'

We're on the same wavelength to the degree that Stephen knows this is a joke. He doesn't laugh. 'I don't think this is a good idea,' he says. 'How are you going to get into this woman's house?'

'She keeps the back door open for the cat. She said the cat flap was broken. I'll just walk in.'

'What if she's shut the door?'

'Then I guess I won't go in – and we'll go home.'

Stephen pauses for a moment as a small group of girls come up to him and point at me. I can tell without knowing any of them that the tallest is the one to watch.

'Is that your wife?' she asks.

Stephen looks to me with a wicked smirk and then back to the girl.

'She wishes.'

The tallest girl is looking at me now. 'What's your name?' she asks.

'Beyoncé.'

'Is it really?'

'Yep. I had the name first and she borrowed it off me.'

The girl frowns in the way children do when they think an adult might be lying but they're not completely certain.

'Do you *love* Mr Evans?' she asks.

I look to Stephen, ready for revenge. 'No way,' I say. 'He's got a really hairy back, like a bear's – and he smells like a bear, too.'

The girl sniffs the air and takes half a step away from Stephen. 'What does a bear smell like?'

'Like the toilet before you flush it. I call him Mr Toilet.'

The group takes a step away as one, making a communal 'ugh' sound.

'Can I call you Mr Toilet?' the tallest girl asks.

'No you cannot.'

That is, obviously, the signal for the girls to turn and run away, each of them chanting 'Mr Toilet' in unison.

Stephen looks to me with a grimace. 'Thanks for that, Beyoncé.'

'You are very welcome. Us girls stick together.'

He sighs as the girls run to the other corner of the playground, still chanting.

'How do you know she lives alone?' he asks.

It takes me a second to realise he's talking about Nikki. 'She said she was alone after Stella left. I didn't see anyone there.'

The cry of 'Mr Toilet' increases on the far side of the playground. In barely seconds, someone has invented a song about it.

Stephen looks between me and the playground again. 'I don't see how it helps,' he says.

'Stella told me she found documents in a cupboard at the top of the stairs. That's where the article that came through my door is from. I found something online about another boy who was stolen from the same area at roughly the same time and I want to see if there's anything about him, too.'

The bit I leave out is that Nikki specifically told me she got rid of the documents after Stella found what she did. The more I think about that, the more I don't believe her. She could have got rid of them at any time – so why wait?

'Wouldn't Stella have said if there were other names?' Stephen asks.

'I don't think she was looking.'

'Maybe ask her to go back to her mum's and look?'

'She's not talking to her mum and I can't ask her that. It's not fair.'

Stephen gives a sideways look to let me know that he's not convinced by Stella and that he still doesn't think I should be trusting her. He doesn't *say* it, though.

He's also not happy that I have answers for his obstacles.

'Do you even know where this cupboard is?' he asks.

'Stella told me top of the stairs. I only need a bit of time – which is where you come in.'

He shakes his head. By now, it feels as if half the playground is singing the 'Mr Toilet' song. It's to the tune of Happy Birthday, except they're singing 'Mr Toilet is here'.

'I'll go anyway,' I tell him, knowing it'll do the trick.

He sighs, although it's unclear if it's because of me, or because of the song.

'Fine,' he says. 'But don't say I didn't warn you.'

THIRTY-NINE

The alley that runs along the rear of Nikki's house is grungy and grim. There are cobbles and cracked patches of tarmac that I doubt have been maintained since it was all laid.

I stand at the back of Nikki's neighbour's place, hidden by an overgrown hedge, and can't help but think of Emma Fletcher. William was taken from her back garden, which was lined by an alley that sounded an awful lot like the one in which I now lurk.

Crisp packets and chocolate wrappers flutter along the path. There is nobody in sight – but the distant sound of a barking dog, and the music I heard from the last time I was here, clings to the breeze. It doesn't feel like the sort of area that ever completely goes quiet.

I look both ways again, double-checking there's nobody around. Everything is clear, so I casually stroll along the lane, slowing as I pass Nikki's where I notice her back door is wide open. I keep walking until I'm hidden by another overgrown hedge, this time on the other side of Nikki's place. Then I take out my phone and text Stephen a thumbs-up emoji.

I'd be lying if I said this didn't excite me and set my heart racing. My life is about routine. It's the various pieces of work leading up to the twice-weekly club sessions – and then the club itself. It's all about emails to councillors, teachers, or creative types. The grant applications and the tax forms. It's definitely not about being a low-level action heroine and/or complete idiot, depending on whether a person listens to me or Stephen.

I count to fifty and then edge along to the rear of Nikki's house. The glare from her kitchen window makes it impossible to see if anyone's there, so I take my chance and walk through the open metal gate into a dusty yard. A broom is lying flat on the ground and there's a rusting lawnmower resting against a wall, despite the lack of a lawn. There are pieces of aluminium and metal scattered around the space, plus a grimy slick of oil, as if someone might have been working on an engine at some point in the past few months.

I've taken a couple of steps towards the house when I hear the sound of a doorbell from inside. It's immediately followed by low-level grumbling and then the noise of a door being pulled open. I edge closer to the house and listen to Stephen's muffled voice. I don't catch every word he says but I do hear him say 'fix your internet'. There's a back and forth between Nikki and Stephen, footsteps, a door closing, a second door closing, and then my phone vibrates. The message from Stephen is a replica of mine – a single thumbs up – which is the signal.

I move quickly through Nikki's back door and into her kitchen. There are voices coming from the living room, where Stephen is supposed to be talking Nikki through speeding up her internet connection. It was Stella who told me that it was terrible and that her mother was always complaining about it. I figured Stephen could be from her provider, turn the modem off and on a few times, unplug a few wires and plug them back in – plus generally keep her in the living room.

The carpet on the stairs is patchy, with large holes showing off the bare wood beneath. I try to stick to the padded areas and get to the top with making minimal noise.

I feel clearer-headed than I did the last time I was here. My emotions were high then and I didn't know what to make of everything. That's probably why I missed the smell of cannabis, which clings to the walls and carpets as if it's built into the house itself. It's not simply the odd joint: Nikki must have been smoking it for years. It's like going into a pub in the days after the smoking ban first came in, when everything still reeked of tobacco and the walls were stained brown.

The cupboard that Stella told me about is immediately obvious when I get to the top of the stairs. There are two doors ahead of me and another open one to the side, in which a white sink is visible. The final door has a different handle to the others. Instead of a push-down horizontal rod, it's a simple pull-open hook.

I pause for a second, making sure I can still hear the faint voices from below, and then I open the door.

Stella was right that there was probably once a boiler in here. It's dark and dank, with no light above, and smells like shoes that have been left out in the rain. It's less of a cupboard, more of a hole in the house. Yellow foam insulation spills from both walls and is scattered in clumps across the floor.

An upright crimson vacuum with a massive bag that has a hole in the side is rammed up against one wall. It looks like something out of the seventies that should've been sent to the tip at least a couple of decades back. Against the other wall, more or less as Stella described, is a series of boxes. I'd been expecting the sort of oblong ones that are used for filing, because they're the ones that Mum has in her attic. Instead, there are a pair of old cereal boxes with the tops cut off. I pull the first towards me and there's almost no weight to it because the content is entirely paper.

As the voices continue below, I finger my way through the box – but there are no full pages. There are envelopes torn in half, plus scraps from notebooks. Many have random single words written on them, like 'Gordon' or 'Mick' – and then a phone number. There are a few half-pages from an old-fashioned phone book, some postage stamps, a note that simply reads: 'Milkman' – and plenty more.

I could spend hours sorting through the various pieces of paper but don't have the time.

The second cereal box is a little more organised than the first. Instead of scraps, there are complete pages pressed into one another. I pull everything out together – and it takes me a couple of seconds to process the top page, because it's almost too perfect. These are the pages Stella told me about. The ones Nikki claimed to have got rid of.

It's a browning-yellow page of lined paper that feels crispy, as if it has got wet and dried out a few times. 'SMITH' is written in faded purple letters in the top corner, with a date from thirty-four years ago in the other corner.

Stella told me the couple who bought her mother's *actual* child – her real sister – was named Smith.

'£3,000' is written in the bottom corner and, above that are varying amounts. There are a few that say '£50' or '£100' – but most payments are for £200.

It's a list of the payments that Nikki and her boyfriend, Robbie, received for the baby. Each is initialled with a tidy 'R' and a tick. It's amazing how clear and organised it all is, as if someone was paying cash towards a car.

The page behind is almost identical to the first, except that 'TAYLOR' is written in large letters in the top corner. The payments are for generally smaller amounts, going as low as £20 and no higher than £140. At the bottom, in the same emotionless type, is the figure £3,000.

It's barely a squiggle. I read somewhere recently that something that cost a pound in the mid-eighties costs around three pounds now. If that's true, then my parents paid the equivalent of £9,000 for me.

They weren't rich and it feels like a huge amount of money… except it also feels like nothing at all.

There's that cliché about everyone having a price – and now I have mine.

Nine grand.

I could get lost in that – except there's a bump from downstairs and I freeze at the sound of a door opening and then Nikki's voice becoming louder. She says something about 'not understanding' but then Stephen calls after her to ask about 'a connection to the wall'. The door closes and then their voices are muffled again.

I should have listened to Stephen about how ridiculous this all is. I'm not sure what came over me, other than a desire for some sort of truth. Perhaps a desire for danger.

The other thing I realise is that there was a chirpiness to Nikki's tone as she was talking to the person she thinks is fixing her internet connection. When I spoke with her, a dark cloud loomed over everything – but she sounds at ease now.

The page about my parents is interesting in one sense but, ultimately, doesn't tell me anything I didn't already know.

I keep looking through the box, where there are receipts for a car, a boiler, for plumbing work and something marked 'guttering'. The years dart back and forth from the eighties through until last year, which at least shows Nikki *knew* all these papers were still in her house.

Deeper into the box and there's a birth certificate for Stella, plus a marriage certificate for Nikki and Robbie, which shows they swapped vows around two years after selling me. There are two old passports with the corners clipped away, both in Nikki's name.

And then, almost at the bottom is a familiar-looking page of paper. It's a browny-yellow lined sheet with 'DON HIPKISS' written in the top right in faded purple type. There's a date from thirty-five years ago and payment amounts from between £40 and £250 that lead down to '£3,000' in the bottom right.

I stare at it, knowing what the characters mean.

Nikki and Robbie didn't sell *two* babies – they sold *three*. The first was a year before I was taken, at around the same time as William Fletcher was snatched.

I wonder how Stella missed this. She told me about the other two and yet this page was here, too. She might not have looked the whole way through the box, or perhaps focused on the article she found that named Jane Craven. I didn't look fully through the first box and there could be more articles in there, perhaps one that names William Fletcher.

I don't get a chance to look because there's another noise from downstairs. Instead of the bump from before, there's a clunk and then a loud click.

Everything happens in a blink – and, as I poke my head around the corner to look down towards the front door, slowly and horrifyingly, it opens.

FORTY

I get the briefest glimpse of a man with dark hair before I rock back around the corner and out of sight. There's no room to hide within the cupboard and, if the man comes up the stairs, there isn't a spot for me to get out of sight.

'Nik?'

His gruff voice echoes around the house, almost a cough than a call. I hold my breath and wait, dreading the sound of foot on step – but then there's a dampened cry of 'in here' – and the living room door opens and almost immediately closes.

I move quickly, shoving the boxes back into the cupboard and then closing it. The moment I've done that, I think about going back in to grab the three invoices – but then the sensible voice in my head finally gets its say.

I move down the stairs as quickly as I can while avoiding the patches where the carpet has worn. I don't bother to hang around, darting around the banister and out through the still open back door, sticking to the side of the fence that's away from the living room. It takes barely seconds and then I'm out and crouching behind the overgrown bush where I first started.

I'm half-expecting footsteps to be following me – or a gruff call of 'oi' – except nothing comes. I've not gone far and yet my chest is tight from the adrenaline and speed. Stephen was right about everything and yet, somehow, I'm in the clear.

As I try to regain my breath, I pat my leg, checking the connection of the prosthetic, though already knowing its fine. I take out my phone and send Stephen a quick thumbs-up emoji. After that, I head along the lane and then loop back around to the front of the houses, where I wait next to a lamp post at the far end of Nikki's street. A couple of kids pass, kicking a can as they go, but neither of them pay me any attention.

It's almost ten minutes later that Stephen pulls up in his car. I barely have my arse on the passenger seat when he starts to ease away and it all happens so quickly that the car beeps its disapproval at my lack of speed in putting on my seat belt.

'I thought you said she lived alone?' he says. Stephen is not happy – and I don't blame him.

'I thought she did,' I reply. 'Who was that guy?'

'I didn't ask – but some sort of boyfriend or husband. He seemed happy enough when Nikki told him I was fixing their internet. He kept saying it was about time.'

'That makes it sound like they live together.'

Stephen turns a little and gives me a full-on side-eye. 'You think?'

There's a quiet between us for a minute or so as I silently run through everything that Stella told me and wonder if she mentioned there was someone else in her mum's house. She said she moved back in but I don't remember any more than that. The mystery man could be her stepdad, or her mum's boyfriend. Perhaps it doesn't matter – except it feels like something that would have come up considering everything else she told me.

It's Stephen who breaks the silence. He glances sideways again and then looks back to the road. 'Did you get what you were looking for?'

'I didn't take anything but I had a look through the cupboard Stella told me about.'

'What did you find?'

'More or less what she told me was there. An invoice with my parents' name on it. I can't believe someone kept it. Mum and

Dad paid three grand for me, all in instalments. Thirty quid here, seventy quid there. That sort of thing. Like paying off something they bought from a catalogue in the old days.'

He doesn't reply at first but then it comes. 'Overpriced.'

I snigger and let it sit. 'Did you fix her internet?'

'I cleared out her internet cache and updated the modem's firmware. Ran a speed test – and she seemed happy enough at that. I left it running an anti-spyware thing that had about two and a half hours left to go. I could've charged her a call-out fee if I wasn't busy covering for you.' He pauses to take a bend and then adds: 'I am *never* doing anything like that again. You should've seen how closely she looked at my fake ID.'

Stephen printed out his photo on a piece of paper, along with a BT logo and a name he made up. With that inside the lanyard which usually houses his ID for the school, it was seemingly authentic. It looked good enough for me. Stephen is one of those people with good looks and a natural confidence to breeze through most things. There was a time when we were trying to get into a sold-out gig at a warehouse and he convinced the bouncer he was the drummer's brother, simply by repeating facts he'd read on Wikipedia.

The enormity of what I've asked of him reveals itself too late. If he'd been found out, he'd have been arrested. He'd have lost his job, his career. And yet he did it because I asked him.

I shouldn't have asked.

The rest of the journey happens largely with the background chatter of the radio. Stephen and I have always been good at sensing the other's mood. It's better that some things are left unsaid and, for now, I'm not sure I want to talk about William Fletcher, let alone what I asked Stephen to do.

He pulls up outside my house and leaves the engine idling. When I don't move, he stops and looks sideways towards me. 'What's up?'

'Do you want to come in for a drink or two?'

'It's a school day tomorrow and I've gotta drive home.'

'I'll get you a taxi.'

'It's still a school day.'

'As if you've never had a drink on a school night…'

There's a hint of a grin and then Stephen pulls on the handbrake and switches off the engine. 'Don't say I never do anything for you.'

'You didn't need your arm twisting *that* hard.'

I don't tell him that, since seeing that man walk so comfortably into Nikki's house, it feels as if something is different with Stella and me. She might not have lied but it feels like an omission that must have been deliberate. Perhaps Stephen was right? He didn't say it explicitly but I made an emotional decision in inviting Stella to stay, when I should have been thinking rationally.

Stephen and I head into the house and Stella calls a chirpy 'in here' from the living room. I catch the momentary look of concern on Stephen's face as he perhaps realises why I wanted him to come in.

Stella is sitting on the sofa with her feet curled underneath herself and her phone in her hand. Except it takes me a moment to realise it's her. When I left this morning, she had long, dark hair – but now it's lighter and shorter, with the ends tucked behind her ears.

'This is Stephen,' I say, poking a thumb towards him as the two of them eye one another. There's an immediate tension in the air, like walking into a room when a conversation has ended abruptly. Not dangerous, as such – but there's a fizz.

Stephen nods a 'hello', which Stella returns with one of her own.

'The hair looks good,' I tell her.

Stella reaches for her head and tugs a strand. 'I needed to sort it out for the interview. I didn't really have the money but it was a friend of a friend…'

I'm not sure why – but I don't believe her. She's looking at me and speaking confidently – but I've gone from hanging on her every word to questioning everything. I probably should have done this days ago.

'How was the interview?' I ask.

'Good, I think. You know what it's like. You can think everything is great but then you never hear back…'

Her eyes dart to Stephen and then back to me, silently querying his presence.

I nod towards the kitchen. 'We're going to crack open some wine.'

Stella nods slowly but doesn't say anything as we disappear back into the hall and then along and into the kitchen. Stephen closes the door behind us, which is the first time in a very long time that this particular door has been shut.

He lowers his voice and leans in closer. 'Did she have her hair cut today?'

'It was long this morning. Why?'

He steps away and then back. His eyes narrow and he starts to say something before stopping himself – and then, eventually, going for it. 'It's just… she's copied your hair.'

Stephen says this as if he's stating that two and two is four – except it's only now he's mentioned it that I realise he's right. It's so obvious and yet I missed it.

'She looks a bit like you,' he adds.

'No she doesn't.'

He raises his eyebrows, not needing to say it, because we both know he's right.

FORTY-ONE

For the first time I can remember, Stephen and I share a bottle of wine in the living room, rather than the kitchen. Now that we're on the comfy seats, surrounded by a cosy carpet, it seems very odd that we've not done this before. There's no real explanation for why the kitchen became our gossip station and minibar but it did.

I've not mentioned my new-found concerns about Stella to Stephen but he either senses it, or has plenty of his own. I hadn't told Stephen that Stella was pregnant – and he offers her a glass of wine that she waves away.

After that, we all settle together in the living room. Stephen has taken it upon himself to ask the questions I should have. He plays the role so well, telling Stella he likes her top and asking about her interview. He tells both of us about a disastrous interview of his own, where he stepped in a puddle outside the office, tried to shake his foot dry, and ended up flipping his slip-on shoe into the chest of the person who it turned out was there to interview him.

I have no idea if it's true – but it gets Stella smiling and, as soon as she's relaxed, he begins.

'Did you grow up around here?' he asks. It's chummy, as if she's a new friend he's met at a bar – but I can sense that edge underneath everything. A feeling that he's analysing all that she says.

'Stoneridge,' Stella replies. She matches his tone, not necessarily keen to engage but not refusing to answer.

'Oh!' He's surprised and interested. 'What school were you at?'

'Stoneridge Primary, then St Catherine's.'

'Really? My cousin was at St Catherine's. You must be more or less the same age. Do you know Lucy Evans?'

If Stephen has a cousin named Lucy, then this is the first time he's mentioned her.

Stella's phone is on the armrest of the chair and she glances towards it, as if willing it to ring. She pauses for a moment, eye twitching. 'Never heard of her,' she says. 'Must have been in different years.'

He looks towards me and asks if I was popular at school. I tell him that I wasn't in with any particular crowd and that I bet he was one of the annoying drama kids, who walked around the halls singing. Stephen doesn't deny it and there's another hint of a smile from Stella.

The more I watch her, the more I realise that she really *does* look like me now that she's had her hair cut. We're around the same height and, although she's skinnier than I am, there's not a lot in it. Nothing that couldn't be hidden with a choice of clothes. I wonder if she opted for this on purpose, or if it was something subconscious because we've been in the same house for a couple of days. Or if it's a coincidence entirely?

'What kind of job are you looking for?'

Stephen pivots effortlessly from talking to me to talking to Stella. It takes her by surprise so much so that she gulps and cranes her neck back before answering.

'Anything with admin,' she says.

'Is that what you've done before?'

'More or less.'

'Where have you worked?'

Stella glances to me and then back to Stephen, perhaps wondering if I'll get her out of answering. 'Mainly agency stuff,' she says stonily. 'They move me around offices covering for maternity leave and things like that. Sometimes it's a week or two, other times it might be a few months. I went where I was sent.'

It's vague but plausible. Stella glances towards me again, probably sensing that the questions are about more than curiosity. Or perhaps it's the mention of 'maternity' and the fact that she's pregnant.

'Everything's moved so fast,' Stephen adds. 'One day that article came through the door and next…' He holds up his hands. '… Here we all are. A new world.'

Stella nods along with this. 'I didn't know how things would pan out.'

'It must've been a tough decision to post the article, though.'

Stella looks across to me for support. 'I didn't think anyone would believe me if I simply went up to them on the street.'

'She's probably right,' I say. 'I don't think I'd have believed a stranger. The article made me look into things for myself.'

Stephen gulps a mouthful of his wine, keeping it casual: 'But how did you find Hope?'

At first, it doesn't look as if Stella will answer. She shuffles on the seat, glancing to her phone once more. 'Her parents were named on a form I found in Mum's house. Her dad's name showed up when I searched for it online – and it mentioned Hope. It didn't take very long.'

I think it's the same thing she told me and, this time, Stephen presses back into his chair, apparently satisfied. He has a little more of his wine and we share the briefest of sideways glances, in which he lets me know that he doesn't have anything else to ask.

Perhaps it's because he's satisfied that the feeling I had the other day about Stella begins to return. She gave up a lot to get me this information.

A strange thing happens after that: the three of us start to get on as a trio. Stephen is always at his charismatic best when he's had a little alcohol – and, before I know it, he's off and telling stories of dates gone wrong. I've heard everything before but it's still funny – and it's not long before Stella is laughing along, too.

Stephen tops up our glasses and then it's as if we've all known each other for years.

It's when I stand to go to the toilet that I realise I've had too much to drink. My head starts to spin and I grab onto the armrest of the chair to help steady myself. There are three empty bottles next to the door, even though I don't remember having anything like that much myself.

Stephen holds my arm and makes a joke of me being too old for all this. I tell him I'm fine – and take another step – except the world swirls again.

There's nervous laughter between Stella and Stephen and they say something to each other that I don't quite take in. Stephen hooks a hand underneath my armpit and says it's probably time for bed. There seems little point in fighting the obvious, so I let him help me up the stairs for what is not the first time. He opens the bedroom door for me and then tells me to close my eyes as he flicks on the light. After that, he leads me over to the bed, where I sit on the corner, eyes still closed.

'I drank too much,' I say with a croak.

'It's been a long week and you've been through a lot.'

He rubs my back and his touch is comforting, even though it's only there for a moment.

'I should get off,' he says.

'Stay,' I tell him.

'Stella's in the other room.'

'Sleep here.' I try to pat the side of the bed opposite to where I sleep – except I miss and waft the air, almost overbalancing.

'You're too much of a snorer,' Stephen says. 'If I wanted to sleep through noise like that, I'd move next to an airport.'

Neither of us laugh but, in my case, it's because I'm swaying slightly. Stephen helps right me and then I shuffle onto the bed, so that I'm lying down with my head on the pillow.

'Please stay,' I say.

There's quiet for a moment and I pull at the straps for my leg, tugging them free until the prosthetic drops to the floor. I already know what's coming.

'I'll sleep downstairs on the sofa,' Stephen says. 'I'll set an alarm so I can go home in the morning and have a shower before work.'

I reach for him but miss and again find myself fumbling at the air. 'Do you trust her?' I ask.

When I open my eyes, the room has turned a fuzzy grey, with the vague shape of Stephen in the centre of it. It feels as if he's sitting on the edge of the bed but when I reach for him, he's further away and closer to the door. He pokes his head outside and looks down the stairs towards the living room, before stepping back towards me. His voice is quiet enough that only I would be able to hear him.

'Maybe,' he says. 'I trust you more.'

Something shifts in the air and then he's next to me. He brushes hair away from my eyes and rests a hand on my shoulder.

'I think I've forgotten something important,' I say.

'Like what?'

I try to force my brain to filter everything that's been said over the evening but it's like wading through sand. Either Stephen or Stella said something that feels like it should be important – except I'm not sure how everything links together.

'Go to sleep,' Stephen says. 'You might remember in the morning.'

My legs sink deeper into the sand as I try to force the memory and so I let myself succumb to the pull.

'Thank you,' I say. And then it's all a blank.

FORTY-TWO

FRIDAY

The next thing I know, my shoulder is being rocked. The grey fuzz springs into sharp colour and Stephen is kneeling next to me. There are dark bristles across his chin and his usually neat hair is jutting out at angles.

'It doesn't look like you've moved all night,' he whispers.

His breath tickles my ear and I roll onto my back, before pushing myself up until I'm sitting and resting against the headboard. 'What time is it?'

'Five to six.'

'Ugh. When did there start being two six o'clocks?'

'I've got to get home before work,' he replies.

I push myself up a little straighter and try to blink away the delicate haze that sits around the corner of my vision.

'How's the head?' Stephen asks.

'Surprisingly clear. How much did I drink?'

'A bit more than a bottle and a half.'

I breathe out a long wisp of air. 'You should've stopped me.'

'I figured you're old enough to make your own choices…'

He makes it sound like a joke but there's truth there, too. It's not his job to stop me drinking wine in my own house.

'I need to go,' he says.

I tell him I'll see him off and then he watches as I wrestle with the straps to my prosthetic until it's firmly attached. He waits for me to stand, checking I'm steady, and then I trail him down the stairs until we're at the bottom. He gives me a hug and I thank him for coming in and staying over. I'm not sure why it felt like I needed him in the house – but he was there when I needed him. I watch him shuffle along the driveway and get into his car, then I shut the door.

There's no sign of Stella in the living room or the kitchen. Someone – probably Stephen – has cleaned up from the night before. The three wine bottles are neatly piled in the recycling box near the back door – and the glasses we used are upside down on the draining board, having been cleaned.

I set the coffee machine running and then slump onto my usual stool and close my eyes for a minute or what turns out to be ten.

When I next open them, my head feels clearer. My laptop is on the counter in front of me and I suddenly know what I want to do.

'Don Hipkiss' was the name written in the corner of the page at Nikki's house – and, if it's the same person, according to Google, he's a former local councillor who lives on the far side of the country.

I look for other potential Don or Donald Hipkisses – but it's a rare name and the only other matches are outside the UK.

Don's wife is Valerie, and also an ex-councillor from the same area. She is often referred to as 'Val' – and they have both worked in public services over the course of forty years or so. There is a lot of information about the pair online, including numerous interviews and photographs. When Don and Val retired at the same time a little over four years back, there was a large feature in their local newspaper to mark the occasion.

It's there that I find out their son, Thomas, had just turned thirty-one at the time. It's the same age as William Fletcher would have been, had he not been stolen from his mother's back garden a year before Jane was taken.

I keep scrolling through the search results – which is when I stumble across the obituary for Don Hipkiss. He died less than a year after his retirement celebration with what is described as a 'short illness'. Considering the length of his career, the tributes are unsurprising.

Val Hipkiss died around a month later – and it's within the articles that accompany her obituary that I find a line that says Thomas Hipkiss studied at Cambridge University and was due to open a bookshop in the town where his parents were councillors. He says he 'wanted to put something back into the community his parents loved' and there's a photo of him standing proudly outside a small shop with a book in each hand.

He's remarkably unremarkable. The sort of man who could be passed three or four times while he pushes a trolley along a Tesco aisle – and yet nobody would be quite sure if it was the same person.

I wonder if Thomas truly *is* William Fletcher and, if so, whether he'd want to know what I know about myself. Who he really is. What his parents did. His possible birth mother, Emma, is dead – and so are the people who raised him.

There's a bump from the stairs and I close the laptop lid as Stella yawns her way into the kitchen.

She waves away the tiredness and then slips onto the stool next to me with a slim smile. 'How's the head?' she asks.

'It's been worse.'

'Did Stephen get off okay…?'

'He woke me up and then went home to get a shower before school.'

Stella puts her phone down on the counter. 'He seems nice,' she says – and it feels as if she means it.

'He is,' I reply.

'He's very protective of you.' A pause. 'All those questions…'

Stella's more perceptive than I thought. Either that, or Stephen's approach was more of a sledgehammer than my booze-addled brain believed it to be.

'We've been friends for a long while,' I say.

'I thought it was quite sweet that he put you to bed.'

There is a touch of something in her tone that's not easy to decipher. Perhaps a longing that she doesn't have this sort of relationship with someone.

'It's not the first time,' I tell her. 'But it's happened in reverse, too.'

Stella nods solemnly and then pushes her hair back. I consider asking whether she copied mine on purpose. I almost do – except it feels too personal a question.

'When are you likely to hear about the job interview?' I ask.

She blinks back into the kitchen. 'They said they might take the weekend to think things over. Other people are being looked at today.'

'I should've asked last night but it slipped my mind. Did you see any more of Wayne yesterday…?'

A shake of the head. 'No. It might not have been him the other night. Maybe I was seeing things.'

She sounds unsure, which I suppose isn't a surprise if she's trying to escape him. Her bruises have more or less gone and, if I hadn't seen them on the first day we met, I wouldn't know to look for the faded remains.

We sit quietly for a little while and there's a genuine peace until I remember what's in my plans for the day.

'I'm going to be out for a lot of today,' I say. 'Feel free to call if you need anything.'

'I don't want to be a burden on you.'

'You're not.'

I push myself up and the world sits mercifully still and unblurred. Having a shower helps wake me up even further and, after that, I change and drink a glass of water before telling Stella I'll see her later. She asks if I know what time I'll be back and I say it'll likely be the evening, before I head out to the car.

I don't know where I'm heading, so plug my phone into the car and rely on its directions. It tells me my destination is almost two hours' drive away, so I find something on the radio that's easy to ignore and then set off.

I've been driving for a little over an hour when I remember the thing I was trying to tell Stephen the night before. It falls into my head as unexpectedly as it fell out.

When Stephen asked Stella how she found me, she said that my dad's name had been on the paper she found in her mother's cupboard. But I saw that page – and all it said was the word 'TAYLOR' – in the same way the others said 'SMITH' and then 'DON HIPKISS'. The reason the final page stood out is *because* it listed a first name.

I pull over into the next lay-by to think it through, trying to remember the pages. I should have taken a photo of them – but it's a bit late now. I'm certain I know what they said in any case. I could see myself misremembering one page – but not all three.

And all that leaves one major question: How *did* Stella find me?

FORTY-THREE

A mother holds open the door as her young son toddles out of Tommy's Books. He's at the age where he must be starting school at some point in the near future. Old enough to question everything but young enough to still want to stay near to his mother. He's clutching a thin book with a colourful cover, which he has open as he walks. I don't catch what he says but he's trying to read part of the book to his mother, who tells him he can read it to her when they get home.

Thomas Hipkiss's bookshop is on an old-fashioned cobbled alley close to the centre of the town where both his parents were councillors. The familiar chain stores are along the high street but there are only small independent shops here, each with trip-overable sandwich boards cluttering up the walkway. It's the sort of street that doesn't exist in too many places any longer. The smell of sausage rolls leaks out of the bakery to one side of the bookstore, which battles with the scent of handmade soaps from the other.

In the window of the bookstore is a line of posters advertising pub gigs – and then a couple advertising in-store signings from local authors over the next month. There's an unquestionable home-grown focus to everything, which I guess would be natural from someone who grew up with parents as central parts of the community.

The door jangles as I head inside and the man behind the counter looks up and smiles at me. He's instantly recognisable as Thomas from the photo of him standing outside with the pair of books. In person, he is much more striking than he was in the picture. He's taller and fitter, with a dusting of sandy stubble. He's also wearing an old-man light-blue jumper, with a small hole in one of the elbows. I can imagine it being his dad's.

He asks if he can help and his tone is well-spoken, rather than posh.

'I'm just browsing,' I say. He says to let him know if I need any help and then I disappear around to the other side of a bookshelf, where I pick off the nearest hardback and open it.

Instead of reading, I peer through the gap between shelves and watch as Thomas types on a keyboard. There's an indescribable quality about him that means I could easily see him paying for someone's shopping if they've forgotten their wallet. Something personable and pleasant.

After a short while, I return the book to the shelf and then head across to the next stack, closer to the till. Thomas glances up and takes me in.

'I don't suppose you know anything about wedding venues, do you?' he asks.

There's a hint of mischievousness about him.

'One of my friends from school got married in a waterpark in Corfu,' I say. 'They had the priest waiting at the bottom of a water slide and both came down and swapped vows at the bottom.'

His eyes widen and then he laughs. 'That's not quite what I meant.'

Thomas twists his monitor around partway and then I step to the side of the counter where I can see the screen. On it, is a picture of a large marquee.

'My fiancée has sent me links to half a dozen potential venues,' he says. 'She wants me to help narrow it down to three before we do visits.'

'That doesn't sound like it should be too hard.'

Thomas clicks the mouse and changes the page away from the marquee and onto what looks like a large village green with a cricket pavilion on the far side.

'I suspect she's already chosen her three, so what she *really* wants me to do is match her picks.'

I laugh at that and he mirrors it with a grin of his own.

'It feels like some sort of test,' he adds.

'No pressure then,' I reply. 'Only your entire life.'

He takes the joke in the spirit it was meant and laughs along, before twisting the monitor back to himself.

'Do you know St Stephen's Hall?' he asks.

'I don't come from round here, I'm afraid.'

He nods at that. 'I think it's her number one pick. There's an orchard at the back and she told me about how she and her best friend growing up used to practise getting married under an apple tree in her back garden when they were younger.'

'It sounds like you already know the answer…?'

A glimmer of a smile crosses his face as he nods along. 'I just want it to be good…' He tails off and then seemingly realises where we are. He looks around the shop and then focuses back on me. 'Sorry, was there something I could help with?'

'I'm not sure.' It takes me a moment to weigh up the situation, wondering what I should do. 'Are you Thomas?' I ask.

His brow crinkles a little. 'Does my reputation precede me?'

'The name of the shop gives it away.'

He gives a gentle laugh. 'Ah! Good point.'

'I think I remember reading an article from a little while back about this shop opening.'

Thomas turns and nods towards the wall, where the exact article I read a few hours before has been clipped from the paper and framed.

'How did you manage to see it?' he asks.

'Huh?'

'You said you weren't from around here…?'

It takes me a second to realise the inconsistency. The clipping is from a local paper that I wouldn't have seen if I lived away from here – or if I hadn't explicitly searched for his father.

'I think I must have stopped in for a coffee at some point,' I say. 'Perhaps saw the paper that day…?'

It's plausible enough that he doesn't question this. There's a few seconds where we stand a couple paces away from each other and I almost blurt out everything I've found from the past week or so. Not just about *my* parents but his, too.

Thomas is still eyeing the article on the wall and a smile creeps across his face – which is when I realise that I can't.

He's happy.

He has this shop, he's getting married – and I know from everything I've been feeling about how hard it is to have a life pulled apart. I came here because I thought he might want to know – except, now I see him, I wonder if *I'd* have been better not knowing. Perhaps Stella had good intentions when it came to me – but I can act with knowledge of what the truth actually means and what it can do.

If I'm right and I were to tell Thomas what I fear to be true about his parents, then it would likely destroy every positive memory he has of them. It's not as if his birth mother, Emma, is still around for any sort of relationship. Nobody would win.

And if I am wrong, things will be even worse.

I suddenly realise that I'm eyeing the article as Thomas looks at me. As I turn back to him, there's a quizzical look on his face.

'Do we know each other?' he asks. 'It suddenly feels like you're familiar.'

I step away from the counter, trying not to show that I'm rattled. 'I don't think so,' I reply, with a shake of the head. I move away faster now, back-pedalling towards the door. 'I hope the wedding goes well,' I say.

He calls a thanks after me – but by that time, I'm already half out the door and on my way back to the car.

FORTY-FOUR

Driving back towards the main road seems to happen without me realising. So much of what's happened leaves me convinced two opposite things can both be true. Telling Thomas would have been for the best – and yet it would also have been the worst. In not telling him, I made the right decision, even though it was wrong.

I'm half an hour into the journey back to the house when my phone rings. For some reason, the car's Bluetooth doesn't kick in, so I end up ignoring it until I get to a lay-by. Stella's name is on the screen as a missed call but, when I call her back, there's no answer. There's also no voicemail, or text.

I set off driving again but am only a few more minutes along the road when it rings once more, before instantly ringing off. There's no lay-by this time, so I keep driving until I reach a set of services, where I pull over a short distance away from the petrol station.

It's another missed call from Stella, with no follow-up. I try calling a second time but it rings and rings until the call drops. I wait for a few minutes and try again – except the outcome is the same. This time, I send her a text saying that I'm on my way and will be about an hour.

The rest of the drive back to Macklebury comes without any other missed calls. Even though I said I was going to be out all day, it's mid-afternoon by the time I pull back onto my driveway.

I'm barely out of the car when I get the sense that something isn't right. There's an itch on the back of my neck and I stop and turn in a circle, feeling watched, even though there is nobody on the street and no one standing in any of the neighbours' windows.

I go to unlock the front door – except it's not locked. I know I secured it when I left this morning, which means Stella must have opened it to leave or answer – and then… I'm not sure.

As soon as I get inside, I can feel something in the air that I can't quite place. Like walking home alone and somehow knowing there's someone following, even though that person isn't in sight. More of a sense than a certainty.

'Hello…?'

My call goes unanswered – but all the doors are closed, including the one that leads into the kitchen, which is always open.

'Stella?'

No answer.

The living room door is nearest, so I nudge that open and stand in the doorway and stare at the scene beyond. Some of the books and magazines that were on the shelf on the far wall have been tossed onto the floor. The box file in which I keep letters and documents usually sits on the bottom shelf – but now it's on the ground, with the top flap open and papers spilling onto the carpet. It's a small thing but there are cushions on the ground, too – plus the table is on its side with two of the wooden legs snapped off and lying in the windowsill.

'Stella…?'

She doesn't answer and I back out of the living room and head along the hall to the kitchen.

I see the pool of red as soon as I open the door. The puddle of oozing crimson has started to set like jelly on the white tiles.

Stella is sitting on the floor next to the oven, her head resting on the handle of the adjacent cupboard. There is blood on her bare knees and more arced across her forehead that has matted into her eyebrow. She jumps when she sees me and then hugs her arms tighter across her front.

Her voice is a croak. 'I called you…'

Before I can reply, her eyelids flicker closed and then she slides sideways to the floor.

FORTY-FIVE

I step quickly across the kitchen as Stella blinks herself awake and then pulls herself into a sitting position.

I crouch at her side and rest an arm on her shoulder. 'What happened?' I ask.

She continues to blink and then rubs her head before pulling away her hand and looking at the blood she's now smeared across her brow.

'Did you see him?' she asks, breathily.

'See who?'

'Wayne.'

I follow her stare towards the door that leads into the hall – but there's nobody there.

'I don't know how he found me,' she adds. 'There was a knock on the door and I thought it was the postman. I unlocked it and the moment I opened it, he burst in.'

She blinks again and then focuses in on me as I help her to her feet. I guide her across to the stool and help her sit, before grabbing a cloth and dabbing away the blood from her hand, face and knees. There's a slim cut above her eye. It's not too deep but has produced enough blood.

'I'm going to check he's gone.'

Stella nods slightly but I'm not certain she's taken it in.

I double-check the back door is locked and then step over the puddle of blood before returning to the hall. I relock the front door and then check the empty living room, before going up the stairs. There are three doors from which to choose and I nudge open the one to the bathroom first. The hairs stand on my arms and it's hard to ignore the tingle of agitation that tells me I'm that crazy woman at the beginning of every horror movie.

There's no one in the bathroom, so I check the spare room. I've not been in here since Stella moved her backpack upstairs – and there's nothing untoward to see. The bed is made and her bag is on the floor at the bottom.

I try my room last. Everything tells me that Wayne will be in here. I've never met him but I can picture him in my mind: roughly shaven, with thick arms and a bulldog neck. I realise it's all my own projection but the unknown is almost always worse than the known.

Inside, and there is nobody in sight. I check my wardrobe but there's only clothes; then under the bed, where there's dust and clutter. There's a cupboard in the hall and I check that, too – then I'm back in the kitchen with Stella, who is holding the cloth to her head.

'There's no one here,' I say. 'I looked everywhere but he's gone.'

She nods slowly and continues blinking. 'I backed away into the living room and he was shouting about me not being able to hide from him. That he'd always find me, that sort of thing. He started throwing things and—'

'It's only stuff,' I tell her. 'None of it matters.'

'I managed to get out but he cornered me in here. He kept saying that I was his. When I went for the back door, he punched me in the stomach. He hit me a couple more times and then I guess I smacked my head on the way down…'

She groans and there's a croak to her voice when she speaks. I picture the blood on her knees and the pool on the floor which I now realise, belatedly, did not come from her head. Our eyes lock and there's recognition.

'Did you…?'

Stella closes her legs and touches her stomach. 'He saw the blood and I think it spooked him. He's hit me before but it usually only bruises. He backed out of the kitchen and I wasn't sure where he went. I remember being upstairs all of a sudden. I was on the toilet and there was blood. When I came down, he wasn't in the kitchen. I didn't know if he'd left, or…' She stares towards the puddle of sticky red on the floor and sighs. 'Sorry…'

I put an arm around her and pull her onto my shoulder. 'You don't have to be sorry.'

Stella wraps her arms through mine and then we stand together for a while. She doesn't cry or talk. She doesn't do anything other than hold me. I don't know enough about babies and pregnancies to know what a miscarriage might be like at this early stage – although the blood is a bad enough sign.

When Stella unfurls herself and slots back onto the stool, she hugs her arms around her front again.

'Did you call the police?' I ask.

She shakes her head.

'An ambulance?'

Another shake. 'Just you.'

'I'll call nine-nine-nine.'

Stella reaches for me, grabbing my wrist before I can get to my phone. 'No.'

'We need to call someone.'

'You'll make it worse. He said he won't come back. I think he knew he'd gone too far.'

She's avoiding eye contact and still staring at the blood on the floor.

'He attacked you,' I say. 'You were pregnant and now…'

One more shake of the head. 'I don't— I just—' She stares off towards the wall and slumps lower. 'I want to clean up and—'

'The hospital will need to look you over.'

Stella takes a long, deep breath. 'It's not like they can do anything now…'

I try to think of something to say to this – except there aren't words. It's not my body, nor my loss. It was only a few days ago that I was insisting that I didn't want to go to the police and now I'm saying that someone else should.

'You should probably have a doctor look at you.'

She nods a little to acknowledge she's heard, although there's no immediate response. She presses into me and I feel her chest rising and falling until she eases herself away and rubs her eyes.

'I got the job,' she says, with a wheeze.

It takes me a few moments to realise what she's talking about – and then I remember the interview she had yesterday.

'I can start on Monday,' she adds. Her tone is flat, more informative than excited.

'That's amazing news.'

'I've also been talking to one of my friends. That was before all this.' She glances towards the blood on the floor again. 'She's just moved into a two-bed place and I can stay with her. I was about to start packing up when Wayne knocked.'

This leaves me speechless for a different reason. It's not because I'm struggling to find words of comfort, it's because this has taken me by surprise.

'Stephen didn't mean anything with the questions last night,' I say.

'It's not that. I didn't really want to stay in the first place.' A pause, then: 'No offence.'

I know she doesn't mean it harshly but 'no offence' only ever seems to mean the opposite. I suddenly feel that returning sense of loss that I don't want her to go.

'I was going to wait for you to get home,' she says, perhaps picking up on my unease. 'I wasn't going to walk out.'

Stella pushes herself up until she's standing and then straightens her clothes. 'I'm going to clean myself up,' she says.

She puts the cloth on the counter and then stands over the blood on the floor. I tell her I'll clean it – and then she steps across it before heading slowly for the stairs. I listen to her footsteps and then the sound of the bathroom door opening. When it closes, I grab a bucket from under the sink and set it filling with water as I fish out the mop from the cubby near the back door.

Everything always seems to happen so quickly that I barely have a moment to get on top of something before the world turns again. It wasn't that long ago I was with Thomas in his bookshop and now there's this.

I squirt some washing-up liquid into the bucket and give it a swirl before clearing away the blood from the floor. It's already gone when I realise I should have probably taken a photo first – if only because Stella might change her mind about calling the police. Not that I'd know because she's leaving.

Because I've started, I mop the rest of the kitchen floor and then tip the murky brown water down the sink before heading into the living room and putting things back to how they were. Aside from the table with the broken legs, there's nothing that isn't easily returned to its spot – and even the table isn't expensive. The papers are going to take a bit more time to sort but, for now, I stuff them all back into the folder, figuring I'll deal with them properly another day.

There is noise from the stairs, so I head into the hallway, where Stella emerges onto the bottom step with her backpack in her hand. She's wearing clean clothes and her hair is wet.

I look down to the backpack: 'I can still call an ambulance…?'

She ignores this. 'I'm going to go to my friend's. She moved in yesterday and has unpacked, so there's a room going.' She glances towards the kitchen. 'I can help clean up first if you want.'

'It's more or less done – and you don't have to do that anyway.'

We stand awkwardly across from each other and she suddenly feels like a stranger again. 'Where does your friend live?' I ask. 'I can give you a lift, or…'

She lets the sentence tail off without interrupting. 'Everything's sorted,' she says.

'It's just…'

'What?'

'I really think you should see a doctor, if nothing else.'

Stella hoists her bag onto her shoulder. 'I might – but not today.' She gives another smile that isn't really a smile.

'How do you know Wayne won't follow you to your friend's?'

'I don't. But he knows I was here, so anywhere has to be safer.'

I realise it's not a dig at me – but it feels like one. That my house isn't safe.

'You don't have to go,' I say.

Another smile that's not.

Stella hoists her bag higher and then steps around me and opens the front door. 'Sorry about the mess,' she says. 'And everything else.'

Then she steps outside and walks along the drive, onto the pavement. She passes a man with a dog, stops to ruffle the pet's ears, and, by the time she gets to the corner, she hasn't once looked back.

FORTY-SIX

As Stella disappears out of sight, I stand on the front step and watch, with a large part of me hoping that she'll return. The man with the dog continues walking along the street, passing the front of my house and nodding towards me as he scolds the animal for sniffing at something on the pavement.

I move across to the fence and step over it before knocking at Mr Bonner's door. There's the familiar wait and then the door is pulled inwards and he stands and takes me in.

He's leaning on his walking stick and then pushes away from it to angle his weight onto the wall. 'Knee giving me gyp today,' he says. 'I could do with a bionic one like yours.'

I laugh – more for his benefit than mine. 'Did you see anyone coming to the house earlier?' I ask.

'When?'

'Anytime. I've been out.'

He looks sideways towards my house and then focuses back on me. 'Nobody, love. Even the postman kept going. Nothing for either of us today.'

It makes me stop and think, remembering that Stella specifically said Wayne came to the front. The back door was locked.

'Were you in your living room all day?' I ask.

'More or less. Bladder's not what it was but you don't want to hear about that.'

'And you didn't see anyone coming *or* going?'

'Should I have?'

I turn between him and my house, unsure of whether it means anything. Mr Bonner could easily have been in another room at the times when Wayne arrived and left.

I say that there's no problem and promise that elusive Scrabble game for another night – and then I return to the house.

I've done much of the tidying but check back into my box file of papers, making sure the basics like my passport and birth certificate are still there. Dad always used to nag me to get a safe, although I'd tell him that, given I'd only be getting a small one, a thief could simply steal the safe and find a way to open it away from my house.

There's nothing obvious that's missing from the stack, although I don't pay too much attention to this sort of thing. There are bills and letters from the bank. The usual sort of correspondence that people stick in a pile and eventually shred a few years along the line.

Back in the kitchen and, now the floor has almost dried, I realise there is still the faintest reddy-black stain on the floor. I could try cleaning it again but I'd have to be in the mood to do that – which is something I'm certainly not. Of everything, it feels like I need company, which is why I grab my car keys and head back outside. This time, I'm careful to set the alarm before I leave.

By the time I get to the school gates, Stephen is already leaning against them, flirting with one of the mums. I know it's not a sexual thing, more of a Stephen thing. He likes the attention.

When he spots me, he says something to the woman, waves goodbye to her two children and then bounds across. It's only as he does this that I remember it's a Friday. No wonder he's full of energy.

I nod towards the woman, who is shooing her children into one of those urban tank/people carrier things. 'Have you turned straight on me?' I ask.

'You wish.'

'I knew this whole thing was a charade to hide your rampant heterosexuality.'

'Got me.' He grins – but it doesn't last long as he realises I'm not joining in. 'What happened?'

I tell him about arriving home to find Stella, the blood, and the damage. Then how she left so abruptly.

Stephen listens and a cloud passes across his face. His eyes narrow and I can feel him readying himself to ask the question I've been asking myself.

'Have you ever actually *seen* Wayne?' he asks.

'No.'

'Heard him on the phone? Seen any sign that he exists?'

Stephen already knows the answer and I don't reply.

'You never told me she was pregnant,' he says.

'It wasn't deliberate.'

'I offered her some wine last night.'

'I didn't think it was my thing to tell. I figured if she wanted you to know, she'd have said.'

Stephen doesn't reply immediately but his eyes narrow a little and it's almost as if I can see cogs turning. 'Did you see any proof that she was ever pregnant?'

'You saw her last night.'

He raises his eyebrows, like someone waiting for the penny to drop. 'Exactly.'

I try to think back, wondering if I ever actually did see Stella's belly. She is skinny, and not far along, so wouldn't necessarily be showing.

Stephen is already ahead of me. 'Was there a scan?' he asks.

'Not that she showed me. There's no reason why she would have done.'

'Do women get morning sickness that early? Was she ever sick?'

'It's one of the first signs,' I say. 'I don't think she was ever sick in the morning... but not everybody gets it like that.'

Stephen doesn't say anything right away. He doesn't need to.

'Why would she lie?' I ask. It's a question more to myself than anyone else – and then I remember the key part. 'Stella wasn't the one who told me she was pregnant,' I say. 'It was her mum.'

Stephen frowns at this as it doesn't quite fit with the narrative.

'If this is all some illusion, why now?' I ask. 'Why trash the house while I was out today?'

Stephen doesn't respond immediately, although, when it comes, it makes some sense. 'Perhaps I spooked her last night. I did ask a lot of questions.'

'But why do any of this?'

'There's one obvious thing. It comes up whenever anyone googles you…'

He's only telling me what I already know. The thing that usually means a barrier goes up whenever I meet someone new.

'Stella never asked me about money,' I say.

'Perhaps she didn't *intend* to ask…' He waits for that to sink in and then adds: 'If someone wants to steal money, they don't usually ask first.'

He's right and there's no question I let Stella into my life in a way I wouldn't usually.

Then it clicks.

'She said she was allergic to dogs,' I say, slowly.

'Did she?'

'When she left today, there was a dog on the street and she patted it on the head…'

It hangs between us. Something small yet something huge. The biggest lies are built on the smallest.

'Then she told us last night that she found me because of my parents' name on the page at her mum's house. Except I saw that page, too – and it only had a last name. If she was telling the truth, then all she had to go on was "Taylor".'

Stephen continues to stare and the look is so intense that I have to turn away.

'You need to change the locks,' he says.

'But it's true,' I reply. 'She told me about the papers in her mother's house and they're there. She gave me that article and it's a fact. I have Jane's ear. Mum admitted I was paid for. The only thing I don't know is whether Mum and Dad knew I was kidnapped.'

I stop and then realise there's another thing I've skimmed past. If Nikki and her boyfriend stole a child – Thomas – to sell a year before Jane, then they wouldn't have needed my parents to give them the idea.

Stephen takes this in with a large inhalation and a glance back towards the school. The caretaker is locking up for the weekend and offers a wave across the playground, which Stephen returns.

'All the best lies are based on truth,' he says.

I let it sit, not knowing how to reply. He tells me he's parked at the back of the school, which is close to where I am, so we set off along the street. With it being a Friday, there's little hanging around, so all the kids and their parents have drifted home, ready for the weekend. The roads feel quiet and we walk in silence, which only adds to my growing unease.

It's Stephen who breaks our impasse. 'Did Stella steal anything?' he asks.

'Not that I noticed. There was a mess in the living room and blood in the kitchen.'

'You *really* need to change the locks.'

He's said that but I let him have the moment. At least it's not *I told you so*. It doesn't mean he's right about Stella and yet there's a definite contradiction. She has given me facts about my past and yet *a* truth isn't an *entire* truth.

'Have you heard back from the police about your assault?' I ask.

'No.'

'Are you still having those... *thoughts?*'

I remember the way Stephen made fists the other night and the anger he described that feels so far away from the person I know.

'I've been trying to ignore them.'

We get to Stephen's car. He fishes for his keys in his manbag and then tosses them from one hand to the other.

'Do you want me to stay over tonight?' he asks.

'I'm a big girl.'

I want him to laugh but he doesn't. Instead, he leans forward and pulls me in for a hug. His grip is tight and comforting, which says more than any words might.

He pulls away and unlocks his car. 'Call if you need me,' he says – and, just for a moment, I almost ask him to stay.

'Same,' I tell him.

FORTY-SEVEN

The house feels empty. I wonder if it's healthy for me to swing so rapidly from one extreme to another. I was used to living alone and content in my own bubble – and then, from nowhere, I liked having Stella around. There was comfort at hearing someone else's footsteps on the stairs or the landing. In knowing someone was going to offer to make me a drink, or ask how I was.

Now she's gone, that sense I once had of contentment by myself has gone and I feel alone.

But I also wonder if Stephen was right and it was all an illusion. Or if I'm looking for fault in a person who gave up so much for me and who ended up being assaulted by their ex, which led to her leaving. It was me who asked Stella to stay. She said, repeatedly, that she would leave.

Unless that was all part of it. What better way to make a person do something than by convincing them it was all their own idea?

I will have the locks changed over the weekend, even though it feels like an overreaction. I want to believe that Stella told me the truth.

I spend the evening rechecking the rooms to see if Wayne caused any further destruction that I missed. Or 'Wayne', of course. I am struggling to get past where Stephen said that the best lies are based on truth. I was so desperate to believe everything Stella told me because she'd already shown me a truth I hadn't known.

If Stephen is right, there's one big concern that is difficult to get past. Nikki told me about Stella's pregnancy – which means that there has to be a chance she and her daughter were in contact all along. And, if that *is* the case, then how much of all this is a lie?

All the best lies are based on truth.

I don't think Stephen has ever said anything more profound. It could be true that I'm Jane Craven *and* that my parents never knew. Nikki could have told me one truth and one lie but, because the truth was so big, the lie went unquestioned.

I picture Mum, sitting alone in her house, surrounded by those photos of Dad, tormented by the fact that I haven't spoken to her in days. I could call her now, perhaps *should*, except that I can't. Not yet. Not today.

I go into the room where Stella has been staying and re-find Dad's scrapbook that I went through what seems like weeks ago. The one that contained the receipt for the car he bought a short distance from when Jane was stolen.

At the front is that grainy photo of Mum and Dad's wedding day. Mum's simple dress and Dad's suit that's too big. It's unnerving to see them younger than I am now. Seeing them so youthful and hopeful for the future has me wondering if what they did was quite so awful. They wanted a child so badly, wanted to *love* a child so much, that they spent what would have been an enormous amount to them.

They even called me Hope.

And perhaps there might have been alternative ways to do things – adoption, fostering – I don't know. But there is one absolute fact in everything.

They brought me up well.

They loved me. Mum *loves* me.

But there's Penny, too. She probably wanted a child just as much. Could have given it the same amount of love – but it was stolen from her.

A hateful, unforgiveable act that's defined by love.

I continue going through the pages, re-looking at the tickets, the receipts and photos. I wish I had something like this: a chronicle of my life, for better and worse.

As I'm flipping pages, a photo of Mum drops out the bottom onto my lap. The picture has a very eighties' look about it. She's in a pink dress with shoulder pads so sharp, I can almost feel them stinging my eyes. She has a heavily hairsprayed perm, like someone from a Vaseline-lensed American soap at the time.

It's only as I'm sticking the photo back in that I realise Mum was ahead of her time. It's actually a picture from before she was married, with 'Barbara Paisley' written underneath. Mum's maiden name.

I continue looking through the book, wondering if I should call Mum. It's almost a question of asking if I forgive her and I'm not sure that I do. I return the book to the box and figure I will sleep on it and decide in the morning.

With the house empty and no Creators' Club in the morning, I struggle to remember what I used to do on quiet Friday evenings like this. The truth is, I probably would have spent them with Stephen, or Aki when we were together. Or at Mum's.

I find myself sitting in bed, thinking about that photo of Mum, with her maiden name written so tidily underneath in Dad's handwriting. It makes me realise that I don't know either Stella or Nikki's last name. It might not matter – but maybe it does?

Searching online for 'Nikki Stoneridge' throws up nothing. I try it with 'Nicky' to cover a misspelling but the only hit is the results from a 5K race that took place two years ago. There is a long list of competitors, with no way of knowing who each individual might be. From my one meeting with her, it also doesn't seem that Nikki is the type to finish fifteenth out of almost two hundred in a 5K race.

With that ruled out, I try 'Nicola Stoneridge' – and this does get a result. There is a picture from almost ten years ago, taken at the Stoneridge Summer Fete, that's captioned as 'local residents Nicola and Robbie Brittan'. The photo shows Nikki looking bony and gaunt – more or less identical to how she did when she let me into her house. There's a man at her side and they're standing next to a candy floss machine as a Ferris wheel sits in the distance behind them. Neither of them are smiling and I get the sense they didn't know the photo was being taken, despite them being named in the caption.

I know her last name now and almost go back and try searching for that – except there's more to the photo than that. First, nobody mentioned Nikki and Robbie being married. Second, Nikki told me that Robbie had fallen off some scaffolding about ten years ago and that they weren't together at the time. Except this picture was taken a little under ten years ago. I suppose 'ten years' is vague enough that it doesn't mean she lied – but something feels off about it. I can't quite remember her wording but Nikki told me she and Robbie broke up not long after everything happened with – and then I think she tailed off. She never actually said they broke up after Jane was stolen but that's what I assumed. And, because I assumed that, I figured Robbie wasn't Stella's father.

That's not the only curious thing about the photograph. I recognise the man next to her. I recognise Robbie. Nikki said he died in that scaffolding accident, except an older, more wrinkled version of that man is the person who let himself in through the front door when I was on the landing upstairs, searching through Nikki's cupboard.

All of which means that Robbie – the apparent mastermind – is very much still alive and very much still living with Nikki.

FORTY-EIGHT

SATURDAY

My routine is always thrown off on the weekends where there is no Saturday Creators' Club. It's usually when something like Christmas or Easter comes around – but there are also these oddities dotted through the year. I'm usually particular about getting up at a set time and then checking over my notes for the day. I'll have my attendance sheets and the various insurance forms that sometimes need filling in. Even though I'd have already done those things earlier in the week, there's a sense of calm about double-checking it all.

On the other days, my sleep is all over the place. Some Saturdays, I can sleep in past lunchtime, as if I'm a teenager again. Others, I'm up at four or five, pacing the house, not knowing what to do with myself.

Today is one of *those* days. I barely sleep before dragging myself down to the empty kitchen and setting the coffee machine going.

It's hard to process that the man who supposedly snatched Jane Craven thirty-four years ago, the man who snatched *me*, was standing at the bottom of the stairs while I was at the top. He didn't die in a scaffolding fall and he's still with Nikki all these years on.

I should go to the police – except I'm not sure what evidence I have. Not much. There's a cutting, which shows Jane and I share the damaged ear. I could do a DNA test to show Penny and I are related – but none of that implicates Robbie, Nikki, or,

I suppose, Stella. So much of what I think I know is based upon their versions of events – and yet Stephen was right that the best lies are hidden in truth.

I have no idea which parts were lies and which were truths.

Besides, if I do go to the police, all it does is potentially get Mum into trouble for her role in whatever happened.

Time passes. I pace, drinking coffee and worrying. I could tell Penny everything that I know, although I'm not sure what that would achieve. It could also still end with Mum getting into trouble and I know I don't want that.

It's as I'm pacing that I end up back at the door into the kitchen from the hall. There's still the faintest of blackened stains on the ground, from where I cleaned up Stella's blood. There was definitely a small graze above her eye but the only other blood I saw was on her knees. There was nothing up or down the stairs, or around the living room.

Stephen asked if I'd ever met or seen Wayne, which I haven't. I only have Stella's word for it that he exists. I believed her that he does – perhaps I still do… it's just…

I check the kitchen bin and then remember that I emptied it into the main wheelie bin outside. I head outside, knowing the grim job that's ahead of me, as I tip the bin onto its side and allow the contents to spill onto the ground at the side of my house. The tied-up bags are fine, it's the loose odds and ends that make me gag. I'm definitely regretting putting in eggshells directly. I nudge things around with my foot, knowing that I'm going to have to use my hands at some stage. It's as I'm coming around to that thought that my phone begins to ring. It's a little after eleven and, with Stephen's name on the screen, my first thought is that he's forgotten there's no club today.

I answer cheerily, ready to make fun, except that his tone is instantly foreboding as he asks where I am.

'At home,' I say. 'Where are you?'

'Elwood centre.'

It's where I grew up. Where Mum lives. 'What are you doing there?' I ask.

He doesn't answer but I can hear him breathing heavily through the speaker.

'What's wrong?' I ask.

'I'm looking at him.'

'Looking at who?'

'One of the guys who beat me up.'

There's a tremble in Stephen's tone that is pure rage. I can feel the injustice burning through the phone.

'He's just walking around,' Stephen says. 'He went into the bank first and now he's in the Co-op. Just walking around as if everything's normal…'

'Steve…'

He doesn't reply, so I say his name again.

'Listen to me,' I add.

'What?'

'Don't do anything stupid.'

'Like what?'

'You know. I'm going to come to you. I'll get in the car now and it won't take long. Wait for me, okay?'

He doesn't reply, so I repeat the last bit, which gets the gentlest of grumbles that's as close to an affirmative as I'm going to get. Then the call drops and the screen is black.

I picture Stephen clenching his fists, with that raw fury in his voice that I'd never heard before. I've never thought of him as violent in any way but there was something about the 'like what?' that felt dangerous.

I stare down at the rubbish on the ground, knowing I'm going to have to pick everything back up before going, else rats will be along.

It's as I'm reaching for the first bag that I see the packet on the floor, half hidden in a brown bag that once contained curry takeaway.

I crouch and pull out the packet fully – although the main thing that does is squirt the remnants of gooey red out of the clear sachet and onto my hand. I sniff it, although I already know what it is. It doesn't particularly smell of anything but then I suppose, if it did, it would be a clearer giveaway.

Buried in my bin – and most definitely not put there by me – is an almost empty pouch of fake blood.

FORTY-NINE

It takes me between fifteen and twenty minutes to pick up the bin bags, wash my hands – and then drive to Elwood. I know the route so well that much of it is done on autopilot until I'm pulling into one of the one-hour spots outside the pharmacy.

I take out my phone to call Stephen, except that I don't have to because, as I hurry along the street, I spot him sitting on a bench next to the war memorial. It's the place where I used to gather with my friends when I was at that glorious age of being young enough to still be doing A-levels and not need a job, while old enough to be allowed out by myself more or less whenever I wanted. My friends and I would sit on the bench for hours and talk about nothing.

Now, Stephen is there by himself, staring towards the other end of the High Street. I slot in next to him but he doesn't acknowledge me and doesn't turn away from his gaze.

'He's in the betting shop,' Stephen says. 'I watched him go in just after I got off the phone with you.'

Stephen's fists are clenched again and his jaw is tight. I touch his arm but he pulls away.

'Steve…'

He ignores me and continues glaring into the distance before, almost as if it's been cued, the doors to the betting shop open and out steps a man in jeans and a hoody. He is bald but, with the tufts around his ears, it looks more through nature than choice.

Stephen immediately pops up into a standing position and I can feel the fire in him.

'Steve…'

He doesn't react to me – but he also doesn't set off to follow the guy who assaulted him. We watch together as the man crosses the road, gives a brief wave towards the driver who slowed for him, and then ducks into the Wetherspoon's.

Stephen takes a step away from the bench but I put both hands on his chest and then stand directly in front of him.

'You're a teacher,' I say. 'A *primary* school teacher. What do you think will happen if you're done for assault?'

He takes a breath but he doesn't back away, or return to the bench. 'He deserves something.'

'Maybe he does – but it's not about him, it's about you. There's no point in destroying your own career and life.'

Stephen takes another breath and then he slouches a little, staring at his feet. 'I thought he was going to kill me.'

There's such pain in his voice that I almost step out of the way. He's my friend, my *best* friend, and I know I can't make that better. He sounds haunted.

'I was on the floor, trying to cover my head, and they were kicking. Someone's boot caught me under the chin and then the other one kicked me in the back of the head. I closed my eyes and didn't think I'd get up.'

He jolts up and takes a step forward, which forces me to move backwards a little – but I don't get out of his way.

'It's about *you*,' I say. 'If you go and do something now, it's your life that will be ruined. You'll be arrested. You'll be in court. You'll never be able to teach again.'

'So what do you suggest?'

He doesn't look at me and his teeth are still clenched.

'Call the police. You know where he is. If he's gone in for a drink, or lunch, he'll be there for a while. They can come now and get him.'

'What if he gets away with it anyway?'

'What if he doesn't?'

Stephen stands rigidly, like a guard on duty outside the palace. It feels as if he's about to step around me and charge towards the pub – and I know I'll be able to do nothing about this.

He strains forward… and then, slowly, reluctantly, reaches into his pocket for his phone.

We sit as one and I feel such relief that I want to hug him.

'Should I call 999?' he asks. 'It doesn't feel like an emergency.'

I tell him to call 101 instead but, as I'm finishing, I spot the pair standing on the corner outside the bank that's next to the betting shop.

Stephen has his phone in his hand but follows my stare.

'What?' he asks.

'It's Stella,' I say.

He cranes his neck, peering closer – although I'm not sure what good it does, given the distance. 'Who's she with?' he asks.

'Her mum,' I reply. 'She's with Nikki.'

FIFTY

The strange thing is that I know what's about to happen before it actually does. Mum's photo slipped out of Dad's scrapbook – and it was the one that listed her maiden name underneath. I told Stella voluntarily where I grew up, which included where I opened my first bank account. My documents, which were always kept in the living room, had been scattered around and I didn't check them completely before dumping everything back into the folder.

And then the most important point of all: Stella has gone out of her way to look like me.

I stand and take a step towards the road and the bank beyond. Stella has now gone into the bank, leaving her mum on the pavement behind.

'Where are you going?' Stephen asks.

I don't turn to look at him, because I can't take my eyes from Nikki. She's eyeing her phone and then stops to turn around, as if she knows she's being watched. I freeze on the spot but she looks through me and continues turning until she glances back to her phone.

'Promise you'll call the police,' I say.

'Where are you going?'

'Just call the police and tell them about the guy who assaulted you. Don't do anything until they're here.' I risk a look backwards towards him. 'Promise me,' I add.

'Okay.'

I turn back – and Nikki is still looking at her phone. Stella has a head-start of close to a minute. I stride across the road and then walk as quickly as I can along the street.

I vaguely sense someone shouting, a woman, but pay little attention as I stride past Nikki, who doesn't seem to notice me, and then into the bank.

This is the place where I opened my first account twenty or so years ago. The manager came into our school for a careers presentation, which somehow ended up with more or less everyone in my year opening their first current account here. Looking back, I'm not sure how it was allowed to happen like that. Perhaps the school got some sort of kickback?

I've not been into the branch for years – but it's all open-plan now. There's a woman standing at the front with a clipboard and no sign of the old closed booths that used to run along the side. Instead, there are people at desks and posters along the walls advertising mortgage and loan rates. At the far end, standing at the empty counter, is Stella.

I ignore the woman at the front, who's asking how she can help – and instead move quickly towards the counter, where I slot in at the side of Stella.

She jumps at the intrusion and turns sideways to look at me – although I'm focusing on the wide-eyed teller with the slip of paper in her hand.

'Is that a withdrawal?' I ask.

The teller says nothing – but she looks from my driving licence on the counter in front of her up to me. My debit card is there, too. Both, presumably, taken from my wallet. It wouldn't be the sort of thing I'd notice until I had to use either.

'I'm Hope Taylor,' I say – and it feels powerful. Not Jane Craven. I'm Hope Taylor and I always will be.

The teller looks between Stella and me – and there's panic in her face. There's a moment in which she's frozen in time but then she turns to her side and starts to say something to the man sitting next to her.

This is all it takes for Stella to bolt. She says nothing to me as she runs past and darts for the door. Nikki is there now – which makes me think she actually did see me as I went past her on the pavement. She holds the door open as Stella races past and then she focuses in on me, her eyes narrow with hatred.

'You'd have *none* of this without me.'

Nikki spits the words towards me – and then doesn't wait for a reply as she spins and follows her daughter out of the bank.

Everything has happened so quickly and yet it was almost in slow-motion. As if the moment I saw them across the street, I knew how everything was going to occur.

I turn back to the teller and my driving licence and debit card are still on the counter in front of her. There's a bill from the electricity company there, too. Every piece of ID Stella might have needed, along with knowledge of my mother's maiden name and – of course – the right look.

'How much did she try to take out?' I ask.

The teller's mouth bobs, so I pull out my wallet from my bag and flip through the empty slots, trying to figure out when Stella might have taken them. I pass across a credit card, then a library card, then a Nectar card. All with my name on the front.

'I'm Hope,' I say. Again.

The teller finally replies this time. 'Is she your sister? She knew your security info.'

'I don't have a sister,' I say – and then I look up to take in the woman. 'Do I call the police, or do you?'

She doesn't get a chance to answer because there's a loud howl from somewhere outside the front doors.

I leave the counter, somehow knowing whatever's outside is more important than what's in.

As I get onto the pavement, there is a sprawl of arms and legs outside the betting shop. Nikki is standing over a pair of women on the pavement below her, shouting for help as two women claw at one another.

It's Angel I spot first. She's sild, nails flailing through the air as she screams 'Don't you dare ignore me' towards Stella, who's throwing her elbows back and forth in an attempt to free herself.

Aki appears from nowhere and grabs Angel around the waist before pulling her up.

'It's not her,' he says loudly, as Angel aims a kick towards Stella.

The free show has attracted a small crowd of onlookers, some of whom are filming on their phones as, slowly, Angel, Aki, Stella and Nikki all turn to take me in. I suppose it was Angel who was shouting and trying to get my attention as I headed into the bank. As Stella ran out, Angel assumed she was me.

'Hi,' I say, giving the smallest of waves.

And then, as if summoned, a police car pulls into the empty parking space on the opposite side of the street.

FIFTY-ONE

It feels right that Mum is back in her chair in the living room. She's literally at home – but she's also *at home*. In the place she's supposed to be. She's aged since she was in my hallway. She was grey anyway but her hair somehow seems lighter, perhaps patchier. The wrinkles are deeper, especially around her eyes. It doesn't look as if she's slept in a long while.

'She tried to withdraw fifty thousand,' I say.

'*Fifty…*' Mum says this in the way mums do – or certainly the way *mine* does. Something sounds so completely unbelievable that she'll repeat it, as if to tell herself that it's true.

'She went in the day before to ask for enough funds. I didn't know this but you can ask for an unlimited withdrawal amount at a bank, as long as you give them twenty-four hours' notice. They need that because hardly any of them have enough cash otherwise. When I caught her at the bank, she was on the return visit to actually take the money.'

'*Fifty…*' Mum repeats.

'She had all the ID and passed the security checks. She looks like me, so they didn't question her any further. I assumed someone wanting fifty thousand in cash would raise a few more flags but apparently not. They said it's not completely uncommon.'

Mum stares back at me in a mix of shock and disbelief. If the bank manager hadn't explained it to me himself, I'm not sure I would have believed it, either.

'The police told me there was no sign of Robbie at the house in Stoneridge – but they've got Stella and Nikki. They've also got footage from the bank and my statements…'

I tail off. It's not only the money I had to tell the police about.

'I changed the locks,' I add. 'More of a just-in-case thing than anything else. A twenty-four-hour guy came out last night and did everything.'

I push myself up from the seat and cross the room, then press a shiny new key into Mum's hand. She stares at it and then gulps, before rubbing her nose with the back of her hand. I return to the chair and she's croaky when she next speaks.

'Is this for me?'

'I wouldn't have given it to you otherwise.'

'It's just I thought…'

She doesn't finish the sentence but I know what she thought. It's what I did, too: that we were done with this sort of thing.

'I had to tell the police everything,' I say. 'They needed the full story. All of it. About you and Dad. About Penny and Jane. There's a chance – probably a good one – that they're going to have to take a statement from you.'

Mum bows her head, perhaps to acknowledge what I've said but I think because she's known that this was coming. Perhaps she's known for decades.

'I don't know what will happen after that,' I say.

'I understand.'

'I want to say that everything will work out and all be fine – but I don't know that for sure.'

Another nod but no words.

'It's impossible for them to investigate an attempted fraud without looking at the rest,' I say. 'I'm sorry.'

Mum looks up and takes me in. She's blinking, trying to keep away the tears. 'It's not you who has to be sorry.'

'I've been messaging Penny as well,' I say. 'I'm probably going to visit her on Tuesday. I thought you should know. It doesn't mean I don't appreciate you bringing me up, or everything that you and Dad did, it's just…'

I can't finish the sentence because it doesn't feel as if the words are there.

There's a lump in Mum's throat that I can hear as she replies. 'I know…'

I don't tell her that I'm going to ask Penny outright what's going on with Chris. Then, if she needs it, I'll offer her whatever money she might need if she wants to leave him. I have a feeling she'll say no – but I have to ask.

'What about Dad and the car he bought?' I ask. 'We never had a car growing up.'

Mum pouts a lip, remembering. 'We had one for a little while but I wasn't involved in what it was, or where he got it. It kept breaking down and only lasted a few months. Your father sold it for scrap and we made do after that.

'I need to tell you something,' she adds, shifting my thoughts back into the room.

She pauses for breath and that moment seems to last a lifetime. As if anything could come next.

'I was telling the truth,' she says. 'When I told you that we didn't know you were stolen, that was the truth. I know you might not believe me – but we didn't know. We *never* would have gone through with everything otherwise. I'm not saying that what your father and I did was right but we thought we were getting a child that was unwanted. We knew we could care for you and love you.

If we had any idea where you'd come from, we would never have gone through with it…'

The final few words are more of a sob than anything else. She stares at me through watery eyes and I know this is the truth. Perhaps I always knew?

'Stephen helped me see it,' I say. 'Stella was so convincing – about all of it. She told me about a boyfriend, who I doubt exists. There were actual bruises on her body. Her mum told me about a pregnancy that didn't exist. They must have practised and practised.'

'You needed to believe,' Mum says.

I almost say Thomas's name, to point out that Nikki and Robbie stole a child previously, so it had to be their idea, not Mum and Dad's. I stop myself because it feels like a secret that should only be mine.

Mum's right. There was enough truth in what Stella and Nikki told me that I wanted to believe the rest, regardless of what it meant. Crappy internet or not, they really did their homework – and, what's more, they let me find out things for myself. They didn't dump everything on me in one go.

All that to steal fifty thousand… although, as the bank manager mentioned, they could have gone back for more on another day.

It's all left me wondering whether Robbie and Nikki kept an eye on this family through the years. They had no reason to know that I was called 'Hope' – but perhaps they drove past a few times? Looked out for any news in which Mum or Dad were featured? Perhaps they know far more about the other daughter, their own child, that Robbie sold? Perhaps they know all about Thomas and his bookshop? I guess it helped that Mum and Dad never moved from here.

I don't know the whys and the details – but I do have Nikki's angry 'You'd have *none* of this without me' to go on. That probably says more than anything else.

'How's Stephen?' Mum asks.

'They got the guy who assaulted him. Turns out one of the neighbouring forces were looking for him, too. They reckon he might have done something similar a few times.'

Mum nods along, only partly taking it in. The key is still in her hand and she looks down to take it in, before clamping her fingers around it.

'I'm so sorry,' she says.

'I know.'

FIFTY-TWO

I pull onto my driveway and, as I get out of the car, Mr Bonner comes out of his house. He raises a hand to get my attention and then I cross to the fence, where he's leaning on his stick.

'I saw the police around last night,' he says.

'It's all fine,' I reply. 'Well, not fine – but it will be.'

I'll tell him everything one of these days but not today.

He seems to recognise this as he nods back towards his house. 'I don't suppose I can tempt you with a game, can I?'

I almost say 'no', partly through reflex, except I stop myself – because it's precisely what I need. I tell him I'll be over shortly and then hover as he disappears back into his house with a newly found bounce in his step. As he disappears, I head into my own house and pick up the mail from the mat. There's only one letter – and this is for Aki. I could text him to say there's something but I know what it led to last time and can't face that again so soon. Perhaps it was Angel who scratched my car, or perhaps it was Stella before I knew who she was. Maybe it doesn't matter? I don't fancy asking Angel again.

The letter is left on the kitchen counter and then I relock the door. After that, I step over the fence and knock on Mr Bonner's door. There's a loud call of 'it's open', so I head inside, into the living room, where he is sitting at the table in the window. The Scrabble board is already open in the middle and there's a dictionary primed at the side. He's turning over the tiles as I take the seat opposite him.

'Oldest goes first,' he says.

'We play youngest goes first in my family.'

He grins and catches my eye, letting me know it's a joke. 'Such an entitled generation.'

We pick our tiles and arrange them on our boards and then spend a good minute trying to make the other go first. In the end, I play 'fever' across the centre square, leaving it for Mr Bonner to add up the score. It's as he's writing the number on his pad that I notice a flicker of movement from the window. He sees it, too, and we watch as three boys stop at the end of my drive and then chat to one another.

I tell Mr Bonner I need a minute and then quickly head outside, stepping over the fence and approaching Oliver who is with friends that I don't recognise.

'Everything all right?' I ask. I haven't seen him since the Saturday I 'lent' him the tin of pencils that his mother ended up throwing at me.

Oliver looks to his friends, as if asking for a silent permission. 'Mum doesn't know I'm here,' he says.

'Why *are* you here?'

'Just to say that I hate her. That she's an idiot. She won't let me come to club any more. She says we don't need charity.'

There's determination and anger in there and I feel it, too.

'Some people find it hard to accept help,' I say. 'They think it makes you seem weak if you need other people. I'm sure she means well. She wouldn't have let you come at all if she didn't.'

Oliver looks up to me and I can almost see the cogs turning as he processes this. If nothing else, she drives him in each weekend – so she can't be *that* against the club. She probably has a point in that I went behind her back to gift her son something. There were better ways.

'Can you talk to her?' he says, quieter now. 'Ask if I can come back?'

'Maybe not me. I'll ask Stephen. You know him. He's good with things like that.' A pause. 'You shouldn't hate your mum,' I add.

'Why?'

'Because you only get one.'

He doesn't reply – but then he doesn't know what I do: that, perhaps, one is more than enough.

The Child in the Photo publishing team

Editorial
Ellen Gleeson

Line edits and copyeditor
Jade Craddock

Proofreader
Liz Hatherell

Production
Alexandra Holmes
Rhianna Louise
Ramesh Kumar Pitchai

Design
Lisa Horton

Marketing
Alex Crow
Hannah Deuce

Publicity
Noelle Holten
Kim Nash
Sarah Hardy

Distribution
Chris Lucraft
Marina Valles

Audio
Rhianna Louise
Nina Winters
Alba Proko
Arran Dutton & Dave Perry –
    Audio Factory
Alison Campbell

Rights and contracts
Peta Nightingale
Saidah Graham

Lightning Source UK Ltd.
Milton Keynes UK
UKHW010813040721
386577UK00001B/154

9 781800 195042